A. M. DARLING

11 AM Publishing
An imprint of 11 AM Publishing LLC
its11am.com

Copyright © 2023 by A.M. Darling

First paperback edition February 2023
Book design by A. M. Darling

ISBN: 979-8-9877914-0-0 (paperback)
ISBN: 979-8-9877914-1-7 (eBook)

To my younger self,

See? Dreams do come true!

PLAYLIST

Wide Awake- Roniit

Measure Of A Man- FKA twigs ft. Central Cee

Trust Issues- The Weekend

Trouble- Valerie Broussard

Love Story- Indila

Hurricane- Tommee Profitt feat. Fleurie

Alone With You- Ashlee

Somebody Like You- Bree Runway

Storm- Ruelle

Veins- Jazmine Sullivan

Lose Face- Daniel Di Angelo

Dirty Mind- Boy Epic

All Night- Zanderr

Ashes- Claire Guerreso

Minefields- Faouzia & John Legend

IMPORTANT NOTE

Please be advised that this book
contains themes and references that
may be sensitive to certain audiences
such as death, murder, suicide,
trauma, panic attacks, explicit
language as well as sexual harassment
and assault.

1

It's a somber morning in Paris. Rain patters against the windows of the small corner cafe I sit in. A cozy and quaint spot with a nineteen-twenties vibe and a fireplace at one end that is the main source of warmth, besides the drinks that is. Wreaths and lights still decorate the walls, echoing the holiday spirit from a few weeks ago. Usually, I'm here to dive into my work amidst such a relaxed atmosphere, but my motives are different today.

I occupy a table for two near a window in the far back, close enough to the fire, while biting my nails and tapping my pen in anticipation. Upon catching myself in the nasty habit, I'm quick to remove my hand from my mouth. Clearing my throat, I return to what I've become a pro at– people watching. My eyes are drawn to a regular customer currently at the counter ordering what I'm sure will be the same thing he orders here every morning.

A small, knowing smile slides up the side of my face and I bring my cooled off cup of café au lait to my lips as he proves me right. I blow a loose strand of blonde hair from underneath my black rimmed glasses– which I wear for aesthetic– and make a move to sweep it behind my ear with the rest of the disobedient hairs. Within a few minutes, the gentleman collects his order and proceeds toward the exit. He spots me and beams, "Ah, Bonjour, Jess!"

"Bonjour, Monsieur Marcel! Bonne journée." He's happier and much more alert than when he strode in. Amazing what a sip or two of espresso can do, and so damn fast! As my gaze follows him out, something catches my attention from the corner of my eye. I look out the window next to me in time to see the rain distorted view of a figure under a red umbrella walk past him and in through the front door. The tiny bells alert everyone of the new arrival.

The umbrella retracts into itself, revealing the mysterious individual with her long auburn tresses cascading around her shoulders and halfway down the back of the knee length black trench coat that adorns her. I've noticed this woman has frequented this café quite a bit as of late. And she happens to be the very person I've been anxiously waiting to get a glimpse of today. Her deep, red lipstick is the perfect shade against her cream complexion and matches the soles of the pair of black stilettos on her feet that now clack along the tile as she makes her way toward the counter. A diamond studded butterfly rests on the back of each heel. I recall them being the very thing that hooked my attention the first time I'd seen her three weeks prior. I was standing behind her in line and noticed them shimmering while looking down to answer a text.

For some bizarre reason, she always wears these shoes. I haven't seen her without them. And whatever she wears always matches them perfectly, and I do mean perfectly. Black and red outfits must be the only garments in her closet.

There's a certain look about her, fierce yet sweet. She's an exquisite beauty, the type I imagine many women envy. I'd argue that she's almost out of place here, based on appearance alone.

I glance down at my watch, taking note that she's forty minutes later than usual. I had begun to think she wouldn't show. Her presence has become my guilty pleasure. I've developed an odd fascination for her that I can't shake. The most newsworthy person on Earth could walk through those doors right now and my curiosity for them would still pale in comparison to how it piques for her. It's baffling to find that, after weeks of observing her, I still cannot understand why she intrigues me.

Perhaps it's the air she carries about her, a profound confidence and assuredness, that I find most captivating. Perhaps it's the touch of softness in her fiery eyes. Whatever it is has created an epic battle in my mind, an internal conflict raging over my next move. Should I continue to observe from a distance, or should I do something a little different and approach her, ask her questions in hopes she'd be open to answering? This is what I'm good at after all. I mean, yeah, I'm an excellent observer, but I'm known best for my reporting. I consider it one of my great accomplishments to have become generally successful as a freelance journalist here in France. Though, not just here, I do a lot of work for news companies all over Europe; something I've been at for four years now.

I began my career at twenty-two, leaving my modest home life in Nebraska for the Parisian lifestyle. It's the job I've wanted since I was a young girl. I was often found with my face in an autobiography, or with pen to paper, gathering intel and conducting interviews with neighbors and peers. I didn't start off as freelance upon arriving in Paris but, after two years of someone else dictating what I wrote, and ultimately not recognizing me for what I bring to the table, I made it a mission to pave my own way in this fine city and create a name for myself.

It's strange for me, being twenty-seven. I loathe the fact that my age, coupled with my looks, prevents many individuals from taking me seriously, especially when it comes to my job. The way I see it, I've had to work harder than most, especially men, to get where I am and even then, it's still an uphill battle.

In my career, I pride myself on knowing when there's a truly great story to be written. This woman, dressed head to toe in all black and red, has a remarkable story my fingers itch to write, I can sense it. And yet, there's this small worry that I may never get that chance. I cannot comprehend why I've been struggling so greatly with the courage to just go up and ask all the burning questions I'm eager to obtain answers to. But perhaps this is the day I may finally pull it together and chase the story that's beckoning me from her aura; wafting in my direction with the scent of that expensive perfume I know she must be wearing.

I observe her gaze slowly passing through the room as she waits in line, scanning intently until finally, those eyes filled with the promise of depth, fall on me. I suck in a sharp breath in shock. "Shit!" I mutter, immediately looking down. Grabbing my pen, I feverishly scribble on the paper pad in front of me, pretending to appear busy, but my pen produces nothing but a bunch of pathetic squiggles and scratches, proof of my utter mortification. I intended on approaching her, but I don't want it to come across as though I'm stalking her!

My phone buzzes, vibrating loudly on the table and I jump, already a heart pounding mess. It's a text from my friend and colleague, Arthur.

Jess, where are you? PLEASE tell me you didn't forget about the meeting!

Crap, the meeting!

Dante Ritter, the Chief Editor of Eiffel Inc., has requested I attend a meeting in which he will discuss an assignment he wants me to take on. As a freelancer, being requested by Ritter is not only a big deal, but extremely rare. He doesn't usually like to venture outside his company for work on a story.

The meeting starts in ten minutes! I don't know why I thought it started an hour later. If I miss this opportunity, I'm certain I won't see another. In a hurried rush, I gather my things, shoving notebooks and utensils violently in my bag, along with my laptop. Amid grabbing a stack of sheets, I knock my box of paper clips to the ground that had, apparently, been resting on top of them. The little pains in the ass fly everywhere and I scramble onto my hands and knees to scoop up as much as I can to leave the floor decent enough. I don't want to come across as a complete ass at the place I frequent quite often myself.

As I turn on my knees to place the handfuls of clips in the box, I come face to toe with the stilettos that have been at the forefront of my mind for weeks. I was so caught up in the madness I failed to hear the noise they must have made as they approached. Yet, here they are, right in front of me, demanding my full attention, and I give it. I give it all. Paper clips be damned!

My gaze slowly travels from the shoes to the deep blue-green eyes looking down at me. My finger slides my glasses to their proper position on my nose as my eyes stay glued to hers.

"Vous me regardez," she says. Her voice is light as a feather yet holds such strength.

"Uh, pardon?" I reply to her bold statement which I understood in English as, "You've been watching me."

An eyebrow shoots up and she slightly tilts her head to one side. "You are American?" Damn, is my accent that noticeable, even in French?

"Oui–um, yes, I am." Suddenly aware of my awkward position, I rise to my feet, running my hands down my black slacks to smooth out the wrinkles and come almost eye level with her. She's taller than my five-foot-six frame by a few inches. I credit it to the support on her feet. A breeze blows in from the closing front door and confirms what I had guessed about her perfume. I knew it was expensive. A smell like that is one of a kind.

"You've been watching me." Though she has a strong French accent, I can tell she's fluent in English.

I swallow hard and find myself at a loss for words, unable to be as clever as I usually am. What can I possibly say that won't make me look like a loon?

She tips her head, gesturing to a few sheets of paper still scattered on the table. "You're a writer." It isn't a question.

I nod my head, more to snap myself out of my state of shock than to answer. "A journalist, actually."

Her full rouge lips softly part in understanding as she brushes a couple of the pages with her fingertips. Her brow creases as she calculates my words, perhaps with suspicion. "What is it you write about?"

"Well, I'm an entertainment journalist. I cover things like celebrities, events, books, prominent figures in a community, any kind of entertainment that makes for a compelling story."

She smiles softly. "Ah, I see."

"I'm sorry if I've made you nervous at all. I'm very observant. 'Watching people' is kind of a hobby of mine I suppose." Dear God, can I sound any creepier?

"So, you're trying to figure out my story?" Her question catches me off guard, as does my phone buzzing wildly in my hand.

"Uh, excuse me for just a moment." I frantically turn away to answer the call, speaking in a hushed tone. "Arthur, hey–"

"Jess, where the hell are you? I can only make excuses for you for so long before Ritter gets more impatient than he *already is.*"

"I know, I know, I'm so sorry Art. I'm on my way. Give me five." I hang up and spin back around in time to see a red umbrella leave out the door and cross the street.

Welp, I've certainly found my word of the day. "Shit…"

2

I am officially twenty minutes late walking through the front doors of Eiffel. I booked it over here. Lucky for me, the café is close by which helped me out a bit—but only a bit. I still need to make it to the conference room and Eiffel is quite large, as it's not just the paper but the news station as well. The headquarters has fifteen floors and close to eleven hundred staff members in-house! I expect the journey to the twelfth floor is going to take a minute, so I scramble through the rush of busy-bodies and onto an overcrowded elevator, praying to the heavens that this doesn't cost me Dante Ritter's interest in keeping me on his extremely short list of desired freelancers.

The elevator makes multiple stops and I feel the weight of every second that ticks by. Eventually, a large group deboards, providing me with some temporary relief. The crowded elevator was doing very little to alleviate my anxiety! However, that initial relief is replaced with dread when a few more folks get on in their place. I was not prepared for this emotional ride this morning. As the last couple people get off two floors below mine, I whisper a silent prayer of gratitude.

A man shouts in French, "Hold the elevator please!" just as the doors start to close. Despite wanting nothing more than to have a moment of solitude on this godforsaken elevator ride, I quickly stick my arm out and trigger the doors to fully open again. I'm mentally kicking myself. Why do I do this? I mean, I know I didn't want to be perceived as an asshole, but I also could have made it to a meeting I'm already late to if I pretended not to hear him. The man jogs on and thanks me ten times over. His face, along with the pits of his business shirt, are drenched in sweat, and he grips a cup of coffee in each hand. Guess I'm not the only one behind schedule this morning.

As I finally step off onto the floor I need, a familiar voice calls out to me. "Jess!" Arthur takes hurried paces my way. Other than a few long, brown strands of hair coming loose from his slicked back 'do, and the stress evident on his face, he certainly looks more collected than I am. His black vest and pants are nicely pressed—a distinct contrast to my wrinkled beige sweater. The sleeves of his crisp white dress shirt are rolled up to the elbows, showing off his toned and tan forearms. I have to hand it to Art, his classy and professional style never falters and adds to his attractiveness. I'm a sucker for a man with a good fashion sense.

"I know, I know. I really hope I didn't screw myself on this one. Is he still going to see me?"

"I was able to buy you some time. I think he knows how punctual you've been in the past and assumes you have a good reason for being late. He's still in there." I exhale a huge sigh of relief. I can't believe I had allowed myself to get so sidetracked.

Art follows as I walk in the direction of the conference room. "So, what's up?" He asks. "Why so late? It's not like you."

"Honestly, I'm afraid I don't really have a good reason. God, I've been so out of it lately. I need to get it together. Something like this can never happen again."

"For what it's worth, you look great for someone who practically ran over here." A sarcastic smile creeps up his face. "You always have a way of making disheveled look good."

I playfully roll my eyes. "I want to hate you sometimes, but I can't. Thank you for the save. I owe you one."

"I know, and I've already come up with the perfect way you can pay me back. Dinner with me the Tuesday after next at that fancy new bistro that just opened in town. I know you've been wanting to go. It was tight but I was able to make the reservations. What do you say?"

"Hmm, interesting."

"What?"

"Well Arthur Reed, if I didn't know any better, I'd say you conspired with the higher powers that be so that I'd owe you one."

"I'm not usually the type to give away my secrets but what if I did?"

I smirk. "Then I'd say I'm highly impressed."

If there's anyone to thank for my growing success at Eiffel, it's Arthur. Without him, I'm not sure I would have ever got an in. As the Assistant Editor-in-Chief, he's had a lot of sway with getting my publications…well…published! I met him during a wine tasting at a mutual friend's house a little over two years after arriving in Paris. We hit it off instantly, discussing everything from family to politics to the very thing we both loved: journalism. I knew he was American because of his accent but didn't catch on to him being a New Yorker. Living in France must've smoothed out the twang in his native tongue. It was wonderful to have met someone else from the states. Right away, it felt like we'd been friends for ages!

I had no idea just how prominent he was in my field until three glasses of wine later, when I opened up to him about my many horrendous work experiences. He listened intently, afterwards expressing his interest in reading one of my pieces. I ended up pulling out a couple of articles I carried with me in my purse, and he loved them! Next thing I knew, he asked me to bring in something new to present to him and, two weeks later, I found myself in front of not only him, but Ritter too, signing all the right papers to get my story published.

From then on, we've had a great friendship. He was the first person in all of Paris I felt took me seriously, not judging me by anything other than my skills. Because of his generosity, I gained increased notoriety and respect in the field. Given all the ways he's looked out for me, including covering for me today, I suppose accepting his offer to a fancy dinner is the least I can do, even knowing that recently, Arthur has wanted our friendship to blossom into something more.

We reach the door to the conference room and I give him my answer. "Hmm… that sounds fair. Tuesday, it is! Let's chat more after." He nods his head with content.

I proceed to try and sneak my way through the large oak double doors with no success. Two sets of eyes instantly fall on me. Me and my moisture zapped hair, potentially crooked glasses, and a file full of disheveled papers under one arm. Peachy.

Clearing my throat, I set my glasses atop my head and address the two gentlemen, one of whom happens to be my arch nemesis, Charles Deflour, the only other freelance journalist Ritter hires. We keep things professional enough, but we despise each other to the core. Motivated by his major hard on for competition, he constantly aims to beat me to a front-page story.

"My sincere apologies for my tardiness." I don't dare look at Ritter, whose pen tapping cuts through the silence. I, instead, hurry my way to the available seat at his desk.

After what seems like a lengthy period of awkward tension, Charles continues his initial discussion with Ritter in French. "As I was saying, this story will be worthy of the front cover." Insert eye roll.

"I have faith it will be. You never fail to impress, Charles." Ritter may have been smitten with me over the last few years, but he treats Charles like the son he's never had, a fact that makes me loath the young, charming, arrogant man even more. It's hard enough making it this far in the industry being a woman, especially a woman as young as I am and from a different country. I want to be taken just as seriously for my work as he is, but I know in my heart of hearts that a big part of my current success, besides Arthur's connections, is largely credited to my double D breasts, petite hourglass frame and big brown eyes.

I learned the hard way, at the start of my journey here in Paris, that my looks were being far more valued than my skills and expertise in my profession. The first company I worked for was much like this one in terms of popularity and I found it unbearable. Very little creative freedom was given, there was hardly any recognition for the hard work I put in, and to top it all off, the work environment was toxic. I was harassed repeatedly, constantly groped, checked out, talked to as though I was some clueless American bimbo, and a couple times I was even sniffed. SNIFFED! My boss was the most horrendous when it came to the type of perverse treatment I received.

HR was no help at all so, with the understanding that I had no true support in my corner, I made the decision to branch off on my own and make a name for myself. For a while it was a struggle getting my work published, let alone viewed by anyone. Many would pass before they even read the first sentence which was so disheartening.

Ultimately, I discovered that there were typically two roadblocks that stood in the way of me getting to where I wanted to be in the industry: either they didn't see me as experienced and, as such, felt it was a waste of their time to invest in something "juvenile" or they were more invested in my looks than my work.

Because of this, I began to purposely dress in a way that would be considered less attractive, and I altered my appearance to appear more "mature and intellectual". I covered myself up by wearing clothing that fit looser and hid all the assets men and women would gawk over. I also stopped wearing makeup and started pulling my hair back into a basic but decent bun. Right away, there were notable differences in how I was treated. I still receive the occasional interest sand ogling, but things are way better than they were, especially in a work environment. I now feel more seen for the work I cherish so much.

Ritter speaks to the both of us, "I have one last thing I'd like to discuss. I'm sure it comes as a surprise that I brought you both in for this meeting. I'm certain you've heard that Alexander Marc, CEO of Ether Inc., is in town to prepare and host a charity banquet in a few weeks' time. I have asked his permission to send someone in to report on the planning leading up to the event, as well as the turnout.

"However, what I truly want is to know more about who he is; his home life, his inspirations, what his relationships were like with his parents, especially his father. I want to know about his romantic interests, hobbies, the challenges he's had to face in his career. You understand where I'm going with this. It needs to be something that really gives all of Europe a fresh perspective on this man. A story they've never heard before. Who is he? People have been waiting a long time to find out."

Alexander Marc is one of the youngest billionaires alive. He is thirty, but his success took off about eight years ago. An unfortunate event led to him inheriting his father's dwindling mass media marketing company at eighteen and, in three short years, he somehow managed to turn it into one of the most successful companies in the world. He's a true entrepreneur, as well as an extremely secretive man when it comes to his personal life. To tap into the world of Marc was a challenge many journalists would, and have, grabbed at the chance to take on, either to try and get a scoop of dirt that could rock the foundation of his empire or just to satisfy curiosity.

"I could have given this assignment to anyone of my team members here, but after much thought and consideration, I think it best to hire outside the company. Which leads me to the reason you both have been asked to attend this meeting. I'd like to hear each of your pitches for this assignment. Why you?"

Before I can respond, Charles opens his obnoxious mouth. "What you really mean is why her. Ritter, you know me. I have produced twelve highly successful articles for you since my first publication with Eiffel three years ago. Five of those made the front page. If what you want is fresh and enticing information on Alexander Marc, I already have a few ideas on how I can make that happen. I'm sharp, dependable, and not only do I find the facts, I back them with evidence. Not to mention I come with experience, something I believe Jessy here doesn't have enough of." He looks over at me and smirks.

I return the gesture. "Are you done?"

His smirk fades, and I watch the hope of having fulfilled a potential burn fade from his eyes. "Sir, let's be honest for a moment. Everyone knows that Alexander Marc won't open up to just anyone. Charles has far too much ego to approach that man and receive positive results. This assignment needs a woman's touch." Charles snickers but I ignore him. "Think about how many journalists and reporters have tried to pull information from Alexander. He's smart. There's no way he's going to trust that a man with the kind of portfolio and overconfidence that Charles has, will really show up to interview him with the intentions of just covering his event. I believe I have an advantage here. Many men underestimate women. And much of the work I've done in the past aligns with the type of article he believes we're after. If I go in with a gentle and innocent approach, he's more likely to let his guard down."

Ritter brings his clasped hands to rest underneath his chin and glances between myself and Charles before speaking. "Okay. Rivers, this one is yours."

I realize I've been holding my breath as I release a sigh of relief and satisfaction. I take a victory glance toward Mr. Ego as he smooths out his jacket and slicks a hand through his hair trying to mask his disappointment and irritation. I'm shocked. I was sure that Ritter would have gone for Charles, the suck up. This assignment would have been huge for him. But, by some incredible miracle, it's been bestowed to me! I'm beaming! I was not expecting to be offered the opportunity to take on a story this big.

Upon the deepening realization of my task ahead, I feel an overwhelming surge of anticipation and hope. If I can give all of Europe, perhaps even the world, a fresh scoop into the life of one of the biggest and most secluded billionaire bachelors, I may never be taken for granted again. That prospect alone is thrilling!

"Don't disappoint, Jess."

"I won't let you down, Sir." I can't afford to, the rest of my career may very well ride on this.

Ritter switches to broken English momentarily. "Bien. You're both dismissed." We rise from our seats. "Actually, Jess, un moment s'il vous plaît." I pause. Charles gives me a begrudging look and proceeds to walk out.

When the door clicks shut, Ritter walks around his desk and up to me, stopping a mere foot from where I stand. He's so close I can smell the onion soup he had for lunch on his breath. Arthur told me it's the same meal he has for lunch every day. I hate onion soup.

"I don't need to remind you of the importance of this assignment. Remember, it will take some finesse. Incorporate the event of course but, in order to retrieve the information that will shape an even bigger story, you're going to need to make him want to open up about his life. Ask the right questions while making him feel… comfortable. I know you can do that." His hazel eyes find my chest and I see his Adam's apple move in that way that makes me want to punch him across his wide, obtuse jaw for the perverted thoughts I'm sure he must be thinking, but I remain calm. Comfortable, indeed. He's getting all too familiar with the word.

His eyes return to my face, where they should have stayed. "To tell you the truth, I had already chosen you for this. But I had to be sure of how hungry you are for it. I knew seeing Charles here would bring that out of you." He winks. "You'll need to work out the times with Alexander's assistant, but he's expecting you sometime this week. Arthur will send any further details along with the contractual agreement."

"Great, I will get started as soon as possible!" I gather my things hurriedly.

"Wait. You were late today."

Damn! I was really hoping to avoid this conversation. "I know and I sincerely apologize. I misunderstood the time, which hardly ever happens to me."

He places both hands in his pockets. "I know. In fact, I don't recall the last time you've been tardy, if ever. Is there something I need to know about? Something that could interfere with the successful outcome of this assignment?"

My mind briefly flashes back to the earlier events this morning: the rain, the heels, the red and black attire, the soul-searching eyes, my utter mortification. "No sir, everything is fine, I just had a rare moment. It won't happen again."

He moves a hand up to my face, pausing just shy of my cheek, then pulls it back, gently clearing his throat. "You have a few hairs out of place." My fingers move to correct it and then I return to collecting my items.

"Thank you for this opportunity." I say, as I adjust my bag strap. "You won't regret it." I turn to make my retreat out the double doors.

"Jess." He calls out to me. "If you have any problems, let me know." I am unsure how to take his underhanded concern or what problems he thinks I'd inform him about. "Of course." Choosing not to dwell on it, I continue my swift exit.

As I make it out into the small foyer, I notice some other journalists gathered and chatting amongst themselves. Among them is Charles. He's such a bitter, egotistical, little French man, standing about four inches shorter than me. What he lacks in height, however, he certainly makes up for in mouth. The man's vast vocabulary does not contain the word "filter".

Art comes up beside me. "Uh-oh. I know that look."

I let out a frustrated sigh. "You didn't tell me Deflour was in there."

"You'd understand my reasoning if you could see how your eye is twitching like you took a bite out of the bitterest lemon on earth." He chuckles.

"It is not."

"If you insist." He winks and looks over at Charles who's now aware of our presence as he walks toward us. "Why don't you go? I'll preoccupy him. We'll catch up more later."

I don't hesitate. As I expeditiously make my way past Charles, he gives me an over dramatic bow. "No time to stay and chat today, Jessy?" He chortles, and I huff in agitation.

*C*urled up in bed, I throw myself into researching all I can on Alexander Marc, clicking through multiple photographs and articles which mainly speak about his business, his father's death, or his completely private life. Articles with headlines such as, *'Heir to the throne or heir to ruin?'*, *'Who is Marc?'* Or *'Bizarre Bachelor Mystery'*, grace the search engine pages. Absolutely no one seems to really know much detail about his life or how he's managed to turn rubble into an empire so quickly. It's eerie, and certainly does nothing to encourage my confidence in the success of my mission. My determination though, is unwavering. I have been given a significant opportunity. I fully intend to milk it for all it's worth.

An email notification pops up on my screen. Information from Art regarding contacting Marc's assistant for the interview, along with a smiley face and a short message that reads, "*Good luck!*". I let out an exasperated breath. From the looks of things, I'm going to need it

3

Standing outside the Marc estate, I watch the doorman pull away with my car to park it in some designated location, then I turn and gaze up at the massive home with its high, white, stone walls. It has a charm to it that is inviting and very pleasing to the eye. One of the red, front double doors opens and a woman with a rich, dark brown complexion, in a superb navy pinstriped suit, walks out displaying a dazzling smile. "Ms. Rivers, a pleasure!" She extends a hand as she descends the marble stairs to meet me, her jet black curls bouncing with each step. I meet her halfway to shake her hand.

"I'm Carmyn Calloway, Mr. Marc's assistant." She's so gorgeous and has such a graceful, confident air about her. Her greeting brings attention to her British dialect. The same dialect I assume Alexander Marc has, being that he's also from Britain. "I was just about to call you when I was told you arrived."

"Yes, I decided to come a little early in case Mr. Marc had any extra time to spare."

"Punctual. Good for you! Unfortunately, he is running late. His car got into a bit of an accident on its way here which is what I intended to call you about."

"Oh! Is he alright?"

"Perfectly fine. If anything, he's just severely flustered about the incident and the fact that this is putting a dent in his schedule today, but he's well."

If the plan is still to meet him today, flustered isn't going to make for an easy interview. "Would you like me to reschedule our meeting?"

"You're in luck actually. His following appointment cancelled. He approved of the idea to use that time to see you instead. It just may be a wait if that's alright."

I smile, nervous, but grateful. "I'd be more than happy to wait." Carmyn escorts me into the home, leading me through the large entry way, past a grand ballroom and into what looks like a living area with a personal bar.

"Would you like something to drink? Coffee perhaps?"

"Yes. Coffee would be wonderful, thank you." I'm awestruck gazing around the classy room. I'd been to quite a few properties to conduct my interviews with various individuals, but I never quite saw anything so dreamy. Large, glass windows frame the room almost entirely, providing a stunning view of a shimmering lake, framed with breathtaking foliage. It's a sight to behold. Inside, water rains down from the corner of a ceiling into a small pool below with big, healthy Koi circling one another. A white, grand piano sits next to an impressive bar, which appears to have been made from a huge, polished slab of crystal quartz. The library of liquor, wine and various other bar delights are immaculately displayed. The walls that do exist appear to be adorned with the same kind of crystal as the bar. The entire space has a certain charm and elegance to it.

It's clear, from the heavenly aroma in the air, that coffee had already been prepared prior to my arrival. I take a seat at the bar just as Carmyn finishes pouring a cup for me. She slides it my way, along with some cream and sugar, and then pours some for herself. "It's from Guatemala. They have the absolute best coffee in my opinion. I'm usually more of a tea enthusiast, but I'd set aside good tea for this marvel."

I take a sip and revel in the smooth taste. She's right, it's incredible! "Thank you for the hospitality."

"Absolutely. It's the least I can do. Mr. Marc finds it imperative that all his guests be comfortable."

I take this opportunity to see what information I can pull from her about Alexander. The woman is almost always around him, I'm sure. She must know something that could be of value. "When we spoke on the phone, you mentioned that it's rare for Mr. Marc to do interviews. Why is that?"

"Isn't it obvious, Ms. Rivers? He's a private man. Personally, I commend him for it. One would think a man of his age and financial means would be strutting around the world like he's untouchable, but Mr. Marc is very sensible and mature. Like him, I believe that when you run the type of empire he does, it's important for the sake of yourself, your company and those who work for you that your personal life remains…personal."

"I can understand that, but he doesn't even talk much about his own company. Bill Gates gave way more interviews in a year than he's given in his entire career."

"Well, I think you just found another question to ask him." Her face takes on a more serious look. "You seem like a smart woman, Ms. Rivers, and a nice one at that, but I've encountered my fair share of journalists and I know that sniffing out dirty laundry to air can be like heroin to your blood streams. A word of advice? Just do the story you're here for and be grateful he's even allowing a journalist into his home, much less allowing you to interview him."

I'm taken aback by her bold and blunt response. I'm not entirely sure what I was expecting but I've definitely been shut all the way down by her. "Oh, of course! I'm sorry if it came off as baiting." Even though that's exactly what I was doing. "I was simply curious. He seems like such an interesting man and I feel like the world would love to get to know a little more about him someday."

"Mm, I'm certain the world would, because the world doesn't know how to mind their own bloody business."

It becomes clear that I need to back off any further questions regarding her boss. She's going to be just as guarded as he is, if not more, and I can't blame her. No one wants to hire an assistant who spills their whole life story to anyone and everyone. In addition to that, pressing the matter any further will likely make her far more suspicious of my intentions than she already is.

I change the subject, asking a bit about her instead which she's much more open to discussing. She tells me she was born in Wales, the daughter of a Neurology professor and a socialite mother. Becoming an assistant to one of the world's most influential billionaires was never something she grew up expecting, let alone wanting, but after a favor for a family member gave her a chance meeting with him, her world took quite an unexpected turn. She was hired by Alexander Marc a little over three years ago, a day she says was the one of the best days of her life.

"When I started, it seemed like the hardest job in the world, and I'll be the first to admit I majorly screwed up a couple times. I don't know how Mr. Marc had the patience considering there were at least ten assistants before me who all lasted less than four months. He's very particular about who he hires. If he's not satisfied with your work, you're out. I learn quickly though –one of my strengths– and by the fifth month I figured if I was still here, I must be doing something right, or at least better than those before me."

Carmyn refills my cup while she continues before pouring herself another. I'm getting much more comfortable. We both are, I think. It's nice getting into my element of finding out someone's story. I imagine the reason Carmyn was open to telling hers to me is because she may not have much time to socialize with people outside the hectic world of her profession. It's probably nice for her to talk to someone about something besides when she can squeeze them in or other administrative matters.

After a while, one of the three phones she has on her person goes off. "Excuse me." She leaves the room and I sit listening to the droplets of water raining down the serene fall.

I steal a quick glance at my watch. I'm surprised to see I've already been here for about an hour. "Ms. Rivers, my apologies." I'm startled by the baritone voice and spin around on my stool to see the man I've come here to meet walk into the room. "I know you've been waiting quite a while. Thank you for your patience." It's as if an angel has entered, draped in charm and elegance. The photos of this man were attractive but do him no justice at all! Alexander Marc is beyond handsome. I'd place him somewhere around six-foot, dark curly hair that's cut to a fade toward the nape of his neck and an olive complexion that I know is credited to his half Italian heritage.

I rise from my seat and meet him in the middle of the floor, shaking his extended hand, his grip warm and firm. "It's quite alright, Mr. Marc, I was happy to wait, and Ms. Calloway was very hospitable. I should be thanking you for still agreeing to meet with me, even after what I'm sure has been a very stressful day."

He gives a quick and faint smile. "Why don't you follow me to my office, we can talk there."

As he escorts me through an enormous hall, I can't help but admire his tailored navy-blue suit. For someone who had a bit of a bender earlier, he's rather put together. Even his demeanor is calmer than I'd expected. He walks with one hand in his pocket. The other swings by his side and I notice the small silver initials engraved on the cuff of his dress shirt.

A. J. M.

For Alexander James Marc.

Not a word is spoken on the way to his office, and I wonder if I should say something, anything. Is he waiting for me to speak, or does he prefer taking his guests on silent walks? To hell with it, I'm going to take a crack at breaking the ice. "You have a breathtaking home Mr. Marc. I can honestly say I've never seen anything quite like it."

He looks back at me with hooded gray eyes under long lashes, another hint of a smile grazes his lips. "I'm happy you like it. It's one of my many vacation homes. Not my favorite place to dwell but then again, it's not often I spend time in Paris these days." When we reach what I can only assume is his office, he opens the door and holds it for me to enter.

The office, unlike the rest of the home, is practically bare, with the exception of a large oak desk with two plush chairs in front and his leather throne behind it. There are also a couple of tall plants standing on either side of the door; their lush green complimenting the glossy cherry-stained hardwood floor. The walls are white, which reflect what sunshine comes from the large windows behind the desk, making the whole room radiant and bright.

Alexander walks past me to his desk, gesturing for me to have a seat which I gladly take. I smile at him as he takes his seat and I immediately get down to business, whipping out my notebook and pen along with my recorder. I hit the record button. "So, Mr. Marc, the media is buzzing with talk of your presence in the city which I suppose brings us to the reason for our meeting today. As I'm sure you're aware, I'm interested in composing an article on your upcoming charity event. My hope is to provide people with a better grasp on the event and the production leading up to it. Give them a glimpse of what putting together this type of charity is like, what it means to you, and the positive impact you believe it will have."

He leans back in his chair, long steepled fingers resting against his chin lightly shadowed in hair. "Tell me Ms. Rivers, as I'm sure you've done your homework, what positive impact do you think my charity will have?"

I expected there would be some sort of a test like this, and I came ready. "Well for starters, I think it's a phenomenal thing Ether Incorporated is doing, having sustainable relief shelters constructed in high-risk areas across the world. The technology behind the architecture alone is sure to prove very successful but the number of lives that can be saved is far more impressive. There should be a lot more focus on ways to proactively prevent such tragedies rather than planning during the aftermath."

Marc remains silent. His mesmerizing, sultry gray eyes stay fixed on me, studying me hard. I can't tell if it's with fondness or judgment. Maybe both? I shift slightly in my seat, finding it difficult to ignore the small stirring in my nether regions. Keep it together Jess!

"Um. So yes, I- I think this event will not only generate great support, but awareness of something that has the potential to be a serious game changer when it comes to areas of the world that experience the most destruction when mother nature rears her head. I read somewhere that you are looking to build schools as well. If I may ask, what's your motive behind these endeavors?"

He finally responds. "I'd like to make a difference in the world, like anyone else. I certainly have the means to, so why not?"

Not exactly the answer I was hoping for. "Yes, but often people with great means invest it into passion projects, be it family related, past related, experience motivated. How about you? What inspired you to go about this?" I press my pen firmly against the paper. My hand, more than eager to write.

Come on Marc. Give me something. ANYTHING.

"Family. Family inspired me." Yes! Now we are getting somewhere.

"How so?"

"Do you have any other questions for me?" I halt my feverish scribbling and look up, thinking I'd see a mask of irritation to match the slightly clipped tone of his question, but all I see is the same unyielding expression he's kept since taking his seat. The man has a serious poker face.

"Oh, um, yes. Yes, I do." I take a moment to recollect my thoughts that have now become horribly scattered. I proceed by asking about plans for the charity banquet instead, like the anticipated number of attendees and who the speakers will be other than himself. All mundane questions that lead to answers lacking the extra something I've been tasked with finding. I knew it would be a challenge getting him to spill details that were personal in some regard, but I didn't think he'd be this damn guarded! It's proving terribly difficult in fact. Every time I try to direct the conversation to anything remotely about him, he redirects me. What's his deal? Is it necessary to be *this* private?

After about thirty minutes of basic chatter, I bring my interview to a close. "Well, I think I got everything I need for today." As if.

I start packing away my notes when he asks, "Are you sure about that?" Head tilted to one side, he eyes me with suspicion. "You seem a little dissatisfied."

A knot forms in my throat as I put on my most convincing smile. "On the contrary, I find this story intriguing already. We're off to a great start! Thank you for your time, Mr. Marc." We both stand and I extend my hand. "I'll see you next Saturday at the manor to discuss the set up for the banquet?"

"I'll make sure we note it in the schedule. Let me call Carmyn to show you out."

"Oh, no need. I recall the way." I proceed to exit. Hesitation, however, brings me to a pause at the doorway. There is, in fact, something I am still itching to understand, well, besides the totality of who he is.

"Actually, I do have one more question." I look back at him. "Why did you agree to this interview? To my knowledge you very rarely speak with journalists or reporters of any kind."

Still standing, he lays his hands on his desk and leans into their support. "Mm, I suppose you could say I owe Dante a favor."

Ritter? How does such a secretive and prominent man end up owing the Chief Editor of Eiffel a favor? I thought he stayed away from anyone associated with the press. He smirks at my evident confusion. "Perhaps a story for another time, Ms. Rivers."

"Yes…Good day Mr. Marc."

He gives a curt nod and I head out the door. My mind is struggling to accept what happened. With the info I've collected, my piece will, at best case, be handed back to me with a dissatisfied look or two. Knowing Ritter, however, it would end up thrown in the bin right in front of me.

As I enter the large front foyer, my cell vibrates in my bag, and I stop to answer. "Arthur, hey."

"Is everything okay? I was beginning to think things went downhill."

"Everything's fine." God do, I hope so. "Marc had to push the meeting back last minute, so I'd been waiting around for a bit."

The Doorman spots me through the front window and I signal to him that I'm ready, then proceed to lower the tone of my voice, aware that I'm still in the echoing mansion. "This might be way harder than I thought, Art. He doesn't trust me one bit, I can see it all over his body language and I hear it in his tone."

"Well of course he doesn't trust you Jess, what did you expect? You literally just met the man for Christ's sake!"

"I know that, but this feels…different. It's like he suspects me of something. Like he knows I'm not here to only cover this event." I still feel the weight of his gaze on my skin.

"I think you're probably being paranoid. Tell you what, this was a big day for you. Swing by my place? We'll have a couple of drinks and laugh away the stress."

Perhaps he's right. Perhaps it's the guilt of knowing I'm trying to stick my nose where it doesn't really belong that's making me think things that aren't necessarily true. After all, I'm one of the lucky few granted the privilege of interviewing him. If he was that suspicious of me, I'm sure he would have turned me away after ten minutes or refused to meet me next Saturday.

I rub my hand on my neck, attempting to relieve some tension and steady my still worked up heart. "I don't know. It does sound wonderful but I–" A soft clicking noise, like that of a latch, comes from the right of me and I spin in the direction of the sound. There's no one there, but there's, indeed, a door that could have been the source of the noise. My mind immediately wants to write it off as a minute thing, however something overpowers that want– perhaps intuition.

"Jess?"

"I'll call you back."

4

---

*a*s I end the call, my eyes remain fixed on the white, paneled door. I walk up to it, my hand shaking as I reach for the handle. I clasp my other hand around it to get it to stop. Questions flood my mind. Am I going to find someone on the other side of this door? If so, what of my short conversation with Arthur did they hear? And what would I say to Alexander if I get caught wandering where I shouldn't be? Curiosity trumps all at this moment and I make a final attempt at the door handle, pulling it down and walking forward into the room, a dimly lit room.

"Hello?" No answer. My eyes adjust to the light and I now see that I've walked into a large library. Every wall is covered in books apart from the wall facing the front of the house, which has two enormous windows with thick dark curtains drawn shut. A lamp in the far back corner is the only light illuminating the massive area.

"Hello? Is someone in here?" I wander further in, examining the room. My eyes are steady searching for something or someone I'm not even sure of. As I diligently scan the room, one thing becomes clear– if there was, in fact, someone here, they aren't anymore– at least not that I am able to see.

"Pardon, Madame." I whirl around shrieking, throwing my hands over my mouth. The doorman stands in the doorway. Lowering my hands to my chest, I breathe a sigh of relief, but I'm certain the lowlight in the room cannot hide the embarrassment that flushes my face. I'm not supposed to be in here and I believe he knows it too.

"I'm so sorry! You startled me."

"My apologies, Madame. Your car is ready."

"Yes, of course." I follow the man out to my car and thank him big time for dealing with my rudeness and being so cool about it, although I know he probably feels it's not his place to say anything to me concerning the matter, even if he wants to. Either way, I'm appreciative. I secretly pray it doesn't get back to Alexander. I don't need anything adding to the complications I'm already experiencing.

Sluggishly, my eyes open as I'm pulled out of my dreams to the sound of loud rapping at the front door. I sit up and realize I'm on the couch. Wow, I must have been completely wiped after yesterday's affairs. I can't even recall shutting my eyes. The knocking comes again, and I groggily pull myself together and go to answer it.

Art stands bright eyed and bushy tailed on the other side, holding two to-go coffee cups and a white paper bag containing some mysterious item. "Well, well. Don't you look fresh this morning!" I roll my eyes and invite him in.

Arthur isn't just a great friend, he's also a fantastic listener, especially when I find myself in need of a good venting session. He is one of only a handful of Americans I've personally come to know here. I have fallen in love with Paris, a romance that began when I was a teen. Oh, how I do miss home though, and when I'm with him, I feel a bit closer to what I left behind. With Arthur there's an ease, a comfort, and a release of stress that he offers in allowing me to bare my soul and just be who I am.

"When you bailed on the offer for drinks last night, I figured you must have fallen ill so I came with the perfect medicine."

"Coffee?"

"Well, yes, always, that's a given. *But* the perfect elixir is coffee *and* these." He pushes the paper bag he brought with him across the kitchen island toward me and I curiously peek inside.

"Wait. Are these–"

"You're favorite flakey, delicious, chocolate chip croissants from La Peep? Oui, Madame!" He always knows how to get me to crack a smile, even on my toughest of days.

"I seriously appreciate it. And I'm so sorry I didn't call you back yesterday. I came home with a massive headache, sat down on the couch and was out like a light apparently."

"See? I knew you were ill." He winks as I take a giant bite out of one of the croissants, closing my eyes for a moment and reveling in its satisfying and delicious taste. "Better?" Mouth full, I nod in response.

"Wonderful. Now, break down for me what happened yesterday at the interview that had you so worried?" I hold up my finger, taking one more bite before answering with a deep sigh.

"What happened was I got nowhere. The man has zero interest in discussing anything that even remotely branches outside the topic of his event. And before you go on about how that was to be expected, I know that, but it doesn't solve the issue at hand. I need Alexander to give me *something*. I can't screw this up."

"You still have a few weeks to get everything together. You gotta stress less and focus more on how you can get him to be more forthcoming next time."

"Yeah, I suppose you're right. I did find out something interesting though. Did you know he owed Ritter some kind of favor? That's apparently why he agreed to the interview."

"Really? Hm, makes sense."

I stare at him with the same look of confusion that I had when Alexander provided that bit of information. "Does it, really? Because it makes absolutely no sense to me."

"Well, I, too, had wondered how Ritter even got the man to agree to an interview in the first place, but I didn't ask. That's a mighty big favor for Marc standards."

A huge favor! How did a multi-billionaire come to owe Ritter anything? I'm only on day two of this assignment and I'm already on the verge of drowning in the number of complex questions my mind has been piling up. I stare off into the distance, pondering for a while before Art speaks again. "There you go with that look. The super-sleuth-putting-pieces-to-the-puzzle-together look."

"Super Sleuth? HA! To be honest, the more I think about it, the more I'm shocked that I was even considered for this assignment to begin with. Ritter knows that investigative journalism is not my forte."

"I believe that's precisely why he chose you. Your background mostly covers lighthearted entertainment pieces. No doubt, Alexander has done some investigation of his own. If he had, that's most likely all he'd have seen of your work. Not only that, but you aren't actually an employee of the company. The way I see it, he's far more likely to trust that you were a harmless journalist looking to get some fulfilling info on his event based off those reasons alone. More so than the likes of, let's say, Charles DeFlour, who has actually been known to dabble heavily in investigative work."

"Mm, yeah, that's a good point. I'm sure that's it."

He scans my torso while sipping his coffee. "And um, I'm sure it helps that you have quite an amazing rack. I'm speaking purely from his perspective here."

I roll my eyes and I cross my arms in distaste. "Not funny."

"What? Is it not true?"

"Oh, I don't know Arthur Reed. I suppose I'm a bit biased when it comes to rating my own breasts." I grab a newspaper laying on the counter, roll it up and playfully chuck it at him as he dodges with a huge grin on his face. "Honestly, what is it with you men? I could walk around wearing a potato sack and many of you will still find a way to sexualize my existence."

"Oh, come on, don't be like that! You're just an attractive woman is all. You can keep hiding yourself in all the baggy clothes you want Jess, but it's not going to hide the fact that you are desirable."

"And to think I ever thought of you as charming." I joke but I'm quite annoyed by his comment.

"Come now. You still do." He winks and takes another sip of his coffee. A lock of wavy light brown hair comes undone from its place and falls over his eye, making him look like a playful child for a moment until he slicks it back in place. His face glows with amusement. "Look, you're going to make this article happen. If anyone can do it, it's you."

I give a weary smile. Yesterday, I started off with so much confidence. Today, however, I can't fight this nerve-wracking feeling stirring within me. I prop my elbows on the counter and press my clasped hands against my forehead.

"Wanna talk about it?"

"No. I just need to focus and stop worrying so damn much." I stand up straight again and release a held breath. "Do you believe in miracles?"

"Well, when I was a boy, my uncle Joe almost choked to death on a fish bone while the family was out for lunch. Some stranger came by, gave him the Heimlich, and saved him from the horrific clutches of death. I suppose that counts as a miracle." I display a surrendered look of amusement at the overly dramatic ending to his story.

My gaze sweeps across the kitchen and out the window, as if the solution to gaining Alexander's vulnerability could be waiting just outside the glass. "I hope so. I'll need a miracle to pull this off."

Art walks around the island and comes up behind me, placing his hands on my shoulders, right at the base of my neck, and begins to apply medium pressure via deep circular motions. My head falls back a bit, giving in to the painful pleasure his movements evoke. He tells me to take deep, methodical breaths and I obey. "There you go. How does that feel?"

"Fucking amazing." I wish I knew Art was so skilled with his hands all this time. Perhaps I wouldn't be so constantly tense.

He steps closer and I allow my head to fall back to the point that it rests against his chest as he continues. Soon after, one of his hands gently moves down my collar bone, between my breasts and across my belly. The warm trail his fingers leave behind has my body buzzing and my mind unsure of whether to enjoy this or freak out. It's not like I don't want his touch. Art and I have been tiptoeing around our attraction for each other for about two years. Every day, desire radiates from him more intensely. It excites me, but also scares me like hell, and I can never understand why. Why can't I just let my best friend be more?

That same hand finds its way up and under my breast as he cups it, giving it gentle squeezes. His lips fall to the sacred place between my shoulder and neck, gently kissing and nipping. Dear God, I'm a sopping mess. My breathing is becoming harder to control.

"Art…" I breathe, completely flushed.

He whispers into my ear, "Just enjoy this, babe. You deserve it."

My body, which has been starved of intimacy for a couple years now, is ready to give in completely as he continues to take the lead. With careful swiftness, he bends me over the countertop. I can feel the cool marble through the thin fibers of my white camisole, making my nipples peak instantaneously. And they aren't the only things on the rise. I'm pinned from behind by the immense display of arousal in Arthur's pants.

His breathing, too, becomes heavier. His lips run a trail of delicious kisses across my back and neck as his hand travels to my waist, gripping it firmly while he makes subtle, deliberate motions with his hips. I'd be lying if I said I hadn't masturbated to this fantasy before. This fantasy of us, finally succumbing to our building feelings for one another. I want this! But… "Art, we shouldn't."

"We should." Another kiss is planted on my shoulder. "We really should."

I'm trying to stay in the moment but it's too late. My mind does not give a damn what my body wants. It has made the decision to freak out. "No, Art, wait!" With much force I push myself off the counter sending both of us flying back, dispersing ourselves to separate parts of the kitchen. "We can't do this. I- I'm not ready. I'm sorry. I'm so sorry. I'm just not ready."

The shock is evident on his face. He takes a moment but brings himself back down to earth and to the realization of my current state. "No, Jess, I'm sorry. I thought– you know what, never mind what I thought."

"It's not that I don't want to. I honestly don't know for sure what's holding me back. And that's the problem. I need to know because I need to be sure of us. Our friendship, what we've built together, means too much to me to not take such a big decision seriously, you know?" God, I hope he does. I hope he understands.

He walks toward me and with arms wide open, proceeds to envelop my petite frame in a thick, comforting embrace, and just holds me. "I understand, Jess. It means the world to me too." Whatever am I to do about this? As much as I feel the pressure to answer that question, I make a mental note to push the figuring out aside for another time. I have entirely too much that requires my attention, and I can't afford to get off track.

Since the interview, I've spent the past week in Milan working on a separate assignment. Now that I'm back, it's full steam ahead with my mission to find out all I can about the billionaire bachelor. After breakfast, I decided to take the opportunity to come to the café, sift through my notes and finally begin work on this article. I sit here at my favorite table, staring at my laptop, trying to figure out how to write the beginning of…the beginning of what? What am I writing the beginning to exactly? An article about an event that's merely an accessory to the real topic of interest? A topic I won't be covering at all if things keep going at this rate.

I groan and run my hands through my hair, as if doing so will bring a moment of comfort and clarity. It brings none. My mind remains as complicated and confused as the second before. "May

I sit?" I look up toward the direction of the voice that comes out of the blue.

When I finally process who stands before me, I fall into disbelief. It's Mystery Woman! The one frequenter in this whole damn café I know absolutely nothing about. Even her orders are never the same, only her shoes, which I take a quick glance down at. "Um, yeah! I mean, sure, it's not taken. Please." I gesture to the empty chair across from me.

"Merci." Her auburn waves bounce as she takes a seat. I notice that her tea is in a teacup today, which suggests she has plans to stay a while. I'm internally rejoicing at the thought that she, perhaps, plans to stay and chat with me a bit, especially since, from the moment she started coming to this café, she has always been a to-go gal. However, I am curious, suspicious even, about her reasoning for seeking a conversation with me. Perhaps she wants to talk about how rude or, possibly even suspicious, she thought I'd been the other day.

I observe her intently as she stirs her tea with impeccable grace. The soft *clink clink* of the spoon against the porcelain is practically rhythmic. Left to me, there would have been splotches of tea over the rim before I could even get it to my lips. Not because I'm clumsy, but because I tend to constantly rush, a bad habit developed with the job.

After a small moment of awkward silence, she peers up at me with a calculating gaze and smiles faintly. "My name is Aralyn."

Finally, I can put a name to her face! "Pleasure to meet you, Aralyn. My name is–"

"I know who you are, Jessica Rivers."

Surely from her point of view my eyes must have turned as big as saucers upon hearing my name escape her lips. A name that I've never told her before, as far as I know. "You can call me Jess..." I trail off, still baffled. "How do you–"

"That's not important. You're writing an article on Alexander Marc." She tilts her head to one side and her eyes slit in suspicion. "Why?"

How the hell does she know I'm writing an article on him? "Uh, yes. He's hosting a charity event in a few weeks. I'm covering the event and the process leading up to it. How did you know I was writing a piece on him?"

"You don't strike me as the type of woman who would settle for reporting boring charity stories."

"Charities are boring to you?" I mentally congratulate myself on a swift deflection.

She shrugs and raises her cup to her lips. "You don't agree?" Damn. Deflection diverted.

"It's for a good cause. And there will be a lot of A-list individuals there."

"Ah, oui. How exciting," she quips with a dull tone and sarcastic smirk. There's this interesting gleam in her eye and I get the sense that she's enjoying this, whatever this happens to be. I haven't a clue what's going on here. What is she on about? More importantly, how is it that Aralyn, a complete stranger to my knowledge, knows this much about me?

"Have you read my work before? Is that how you know of me?"

"I've never read any of your work. And, please take no offense, but I don't intend to. Reading is not one of my life pleasures."

I bite my lip while trying to sort through my mixed emotions to such a response. I've always considered myself fantastic at reading people, yet I struggle picking up on the energy of the woman sitting across from me. It's as though she has intentionally put up a wall that even I can't penetrate. I gather myself before responding. "Is there something you want?" My tone comes out more irritated than I intended.

"Want? No. I suppose it's more of a need." Her expression, previously neutral, falters a bit, and for a split second I could almost swear I catch a hint of pain cross her features, but it disappears before I can be sure.

She reaches into her little red pocketbook and pulls out a slip of folded paper, delicately sliding it to me. "Meet me at this address tomorrow at two."

I'm hesitant, but I do reach out for it. I try to slide the paper toward me but her grip on it holds firm. "Do not look at it until I'm gone. And please, don't be late." With that, she removes her hand and I take the slip in my fist as she stands, putting on her coat and collecting her bag.

She turns to leave but before she can, I speak up. "Why should I meet you?"

Aralyn looks back at me, her face, once again, void of any readable emotion. "You can't afford not to." Then she walks away. The sound of her heels against the wooden floor fade as she exits. I'm left here, staring at her white, porcelain cup half full, remnants of her red lipstick on the rim, as a million thoughts and questions race through my mind.

I look down at my hands and unfold the paper I was given. Inside, the only thing written is an address.

707 Rue Pasteur

Wait…I know this address. It belongs to a high-end salon in the city, owned by the renowned Madame Chérot, one of the most prestigious hair stylists, not only in France, but all of Europe. I wrote a story on the grand opening of one of her newer salons in Versailles about a year ago.

Why on earth would Aralyn want me to meet her there? Is it possible that's how she knows me? Could she have been one of the stylists there at the time of the interview? But if that were true, it still doesn't explain how she knows I'm writing an article on Alexander, or why she's so curious about it. Could it be possible that he's somehow tied to this meetup spot? And how did this whole thing go from something she needed to something I can't afford not to meet up with her about? I haven't a clue where this is headed or if the price of going down this rabbit hole will be worth it, but I don't think I can stop myself from finding out.

Anything for a good story, right?

5

After parking on the same block as the salon, I glance at myself in the rear-view mirror, sweeping my index fingers under my eyes. The bags look as awful as I feel. I got almost no sleep last night. All I could do was toss and turn, restless; the bizarre events that have occurred recently have been wearing on me. The conversation Aralyn and I had relentlessly replayed in my mind, and the stress of getting personal information on Alexander was giving me nightmares of utter failure.

I almost didn't show up to the salon today, disturbed by this sinking feeling when I got out of bed that I might be walking into something I shouldn't. But the curiosity –that desire to find answers to the questions haunting my days– is greater than the voice inside my head. I inhale a long, deep breath, and exhale fully before making my way out of the car. The salon is in a beautiful neighborhood. Large historic buildings line the strip, occupied by various high-end restaurants and boutiques. The lights from Christmas haven't been taken down yet, so they twinkle in the snow dusted trees.

I wrap my coat tighter around me as I make my way to the doors of La Chérot. It looks warm and inviting. Through the large glass windows, I can see stylists hard at work, providing their clients with the trendiest styles. As soon as I open the doors, I am greeted by the flowery and seductive scents of shampoo and styling products. It's only on rare occasions that I find myself in a salon at all. My long and wavy blonde hair isn't the best in the world, but I get by well throwing it up in a slightly messy bun that can still pass for professional, most days.

"Puis-je vous aider, Madame?" The receptionist flashes a bright smile as she asks how she can assist me.

I respond in French. "Yes, um, I'm supposed to be meeting a lady here by the name of Aralyn? Sorry, I don't know her last name. Do you know who I might be referring too?"

Her smile fades, replaced by a look of distaste. Did I say something wrong? "Wait here please." She rises from her seat and walks around the wall that separates the waiting area and the actual salon. I peek around and watch as she strolls to the far back of the room and opens the door to another, then disappears momentarily.

I sigh, loathing the fact that I'm once again left with my multitude of thoughts. Whatever this meeting will bring, it's imperative to me that I obtain legit answers from Aralyn. I'm curious to know how she knows me if it wasn't by reading any of my articles. Have we met before and I somehow failed to commit our meeting to memory? That can't possibly be it though. I wouldn't have forgotten Aralyn. Then, there's the question of what it is she "needs" and if it will even be something I'll be willing, yet alone want, to provide. And what am I supposed to be gaining from this meeting that's so damn important it couldn't be discussed at the café?

My thoughts are interrupted by the sight of the receptionist rounding the corner, followed by the woman I've come to meet. "Jess! I'm glad you made it." Aralyn's smile is bigger and somehow more genuine than the lady at the front desk, whose expression now has a note of sourness.

Aralyn walks up and greets me warmly with a kiss to each cheek. Her hair is up in a bun today too, showing off her striking facial structure, especially highlighting her high cheekbones. "You're early." Only about fifteen minutes ahead of schedule.

"Well, you know what they say. Early is on time, on time is late."

"Ah, oui. Please, follow me." She turns on her adored heels and escorts me through the clouds of hair spray, steam, and the roaring of blow dryers.

No one even looks up at me as we pass through, which I find relieving. Compared to Ms. Incredible-body-high-heels, I feel as though I'm wearing a trash bag. And to think I had actually made a mediocre attempt to impress today with my gray fitted dress suit, two-inch pumps that match and a black knee length coat, which is more than I can say I do most days. I'm certainly not the most vibrantly dressed person in the world but the same could be said for Aralyn with her constant black and red attire. Although I must say, she pulls it off extremely well. Today, she has on a simple, yet elegant, little black dress.

Aralyn leads me through the same door the receptionist had disappeared behind earlier, and we enter a long hallway. It's pitch black except for a lit exit at the end, which I assume is where we are headed. There's soft music playing with a slightly more upbeat tempo than the typical elevator music. Must be to help keep the awkward walks in the dark from being a little less…well…awkward. As ritzy as the place is, you would think they'd invest in lights for a hallway.

"So, no lights?"

"Don't worry. It will get brighter." Like usual, her reply does little to satisfy my blazing curiosity.

We reach the lit exit, which I now see is an entrance into another room. Before walking in, she turns to face me. "You should know I'm taking quite a risk bringing you here, Jess. Your confidentiality is appreciated."

My confidentiality? What the hell am I walking into? "You do recall being the one who invited me here, right? I didn't have to come."

"No. You didn't. All the same, I'm asking you to be discreet. For both our sakes."

"What is this, Aralyn? Where are you taking me?"

She enters the room and calls out to my frozen frame just outside the doorway. "Follow."

Should I? Looking down at the floor, I note the distinct line that separates what I know from whatever it is I'm about to find out. What's waiting for me if I cross this line? I'm intelligent enough to understand that the meaning of confidentiality, when used in this type of situation, is an invitation to harbor secrets. But will these be secrets worth harboring? Are they even worth knowing at all?

I glance back down the dark passage at the door, knowing that on the other side is a normal, posh looking salon. Already, being in any salon is not normal for me. How ironic that if I cross this threshold, I'll be running the risk of La Chérot, in all of its luxury, being the last normal thing I could encounter.

Oh, stop all this Jess. You are thinking too hard about it. You need answers, and they are right there in that room, with that woman. Suck it up and get the story.

With a mental push, I step across the line with my head held high. After all, what's life without a little adventure? When I enter, I'm quite surprised by how the space looks. It's a rather large room that has a Victorian era theme with a modern twist. Plush couches and armchairs look like thrones and paintings and statues adorn the walls of the room cohesively. Black drapes cascade elegantly from the ceilings and there's fresh wood burning in a beautifully crafted stone fireplace; its crackling is the only sound in the room, besides the sound of Aralyn's heels clacking against the dark marble floor.

She makes her way to a black leather sofa near the fireplace and takes a seat before popping a bottle of chilled champagne, pouring it into two flutes, and motioning me to take a seat beside her. I do so hesitantly, taking note of how much uncertainty drives every move I make at present.

"I thank you for meeting with me. I know this must all be very confusing to you. There are reasons for my doing it this way."

"And are you going to tell me what those reasons are?"

Her face, once again, presents a stoic expression. "Not yet."

"Aralyn, forgive me if I come off harsh, but what the hell is this all about? Who are you? Why am I here and where is Madame Chérot? Doesn't she own this place?"

"Madame Chérot is my mentor and she's not here today. That's one of the reasons I suggested meeting here and requested your confidentiality." Oh great, I've been here for less than five minutes and already I discover I'm taking part in unlawful entry.

"And the other reasons?"

"This is all I will say about the matter for now." My mouth opens to argue about the unfairness of this situation, but she interrupts me. "You're going about it all wrong you know. Alexander is a complicated man and if you wish to figure out the life of a complicated man, you need to be his weakness. What you must ask yourself today is whether you are willing to be that weakness."

"I'm sorry, what?" So, this is about Alexander. But what exactly is she suggesting here?

"You need information on who Alexander is, do you not?"

"Well, yes but-"

"Good. Then this must get done today. Marie, Jovana, you can come in now please!" she calls out.

My bewildered gaze follows hers toward black drapes hanging in front of another doorway in the back of the room and watch as two women enter through them. One of them is petite with a short black pixie cut, a gorgeous contour and plum lipstick that looks flawless against her cream skin. She wears a black dress, similar to the one Aralyn is wearing, accept this woman's dress has a raised collar. The second woman is taller by at least a foot. She looks like an Amazon warrior with her caramel skin, long black curls cascading over her shoulders and dark brown eyes like my own. She also wears black by way of a well-fitted blouse and pencil skirt.

The ladies walk toward us with happy smiles that don't quite reach their eyes. They seem a bit nervous. Aralyn rises from her seat and walks over to where they stand. "Jess, this is Marie…" Her hand touches the shoulder of the lady with the pixie cut, then extends toward the warrior woman. "And this is Jovana. They will be preparing you for this evening."

"Uh, what exactly am I preparing for?"

"There's an exhibit tonight, hosted by Monsieur Lebrov. He is an artist who specializes in intriguing body art. Perhaps you've heard of him. Many distinguished individuals from around the world will be there, including Alexander. I've arranged everything. A friend of mine, Marguerite Fraser, will be your escort this evening. Your job, thanks to the work of these two lovely ladies, will be made quite simple. All you must do is impress."

I set my empty flute down on the coffee table. My head spins a bit, both from trying to process what Aralyn is saying to me and from having thrown back the champagne. "What do you mean *you've arranged everything?* You're really going to have to help me out here because I am at a complete loss! An exhibit? An escort? A fucking makeover? What does any of this have to do with me getting information on Alexander Marc? You're telling me that you've set up some elaborate scheme so I can, what, use my looks to get his attention? Hope he'll think I'm pretty enough to pour his soul out too? This plan sounds ludicrous and will probably be a waste of my time quite frankly."

She lets out a sharp exhale sound crosses her arms, stepping toward me. "You think you don't need my help with this, but you do. As I mentioned, gaining the trust of a man like him is not easy. He's not going to freely hand over his life story without strong reason. This 'elaborate scheme' is necessary. You have to get him to fall for you."

I take a step back in shock. "What?"

"I'm not saying it will be easy. In fact, it may prove to be one of the hardest things you'll ever do. Alexander, like most men, appreciates a beautiful woman, but it's rare he encounters one with beauty *and* the right personality to match. You are strong, determined, independent, and I sense you also have a tenderness that he can nurture. He won't realize it right away, but it's those qualities that will make him desire you in the end. So, these ladies are going to give you the bait to your hook. They will turn you into a beauty to die for."

I aggressively shake my head. There's no way I'm going through with this. She's asking me to do the one thing I've been trying to avoid my whole career– using my looks to get ahead. It makes me feel a little sick. I'd like to think that perhaps the bubbly hasn't yet settled in my stomach but, in truth, I'm terrified. I don't want to do this.

"No."

"Jess–"

"No! Do you realize what you're asking me to do? You want *me* to trick one of the most well-to-do yet private men in the world into falling for me, by getting all dolled up and changing who I am!" I snatch my coat and pocketbook off the chair and push past her, heading for the door I should have never walked through to begin with.

"Jess, wait. Wait! If you walk out that door you will fail."

I whirl around just as I reach the entryway. Her words spark an anger inside me I haven't felt in a long time. Who the hell is this woman who presumes to know me well enough to measure my success? God? "How dare you."

"I'm only telling you the truth."

"You don't know me, Aralyn!"

"You're right, I don't. But I know a lot about Alexander. He doesn't just let anyone in, not unless that person is someone he deeply cares for and loves. You want his story; I know how much you crave it. The desire is a strong scent that seeps from your pores and it's hard to ignore. What I'm offering you is the one and only chance at obtaining that desire. You don't have to take it but know if you leave, I won't offer again."

I hold my tongue, uncertain of what to say. My emotions are a mixed bag of confusion and intrigue. I'm really starting to loathe Aralyn for everything I've been presented with since walking into this room and, at the same time, I can't deny that this crazy plan of hers makes some sense. Many people have tried to get a glimpse into Alexander Marc's hidden world and have been unsuccessful. Although I have a lot of hope and drive, I know the harsh truth is that it may not be enough to get me where so many others couldn't reach.

I hate to think she could be on to something in suggesting I become some temptress who lures a man into vulnerability, only to burn his trust with the movement of my pen against paper. It sounds shameful, desperate, and just plain cruel. There must be another way. This can't be my only option.

And something still doesn't add up. I walk back toward her. The other two ladies take a hint and quietly make their way out of the room. "What do you get out of this? Back at the Café, you told me you needed something from me, so I'm guessing there is a catch to this 'helpful' plan of yours?"

"You and I are similar in that we both want something from Alexander. What I want is more…personal."

"And what exactly is it that you want? I assume you must know him somehow to be so sure of this plan of yours. Did he do something to you? Am I delivering your revenge? Because we both know what will happen if this works, he's going to get hurt."

She stares at me, eyes still giving nothing away, increasing my frustration. "What I need isn't important for you to know at this time." Of course not. Why did I think I'd get an answer? Nothing about our conversation today is getting me any closer to understanding what is going on and I'm getting fed up, which she must notice, because before I can get out what's on my mind, she speaks again. "I know a lot of this does not make much sense right now, but I'm asking you to please trust me."

"Wow. You know, for someone who doesn't give much, you sure do ask for a lot." My arms cross my chest as I try hard to keep my composure.

She moves over to the end table, topping off her glass and refilling mine. She brings it over and holds it out to me. I don't take it, instead I stare her down. It's unbelievable to me that I'm even still standing here, I should have left a long time ago. Trust her. She wants me to trust her. Is she crazy? Am I crazy for seriously considering it? I hardly know her. Yet, the idea of not accomplishing the one thing that can set my career ablaze terrifies me more than anything else right now. The more I ponder it in these few eternal seconds, the more I keep hearing haunting voices in my head, echoing louder and louder. Dante Ritter telling me to not disappoint him, Arthur telling me he believes I can do it, and Aralyn insisting that I will fail if I turn down her offer.

"You can't afford not to." What if she's right? Could walking away cost me this story?

"Jess, I promise, when this is all over, you will understand everything. It will all be okay."

With a sigh of surrender I shake my head. "Okay fine. Fine. How do we do this?"

She grins from ear to ear before laying out her master plan. At the event, I'll be going by a different name– Isabella Evans. Not the worst name, I suppose. The makeover I'm intended to receive will not only highlight my sex appeal, but will make it difficult for Alexander to discover my true identity. I'll, unfortunately, be getting a hair color change which I try to argue but Aralyn is having none of it. Says I will be getting a blond wig to utilize on the days where I have to be myself, and that I should dress the way I normally do on those days. The next few weeks of my life will be a constant shift between Jessica Rivers and Isabella Evans.

I'm growing increasingly worried. It's not that I don't think I can pull it off, I'm confident in that. Isabella Evans used to be me once upon a time, before I decided to hide my best assets from the world, particularly from men. I've never cared to be the center of attention, especially now, but I'll do it. What worries me is the repercussions. Not just the repercussions if I get caught, but the repercussions even if I don't. I'll still be intruding on this man's life. I'll be taking any information he gives me in confidence and blabbing about it to everyone. The journalist in me is telling me to suck it up, this is my career on the line. The other, very real, part of me tells me to quit while I'm ahead; this isn't the way.

Aralyn, once again, attempts to hand me the flute of Champagne. I take it from her and she raises her own, gesturing a toast in a rather pleasing mood. "To desire."

I raise mine slightly, while giving her a cautious and questioning glare. I can't trust Aralyn. I'll play along with her little game for the time being, but I plan on keeping a watchful eye and ear on everything. There's something horribly off about this entire situation and I need to be careful, or I might fall deep into a pit I can't climb my way out of, if I haven't done so already.

Six hours. That's how long it takes for Marie and Jovana to get me primed and ready for my nerve-wrecking night. They both worked tirelessly on my makeup, nails and wardrobe. My outfit is beautiful, although completely out of my comfort zone. They cinched me up in a sexy black corset and garter belt. My dress is a long, red, satin dream with a medium length train and a slit up the side. I run my fingers across my waistline a few times, feeling the smoothness of the fabric and wondering if I ever imagined myself in something like this.

Now that the ladies have done all they can for me, I stand in front of a large, covered mirror, twiddling my thumbs, anxiety coursing through my veins. I already felt regretful of my decision to go through with this wild plan the moment Jovana cut the first few strands of my hair. I'd watched the ground with watery eyes as more of my blonde locks fell and laid scattered before me.

Aralyn, who I oddly hadn't seen much of during my transition, walks in the room. Her eyes light up and a bright smile graces her face upon sight of me. This might be the most revealing expression I've seen from her yet. She congratulates Marie and Jovana on a job well done. "Wow! Bravo mesdames! Elle a l'air magnifique!" The women's faces soften, relieved of tension for the first time since we've met. Excited, Aralyn takes position behind me, placing her hands on my shoulders. "Are you ready?"

I swallow hard, nervous as all hell, but ready to just get this over with. For me, the process seemed a bit tortuous, especially since I was given absolutely no control or say in anything that was done to my appearance. My control was completely given up to Aralyn and her team. I wish I could say I trust their judgment, but as I stand here awaiting the sight of my reflection in the mirror, I realize I don't trust them one bit and I'm scared to despise what I see once that cover comes off.

After nodding my head in response, Aralyn signals for Jovana to pull off the cloth. When it falls away, I squint and blink a few times as my eyes adjust to what I'm seeing. My jaw hits the floor. I hardly recognize the woman in the mirror! Gone is my blonde comfort, replaced by a fierce black asymmetrical bob. The right side stops at my jawline and the left falls an inch or two below. My chestnut eyes are highlighted by a smoky palette and my lips are a deep rouge. The dress shows off every curve of my body I've tried to hide for years, almost everything is on display.

"You are breathtaking."

My lip begins to quiver, and I catch myself, holding back the immense emotion rocking my core. She's right. I *am* breathtaking and I am also stunned, excited, sad, terrified and relieved. All these feelings overwhelm me at once. The results are magnificent and yet, at the same time, I'm finding these changes hard to accept. The me I had spent so much time shaping and molding to deflect attention has been swept away and I'm left feeling so damn exposed.

"What do you think?"

I stare, bewildered at the woman in the red dress. "I don't...I don't really have the words to describe it."

Concern etches Aralyn's face. "Do you not like it?"

"No! No. I love it actually. I do, I'm just shocked is all." Relief washes over her. Marie and Jovana also become instantly more relaxed at my reply. My fingers trace the singular diamond that hangs from a silver chain around my neck.

"I have something for you."

In addition to all this? What more could she possibly have? She gives an amused smirk at my puzzled gaze and beckons Marie over, who's holding a firm pillow with an object on top of it covered by a cloth. "There is one last thing you need to complete this look." She pulls off the cover, revealing the mysterious object underneath. It's a gorgeous pair of black heels. They are simple in style, yet elegant. The fabric seems to be suede and the toes are pointed. My head snaps from the shoes up to Aralyn's face. I pick up the heels and turn them over knowing what I'll see before I lay eyes on it. Red soles.

"Beautiful, no?"

"Yes, they're really something. What's the story behind your love for these kind of heels? You wear that pair you have on all the time. I've never seen you without them. Are they an obsession of yours?" I know this brand of shoe to be a symbol of status amongst men and women around the world, but she has a custom pair that the designer doesn't openly sell. I know because I've scoured every online retailer looking for them since meeting Aralyn. No red soled shoes with butterflies made of diamonds on the back.

"Mm, obsession? Not quite."

"Then what?" She grins mischievously before walking away. I take it I'm not getting that answer today either.

"Your car will be here in ten minutes." Before exiting, she turns to me. "Best of luck tonight, Jess. I know you will shine."

6
___

I stare out the back-passenger window in the chic, black SUV that is my chariot for the evening. My driver, who has introduced himself as Jean-Philippe, hasn't said a word to me the whole ride. He seems nice though. I wonder who's covering the cost of all this pampering. If it's Aralyn then it tells me a few things, first that the girl's got serious money. Secondly, what she wants must be pretty damn important for her to go to such great lengths, all so I could potentially seduce and trick the billionaire bachelor.

The storm that was forecasted earlier has arrived and large droplets of rain thunder against the car's windows, obscuring my view of the Paris nightlife. I turn my attention to my phone, checking my emails for what feels like the hundredth time. Nothing new. I stir in my seat, itching to end the silence and distract myself from my compounding nerves.

"So, Jean-Philippe, do you know Aralyn?"

"Oui, Mademoiselle. I have been her chauffeur for four years."

Perfect. If I can't get answers from Marie and Jovana or the woman herself, perhaps her personal driver will oblige me. "Is she always this generous?" He gives me a questioning glance in the rear-view mirror. "I mean, do you normally drive around other people for her?"

"I believe you're the first Mademoiselle. She must be very fond of you." I hold back a snicker. I'm not sure about her feelings toward me honestly, but I've begun to doubt that fond is one of them. It seems far more plausible that Aralyn is simply desperate and using me for some self-serving purpose of which I'm still unaware.

"She must be pretty well-to-do to have hired a Chauffeur." He remains silent; eyes focused on the road ahead. "What exactly does she do?"

"You do not know?"

"She forgot to mention it."

About ten seconds pass before he replies. "I think that's something you should ask her yourself, Mademoiselle."

What the hell is with all the secrets? It's as though she has everyone under her code of confidentiality! It's infuriating. I do respect Jean's silence, however; I know he's just being a loyal employee. Without much luck in my endeavors to obtain more information, I sink further into the leather seat and go back to gazing out the window, even though there isn't much to see. The pattering of the rain calms me, and I surrender to its soothing sound as I am lulled to sleep.

I'm jolted awake by the sound of a door closing. Eyes blurry with sleep, it takes a moment for me to fully take in the figure sitting next to me. The large platinum blonde bun resting on the top of her head is the first thing I notice before anything else. She stares at me with a look of approval one moment and a hint of dissatisfaction the next. "Well, at least you look the part. My name is Marguerite, can you remember that?" Her accent gives away her French origin.

Simple enough. "Yes." I make a move to wipe the sleep from my eyes and stop upon remembering the beautifully done makeup on my face.

"Bien. It's important you don't forget. This isn't the best way to go about one's first time portraying someone else, but time is not something we have much of. Now then, you and I are close friends, we attended Sorbonne together and used to be roommates in a villa up north until I got married to my wonderful husband, Gregoir–" she raises her hand, showing off the rather large sparkling diamond on her ring finger– "whom you will see later tonight. Are you with me so far?"

"I believe so."

"We will not seek Alexander right away. He does not stay long at big events like these unless he needs to, so he will likely show up late and stay at least half an hour before pardoning himself for the evening. We will catch him just as he's about to leave, run into him how do you say… 'spontaneously', and I will introduce you."

It amazes me how elaborate her story is, every detail planned and ready to go. "Wouldn't it be better to catch him well before he's ready to leave? You know, to give us a chance to talk?"

She rolls her eyes. "Such a journalist, always so eager to get the story. You cannot rush Alexander. He's not your average man. Getting a man like that to give you what you're looking for takes a certain…finesse. You need to be the last thing he thinks about at the end of tonight and the first thing he thinks of when he wakes in the morning. Just trust that I know what I'm doing and follow my lead. Oui?"

Once again, I am asked to put my trust in another total stranger today. It's comical, in a way, how everything has played out since I awoke this morning. It's as though I'm living in some surreal dream where I can't take anything seriously because I can't believe anything that's taking place. At this point, I'm throwing all caution to the damn wind and laughing as I do. What the hell, why not add another crazy decision to the list that keeps growing by the hour?

Marguerite continues, briefing me on etiquette and lets me know that I should keep my mouth shut unless spoken to. Obviously, there isn't any trust in *me* to not screw things up and I won't lie, I can't blame her. I'm not too confident in my performance either. She instructs Jean-Philippe, who has parked us in some unfamiliar neighborhood, to continue to the exhibit. We don't drive for too much longer before we arrive at the venue.

Jean-Philippe hops out and comes around to open Marguerite's door. Before exiting, she gives me a faint smile. "Show time."

I follow her lead, scooting out behind her, and grab hold of Jean-Philippes' offered hand as my suede pumps take their first steps onto the long red carpet that leads through the large doorway of the building. I'm thankful for the cover of the umbrella he holds as droplets continue their descent from the sky.

I'm nearly blinded by bright flashes of light. There are yells, shouts, and clicking noises all around us. Paparazzi are everywhere, and I suddenly feel like a deer in headlights. A hand gently presses against the small of my back, guiding me forward. "You'll do wonderful Mademoiselle," the chivalrous chauffeur says to me, taking notice of my obvious discomfort. I'm grateful to him for not adding to it, but rather trying to make me feel more secure. He kindly passes me off to one of the ushers who walks with me the length of the carpet, covering me with an umbrella as best he can.

We meet Marguerite at the entrance. The bell boy takes her long, white fur coat wrapped around her shoulders. Doing so reveals her curvy figure in a stunning periwinkle blue gown that shimmers silver in the light. The color makes her brilliant light blue eyes pop.

After my coat is taken, she hooks her arm around mine. "Stay close," she whispers. We descend the steps into the main hall of the exhibit and I'm completely stunned.

There are bodies– naked bodies –painted, displayed in every direction. Sure, I knew we'd be seeing painted naked bodies, but I had not contemplated that I'd be viewing those painted naked bodies in the midst of sexual acts! Many of the models on display are performing different steamy scenes, amidst various abstract backgrounds. It's simply erotic to say the least! I just know there's rouge rising to my cheeks. This is a first for me! I feel dirty and yet oh so intrigued.

Before long, quite a few people come up to us as we make our way through the exhibit, mostly to say hello to the woman who has me glued tight to her hip, but several are also curious about me; the woman dressed to the nines who they've never seen nor heard of. I have no business being here, but Marguerite and I do what we can to make sure we are the only ones who know it. I'm introduced to everyone we meet, and Marguerite tells the story of how our make-believe friendship began. I smile and give thanks for the flattering comments on my look that I still experience a bit of discomfort about. I also answer questions about my career and upbringing back in the states, all of which is made up and starts to seem mundane after a bit. I loathe repeating myself and my interest is soon stolen by the scandalous works we pass.

I know of the artist, Jacques Lebrov, and have seen short video documentaries on him before, but nothing compares to seeing his genius up close and personal. None of his work I had previously seen had been this X-rated. These models have a hell of a job. No noises escape their lips as they hump, stroke or bend in all sorts of strange positions. A few are even bound in a sensual fashion. Each one of them is magnificent in bringing a certain visionary piece to life. They are painted in a way that visually blends them into one of the painted backgrounds they are each placed in front of. Their movements against the stillness of those very backgrounds give a hypnotic feel that is alluring and awe inspiring.

A male model nearby captures my attention. He is painted gold and blue against a similarly colored backdrop, stroking his member with a methodical pace. His eyes are closed, mouth partially open, as though letting out a pleasurable cry that is muted to the ears of everyone around. It feels so wrong to watch… but I find myself unable to peel myself away. Instead, I'm drawn deeper and deeper into the act set before me.

"Bella!" I'm yanked from my trance by Marguerite's screech of my alter ego's name. I spot her moving toward me with her arm looped around someone else's for a change. I'd been so into the art, I never noticed she'd left my side!

"Bella, I'm sure you know of Monsieur Lebrov. Monsieur, this is my friend I was telling you about, Isabella Evans."

"Ah chérie!" The vibrant gentleman takes both my hands to his lips, planting a quick but warm kiss upon each. "Quel plaisir. Marguerite has been telling me a lot about you. It is truly an honor to meet another beautiful soul." Jacques Lebrov is a handsome man, in his late thirties. He has his long black hair pulled into a braid that ends at the base of his back and he wears a simple, yet fashionable, pair of black rimmed glasses along with a royal purple suit, a nice look against his sun-kissed skin. Needless to say, he stands out, but the style suits him. He looks quite suave.

"Monsieur Lebrov, it is I who feels honored. Your work is stunning and quite tantalizing I must say! I've been to quite a few art shows and I've never seen anything quite like this."

The man's sharp smile meets his warm chestnut eyes. "Ah, merci beaucoup! S'il vous plaît, call me Jacques." He escorts

Marguerite and I on a grand tour of some of his work, providing in-depth detail on the inspirations and motivations behind the vision. This depth of information was what I wished a certain billionaire would have been keener to discuss the previous day.

I become so wrapped up in Jacques' creative world that I, once again, am not aware of any changes in my surroundings. In this case, it's the change in the atmosphere. It isn't until Marguerite alerts me to it that I catch on and take notice of how the chatter in the large hall has died down a few octaves. She nudges me in the side and I look over to where her eyes are signaling for me to turn my attention.

I don't see what the big deal is at first, but then I spot three men in all black huddling together. I soon realize they are bodyguards when they step aside and the man they are guarding appears. Alexander Marc had finally arrived.

"What about you, Bella? What is it that you do?"

"I'm sorry?" I'm late pulling my attention away from my reason for being here.

He peers over to see what I'm looking at as the view of Alexander becomes obscured by others who are trying to get a glimpse. He continues, "Your job. What do you do for work?"

Marguerite swoops in to save me. "She's an author, isn't that right?"

I collect myself. "Um, yes, a journalist actually. I work with many different publishing companies. I'm actually currently on assignment with Eiffel Inc." Marguerite's heated glare sears into the side of my face.

"Really? Magnifique! Do you know Dante Ritter?"

"Yes, he's the one I report to. How do you know him?"

"Dante and I have history. We lived in the same neighborhood as children." Wow. It's strange hearing that. I've never looked at Ritter and thought of him as a man who had a childhood. In fact, I had never really thought of him at all outside of business. To me, he had just been my strict on and off boss with a creeper tendency.

"Small world! I bet you have some intriguing childhood memories. I'd love to write an article on you sometime if you're open to it." Jacques waves to someone behind us and Marguerite continues to eye me disapprovingly. I know I'm being risky going off script, but even she isn't going to stop me from going after a potential opportunity like this.

"I should greet my other guests. It was lovely speaking with you both, and Bella, it was wonderful meeting you. I just might take you up on your offer. Here's my card. When you're ready, we can talk." He winks and kisses our cheeks before departing. "Bonne soirée."

My heart beams with excitement! I slip the card into my little black pocketbook before Marguerite pulls me to the side. "Are you insane?"

"Lucky is more like it. I quite possibly just scored an interview with Jacques Lebrov!"

"We aren't here for you to find other jobs, we are here for you to get started on ONE job and it's that man right over there! Are you trying to sabotage yourself?"

"What the hell is the big deal?"

"You must stay focused, Jess. You seem to get distracted too easily and that's not something you can afford to do right now. There can be no distractions. Vous comprenez?"

I'm finding it difficult to reel in my immense frustration. There's a lot of people telling me what to do lately and I'm growing sick of it. I didn't sign up to be treated like a five-year-old. As Marguerite begins to open her mouth again, I turn on my heels and storm off. "Where are you going?"

"Don't worry, I'm sure you'll figure it out!" Lord knows she's bound to follow me anyway, so she can drag me back to her hip.

When I reach the restroom, I enter the largest stall and pace back and forth, frustrated but trying to calm myself enough to consider my next move. Alexander Marc is out there, and I need to be prepared to approach him. I knew when I was given this assignment that it wouldn't be easy, but I never imagined that everything that has occurred so far would ever become a part of my reality. There's no doubt I'm going above and beyond the call of duty and it both terrifies and excites me.

Men are not my forte, despite what others might assume. I've only ever had two relationships that lasted more than six months and the past few years, dating has not been my top priority. Now, here I am, helping a woman I barely know by seducing a man I barely know and tricking him into spilling his life story. It's an insane feat and how this all ends up helping Aralyn is beyond me, a fact I'm still extremely uneasy about. Hell, the whole damn thing makes me uneasy.

Over the past several hours, I've allowed myself to be transformed for the benefit of four individuals, Aralyn, Dante Ritter, myself and Alexander Marc, whose benefit will surely be short lived and at the expense of what…a front-page article? God, have I become so selfish? How could it be seen as anything but?

I'm not desperate, my work constantly keeps the bills paid, a solid roof over my head and food on the table. So, why am I willing to stoop so low, risk so much?

A knock on the stall door jilts me from my thoughts. "Just a moment." Another knock. "Une minute!"

I'm convinced it's Marguerite when the knock comes again. The fourth knock takes my impatience over the edge. I fling open the door to give a strong verbal lashing to the asshole on the other side. "Ok, seriously? I said give me a–" A little girl of about five or six bolts in. I briefly ask myself how she's even at such an event, as it's my understanding that this is very much adults only. I chalk it up to her possibly being a child of one of the staff members and scurry out, closing the door behind me.

Just outside the bathroom I stop, trying to catch another moment to myself as the music thumps loudly through the hall. It's only me in the corridor that leads back out to the exhibition. I lean my back and head against the cool stone wall to help ease me after getting so worked up. Not many seconds pass when a voice comes from the entryway, and I look over to see a man walk in. I blink a few times to make sure I am not mistaking who I'm seeing.

"I don't care about the cost Carson, just see that it gets done!" His voice is clipped and loud, to drown out the music I'm sure. Alexander hangs up and breathes out heavily, running a stressed hand through a head of dark waves.

The restroom door opens and I watch the little girl, clearly relieved, skip past me down the hall, pushing past Alexander and through the doors to a staff room. After he questioningly watches her go by, his gaze shifts and falls on me, still against the wall, unable to really move or breathe for that matter.

Even from the distance between us, I see him softly cock his head to the side as he gives me a once over, squinting slightly as if trying to put together a piece of a puzzle. Here we both stand, staring at each other for what seems to me like quite a while, that is until a group of ladies walk in. They all give a quick glance back at the gorgeous man in the entryway and coyly giggle amongst themselves as they proceed to the restroom.

I look from them back to him, whose curious eyes are still trained on me. After a few deep breaths, I somehow pull within me the courage to make my move down the hall to him. But as I do, one of his bodyguards enters, whispering something that makes them both turn to leave.

Shit! I pick up my pace. As I round the corner into the exhibition hall, I see him near the back entrance being halted by Marguerite. She smiles and speaks to him in a cheerful manner, all the while her eyes keep darting from him to the room, sweeping it in search of me, no doubt. I hurry over, slowing down as I get closer. As I walk up, I over-hear Alexander hastily say, "It's wonderful to see you Marguerite but I really must—"

"Oh, there you are!" She squeals, cutting him off. Relieved, she extends an arm out to me and I take it, following her lead up the steps to the tall, dapper man in the crisp black suit. "Alexander, this is my good friend, Isabella Evans. She's a well-known erotic author from America." Woah, *erotic* author? That's news to me! When did we agree on that narrative? I try hard to keep the look of utter shock and mortification off my face.

"Is that so?" Alexander casts an incredulous look in my direction, scanning me over once more, fully taking in the "new" woman standing before him.

"Mr. Marc. What a pleasure to meet you."

"The pleasure is mutual." For a quick second, there's a spark in his stormy eyes I haven't seen before. I wonder, briefly, if I imagined it.

My mouth opens to speak but Marguerite beats me to it. "I'm actually surprised you two don't know each other Alex, I was expecting you to tell me you'd already met," she says with a realistic look of surprise. I have to hand it to her, she plays her part extremely well. I need to be just as good if we are going to pull the night off.

"Interesting. I didn't think you had any good friends I haven't met. I can't say we've ever been introduced. Though, you do seem familiar somehow Ms. Evans."

"I met you once." Crap, reverse Jess, reverse! "I mean, not really. We kind of just saw each other in passing at an event a few months ago. I forget which one."

"Ah, oui! Speaking of events, Gregoire and I are looking forward to the banquet, Alex. It will be quite the affair, I'm sure!" Despite my earlier frustration, I really am grateful for her save.

"As always, it will be wonderful to see you both Marguerite." One of his bodyguards comes forward and whispers to him in a low tone. "If you'll pardon me, my car is waiting. I really must be on my way."

Marguerite gives a small pout. "If you must. Don't be a stranger while you're in Paris. I know you aren't here long and you don't come this way often anymore. Perhaps we can find a time to get together before you go. Gregoire would love that."

"I'll have Carmyn check my schedule and give you a call. Bonne soirée." The two exchange cheek kisses and then he faces me. His tall frame is almost overbearing as he steps my way. Just like the first time we met, his scent causes quite the commotion in parts of my anatomy that haven't experienced action in some time. The man smells amazing!

"Ms. Evans." He grabs my hand, bringing it to his lips, planting a soft kiss upon it as his piercing gray eyes make direct contact with mine without faltering. The warmth of his breath against my skin sends signals shooting throughout my body, and the ever-increasing fluttering in my abdomen is hard to ignore. It's the first time in a long time that any man has gotten to me in such a way. Then again, when it comes to most men, I never give them the time of day. Is this what I've allowed myself to miss out on? Men like him who can charm a woman till she's weak in the knees without much more than a look? Here I am with plans to try and seduce him, yet I'm the one being lured in.

I should feel delighted. Afterall, the night gave way to some progress. But, as I watch Alexander get swiftly escorted out of the building, my brow furrows and my chest feels tight. This is a dangerous game I've chosen to play. However, after pulling myself back together, I remind myself of the importance of this assignment. I need to have this article ready in a couple weeks and if Aralyn's plan is working, then that's what matters, no matter the risk.

"Well, that did not go entirely as planned, I had hoped there would be a little more time for conversation, but we got you noticed. It is a start." Marguerite mutters.

"So, what now?"

"Now you find a way to conveniently 'bump into him' again soon, start a conversation, and give him a reason to begin to trust you."

I give her an incredulous look. "That's it? That's the next big plan, to wait for an opportunity to 'bump into him'?"

She cocks an eyebrow and purses her lips. "Do you have a better idea?"

"Look, I didn't sign up to do all this for ten seconds of his time and *maybe* the opportunity to come across him again. There must be something else we can do."

She lets out a sigh. "I'll speak to Aralyn. I'm sure she will offer some advice. For now, my work is done. Enjoy the rest of your evening Jess. Au revoir." She flirtatiously waves over to a tall middle-aged man with short, curly blond hair and a quirky mustache in a corner of the room. By the looks of it I assume he's Gregoire. Marguerite heads his way, leaving me alone on the top of the steps.

I'm beyond irritated! Aralyn and Marguerite might be fine with taking their sweet time, but time is not a luxury I can afford. I'm not sure what comes over me, but I make a hasty decision, and without hesitation I make a beeline for the courtyard exit that Alexander left from.

Time to take matters into my own hands.

7

The courtyard is huge, about the length of a football field. Alexander and his men are all the way on the other side. I wonder, momentarily, why he used the back entrance. Possibly to avoid the paparazzi. In any case, I'm grateful he did. If not for the long walk, he'd be long gone by now. I kick off my heels by a bush, bunch up the front of my dress and book it his direction, praying to all the heavens that I can make it to him in time.

Just as I see him approach the valet area, I shout his name with all the power my already overworked lungs can muster. "Alexander Marc!" To my immense joy, he stops and turns to find me bolting toward him with such desperation he probably thinks me pitiful. After a few short seconds, I catch up, huffing and practically void of breath. Running in a corset is an entirely different beast.

"Ms. Evans? Where's your coat?" His question makes me laugh. Standing before him is a woman who I'm certain appears as though she's lost her goddamn mind, and his concern is her coat. He looks down. "And your shoes?"

I have found my voice, despite the heavy panting, "They would have held me back, so I left them." As I aim to steady my breathing, he takes off his long black overcoat and places it around my shoulders. I thank him and he turns to his men, instructing them to give us a moment. I can tell one of the guards is a bit irritated, but they comply without so much as a word and walk to the car, leaving the two of us alone.

"Do you normally chase after men bare foot?" His question is lighthearted.

"Only the ones fast enough to get away." My shaky attempt at humor causes my cheeks to grow hot with embarrassment, which is quite surprising. After all, I just chased this man down like a maniac, but it's my joke that's got me blushing! I'm even more embarrassed when I realize that I must now explain myself, and I didn't get that far along in my impulsive plan. "I-uh, we-uh, I want to talk to you about something." Oh really, Jess? I'm sure he would never have guessed.

"Indeed." There's that heated look again while examining my body. "You're wet."

My eyes grow wide. "Uh, excuse me?"

"The bottom of your dress. It's wet." I look back at the soaked train of my garment. Wearing dresses like this is really so out of my norm. I totally spaced about the train when I took off along the rain drenched grounds.

"Oh, haha, would you look at that."

"Ms. Evans, any woman who takes it upon herself to brave this weather, with bare feet and nothing but her gown, in the hopes of being granted a modicum of my time is welcome to it. I'm quite impressed. However, I do have some fairly urgent business to attend to at the moment. Perhaps, you'd like to have this discussion of yours over brunch, say Sunday morning?" Two days' time. It dawns on me that I'm supposed to be meeting him as Jessica Rivers tomorrow to go over his vision for the banquet. These meetings are way too close to each other. How will I be able to continue convincing him that I'm an entirely different person? I'm sure sooner, rather than later, he's going to figure me out and it's going to blow up in my face significantly. What to do?

"Um, sure, that sounds great."

"Wonderful. Meet me at the Hotel DuPont at eleven. They have a restaurant there called La Chambre Dorée. Let the host know you are under my reservation. They'll escort you to my table."

I can't believe I'm really going through with this. "I look forward to it."

I prepare to take off his coat, but he holds up a hand bringing me to pause. "Give it back to me on Sunday. Just promise me you'll hurry back in and put on your shoes. You'll catch your death and then I'll not get my coat back at all." He cracks a breathtaking smile. I've never even seen him smile in photos. It's now an additional mystery as to why he doesn't do it more. It's enjoyable seeing this side of him. He was so serious last week; I wasn't sure he had it in him to be this delightful and charming.

I return the smile and he winks. "Good night, Ms. Evans." Then makes his way to the car.

As he's driven away, I'm filled with hope. I had no idea how I'd be received, but the fact that I now have a personal meetup with him, despite it being so close to the interview tomorrow, is magnificent! It's one step closer, and I will take each and every step I can till I make it to the finish line.

*W*hen I arrived home, I immediately shed my clothes, like a snake shedding her skin, eager to embrace her new body. I poured myself a glass of cabernet and laid on the sofa in nothing but my underwear. Soon, one glass turned into three and I drank myself into submission of sleep. That is until being drawn out of it by my phone buzzing repeatedly. Finally, I find the will to answer. "Hello?"

"Bonjour, Jess."

I spring up. "Aralyn?"

"I heard the night went well enough." I pull my phone away for a moment to look at the time. What the fuck! It's three twenty-seven in the morning!

"God, do you know what time it is? How did you get my number anyway? I never gave it to you."

"Marguerite told me you need help planning your next move with Alexander." I rub my eye, wincing at the sting of the eyeliner and shadow I forgot I'd fallen asleep still wearing.

I'm glad she called. During my wino reflections earlier, I determined that I don't want any more of Aralyn's help. I'm already in, I don't even know how deep, and don't care to be pushed further. "She's mistaken. I'll be fine."

"That's not the impression you gave her."

"I could care less about that woman's impressions. I don't know her, Aralyn. Like I said, I'll be fine. The only thing that would be helpful would be some detailed info on Alexander so I can know what to focus on to get into his good graces. You can provide me with that, right? Seeing as you seem to know this guy."

"I never said I knew him."

"Well, you certainly never said you didn't. And if we're being completely honest, I'm not entirely sure why else you'd be helping me with this for our supposed mutual benefit if you didn't somehow know the man." I rise to my feet, immediately holding my head and closing my eyes to stop the slight spinning sensation I'm feeling.

There's a small pause before she answers again. "I'll help you out with another meeting, but you should know that knowing his interests aren't important right now." Little does she know I already have a meeting set up. "After all, his information is what you are trying to find out from him. You just need the right… je ne sais quoi."

I fill a glass with water at the kitchen sink. "Aralyn, if you're not going to give me any of that info then I don't need your help. Besides, your 'je ne sais quoi' sounds like trouble."

I hear her giggle and it startles me, as I didn't intend to say anything that one would find comedic. "Oh, mon chérie, there's nothing wrong with a little trouble. Open up. I'm at your door."

"You're kidding me." The doorbell rings. *Seriously?*

After running to my room to grab a robe, I throw the front door open. There stands the auburn headed devil herself.

"Bonjour," she says with a smirk. I slide out onto the steps, closing the door behind me. There's no way I'm letting her in.

"Aralyn, what the hell are you doing here? How did you know where I live?"

"I retrieved your address from someone you work with."

"You went to my job? What is wrong with you? Are you stalking me?"

"It was before I officially introduced myself to you."

"I'm sorry, is that supposed to make me feel better about this? Cause news flash, it absolutely makes it worse!" It's official. Aralyn is a psychopath. I made a deal with a complete psycho! "You know what, like I told you already, I don't need anymore help from you Aralyn. I can handle this on my own."

"Doesn't seem like it."

"You know, I don't understand why you're doing this, but this seems really wrong and strange. And this plan you put together for me last night? You got me all transformed for four minutes of his time! Most of which involved a back-and-forth convo with Marguerite. Mission totally failed if you ask me!" I think it best to leave out my little encounter with Alexander in the courtyard.

"You're not very patient, are you?"

"Not really, no, not when I'm in a time crunch. And guess what? I'm in a time crunch." Doesn't she know that? Or have I actually found something about myself that Aralyn has no clue about?

She folds her arms in irritation. "I wish you would trust me here."

"Can you blame me? You haven't given me one solid reason why I should! I'm not stupid, Aralyn, I don't hand out blind trust like Halloween candy. Especially to people who go around all sketchy-like collecting information on me."

"And I don't do all this for just anyone, especially someone I've just met." So, there it is. She confirms that we've never met before, adding to the mystery of how she seems to know so much about me. I need her to give me an explanation this instant.

"Tell me why. If you want me to do this for you I need to know why you're so intent on helping me. I need to know what you get out of this."

She exhales a surrendered breath and looks off into the distance, contemplating, I'm sure. Aralyn is such a beautiful woman. Upset or not, she has this complete allure about her. And it isn't just her looks. There's this innocence hidden behind the wall of intensity she's built around herself. There are also secrets, many secrets, their weight visible in her eyes. There is a lot about her I envy, but I don't envy that. That many secrets can't possibly come without a shit load of pain.

She speaks up after a while. "You asked me back at the salon if I was doing this to get back at him. If what I want is revenge." My ears perk with anticipation. "It's true, I want revenge…but not on Alexander. Do you have a cigarette?"

Her question throws me off a bit. I shake my head no. What does she mean she wants revenge but not on Alexander? And how on earth does me writing an article about him help her get revenge?

"It's a terrible habit, I know." Wisps of breath dance from her lips amidst the frigid air as she laughs softly to herself. "I haven't had one in almost eight years. Somehow, I feel like I need one at this moment." Her eyes become watery, but I can see her fight to keep tears from spilling over, something she must have mastered. "Something very bad has happened. My life is forever changed. There's no going back."

The January breeze causes some strands of hair to fly gently across her face. Aralyn bites her lip to keep it from quivering. "Alexander has information that can get me what I need to, at least, grant me some solace in what's happened. Then I can finally be at peace. You see, if you can get close enough to him that he's willing to be open about the information you are looking for then maybe, just maybe, you can get the information I need too."

Even through the emotion, her expression remains controlled. She isn't going to allow me to see her natural soul and to my amazement, I'm okay with that. Whatever happened obviously beat her down, scarred and hardened her. If she isn't willing to show me her truest self, I'm starting to understand that I can't hold it against her, not right now. I know what it's like to want to cower behind an energetic barrier to keep the hurt from getting in. I have done it for so long.

"Okay. Well, thank you for sharing that. I can tell it's not easy for you. But what information am I looking to get out of him that can help you?"

"A name, Jess. The name of the woman he loves."

Oh, so many questions are flooding my mind. The woman he loves? Is she seeking vengeance on this unnamed woman because she has something to do with what happened to her? Could this be a jealousy thing? Does Aralyn love Alexander but his heart is elsewhere so she's after the woman responsible for claiming it? And then there's something else that springs to mind... "If Alexander is already in a loving relationship with someone, then why is the plan for me to seduce him?"

"They aren't together."

"Okay, so then what, exactly, is the goal here?"

"The only way he will trust you is if he cares about you. To care about you, he has to like you, a lot, either as a friend or a potential partner. Last night wasn't supposed to be a big Cinderella moment Jess. Its purpose was simply to get him to notice you, more than he would have in a room, being interviewed."

"So why not find out from him yourself? Doesn't he care about you?"

"You, again, assume I know him. Alexander holds the key to what I need. I know how bizarre all of this must seem to you and I appreciate you for even being willing to follow some strange woman you don't know into a salon and allow your image to be changed. Obviously, you're not doing it for me but thank you still. I only hope we can continue to work this out together."

"You are absolutely correct. This is bizarre. Insane in fact! But you really may be right in that I'll need your help, as much as I hate to admit it. No other journalist has gotten this close to him and I can't stop testing the limits, not yet." Why, oh why, am I doing this? This mission has 'crash and burn' written all over it. But I guess what Carmyn said to me at Alexander's estate was right, sniffing out dirty laundry really is like heroin to a journalist's blood stream; because no matter how much I want to say no, I can't. "Fine. Let's continue to help each other out, but the minute it seems like this is about to go up in flames, I'm jumping ship. Understand?"

"Oui."

"And I know there are some things you don't want to talk about for personal reasons or whatever and I respect that. So, let's keep things strictly business from now on. You don't go snooping into my life like you've apparently been doing, and I'll keep out of yours."

"D'accord." A black SUV pulls up in front of us. The windows were tinted so I can't see who's inside, but if I were to guess, I'd say it's Jean-Philippe, as the car looks identical to the one I was in earlier. "I must go now. I'm glad we had a chance to talk."

"Yeah, but maybe next time swing by at ten and not some god forsaken hour of the morning. I'm begging you. What little sleep I get is important."

Aralyn chuckles as she walks down to the car and then looks back at me. "By the way, remember how I mentioned your impatience?"

"Sure."

"Be a little more patient. One of the things you need to understand about Alex is that, other than business, he lives the rest of his life outside of the public eye. So, if he doesn't express interest in you as quickly as you would like, it does not necessarily mean he is uninterested. If you wish to know his true feelings, you'll have to be alone with him. That's the only way." I know there's some truth in what she's saying. I had felt his interest hours ago when we were alone. Subtle, but definitely present. Whether his interest is romantic or not remains to be seen. But one thing's for certain, I got his attention.

Jean-Philippe comes around and opens the passenger door. Aralyn says goodnight before he shuts it. He smiles at me and tips his hat before walking back around to the driver's seat.

As I watch the car pull away, a bundle of nerves stirs in my gut. Something is still not sitting right with me about this plan. Yes, the identity swap may work but for how long? Later today, I'll have to switch back into a pumpkin and meet Alexander at the location for the charity event. This reminder sparks yet another rather impulsive decision. It's time for operation damage control.

Aralyn's going to be pissed.

8

Anxiously, I wait in the main hallway of the Crescendo venue, resisting the urge to bite my beautifully done nails and play with my now shortened black hair. I don't own much attire to pull off the Isabella Evans persona, but I did keep a few chic outfits from my first couple of years in Paris. Today, I opted for a sweet, white, short-sleeved blouse and a knee length black pencil skirt that shows off my curves in all the best ways. My pair of five-inch white stilettos complete the look.

I had an epiphany before going back to bed last night. I couldn't get Marguerites' words out of my head. *"Now, you find a way to 'run into him' again soon, start a conversation and give him a reason to begin to trust you."*

Give him a reason to trust me. What better way to do that than to tell him the truth about my intentions? Cue impulsive decision! This morning I devised a plan that will either go perfectly right or horribly wrong. Somehow, I need to get Alexander Marc to trust me and how will he trust me if I end up exposed for being a fraud? As a journalist with connections to so many people throughout the city of Paris, I'm bound to run into someone who will figure out I'm not who I'm pretending to be. They'll see me as a woman lying to a wealthy man for a reason unknown to them, and unknown reasons are reason enough to talk. Not only will I soil my chance at victory with Alexander, but I could also majorly hurt my career and there is no way I'm headed down that road. If Alexander is bound to find out, it might as well be today, and it might as well come from my lips.

I won't disclose the whole truth, but some truth must be better than trying to blatantly deceive him with a disguise and hoping he'll never catch on. I need to approach this from a different angle, and I need to move fast. Ritter messaged me this morning telling me to come by the office in a couple days so he can hear about what I have so far, which, at this point, is zilch.

The front double doors open and in walk some familiar faces. Carmyn struts through looking more striking than she did when we first met, followed by Alexander, who appears to be on a business call. Carmyn steals a quick glance in my direction and continues forward. They both stroll right past. She doesn't recognize me at all! And he barely notices that I'm even standing here. I take one last moment to ponder if what I'm doing is wise. Once I do this, there's no going back.

Upon making up my mind, I hurry after the pair. "Mr. Marc!"

Perfectly in sync, the two turn around. As I approach, Carmyn eyes me with heavy curiosity while one of Alexander's eyebrows shoots up in surprise. He may not have seen me before, but he's seeing me now and it's clicking that I'm the mysterious woman from last night.

"I'll call you back." He hangs up and says nothing, just continues to look at me with some confusion.

Carmyn speaks up, however. "I'm sorry, who are you?"

"My apologies. Mr. Marc, I know you seeing me here is a huge shock. I just had to meet you today and come clean. You see, I was presented to you last night as Isabella Evans. I look vastly different, I know, but I'm the journalist covering your story, Jess Rivers. I feel it best to address this now as it may come up in the near future. I'm hoping you'll give me an opportunity to explain myself." I stop and hold my breath, preparing for his wrath; ready to be called out for being a phony and a fake. Ready to be escorted out the door by security. I even glance over my shoulder, expecting to see one of his bodyguards at my back, but they stand in place at the front entry.

Carmyn speaks up again. "I'm confused. You're Jess Rivers? Why the alias, or is Isabella your actual name?"

I respect Carmyn immensely and I completely understand her desire for answers but, as I speak, I maintain eye contact with the man whose opinion means the most to me right now. "Marguerite really wanted me to go to the exhibit with her but, I must admit, those types of events make me incredibly nervous. Mostly because I don't really own adequate attire, and I wasn't sure how much I'd fit in with the crowd. There were so many A-list people attending and I hated to think that, somehow, what I looked like or how I came off would reflect badly upon my friend. Marguerite was so adamant about me going though, she suggested it could be a fun idea to give me a makeover and an alter ego persona. It honestly sounded kind of cool, so I just went with it. When I saw you, I soon realized you didn't recognize me and I knew I'd be seeing you today so, well, here I am."

"Well, kudos to your friend darling, you look brilliant!" I'm thankful for Carmyn's kind and helpful chime in. If my explanation is enough for her, maybe, just maybe, it's satisfactory enough for him too.

Once again, Alexander gives me a quick once over before responding. "Walk with me." He starts toward one of the side doors in the hall. I don my coat and nervously follow.

Carmyn calls out to him. "Uh, Mr. Marc, Monsieur Lauril was expecting us two minutes ago."

He turns to his assistant and briefly continues his walk backwards. "Ms. Calloway, I am sinking a lot of money into the use of this fine facility, I am sure Mr. Lauril can wait a little longer." I don't turn in time to see Carmyn's reaction, but my guess is it's an accepting one given she says nothing else about the matter.

Outside, Alexander leads us through a garden. Each step makes me feel as though I'm walking closer to my doom, as if at any moment he will face me and call me on my bullshit. The further we walk, past tall shrubs and bare bushes still asleep for the season, the more my feeling of dread is compounded by feelings of deep curiosity and confusion. This isn't the first time I've been met with his lengthy silence on a walk but it's certainly the longest, by far.

Attempting to distract myself from the chaotic storm brewing within me, I take the opportunity to study him intently—this beautiful enigma in a perfectly tailored suit. He appears to have all the physical perfections of a God, along with the intense inner workings of one too. I get so distracted admiring his physique that I almost smack into him when he finally comes to a stop.

He faces me. "I suppose this is what you were going to tell me at brunch tomorrow." I hadn't a clue what I was going to tell him at all, but, yeah, let's go with that.

"I'm sorry. I wish I would have told you the moment Marguerite introduced me to you."

"Who are you?"

My heart stills at his words. "What do you mean?"

"I knew who you were the moment I saw you in that hallway back at the exhibit, Ms. Rivers." Wow! Okay, this is certainly unexpected. "Your eyes gave it away. You had that same look you gave me when we first met at my home." Oh god, I hope it wasn't the look of intrigue and lustful desire which I tried hard to reign in.

"You knew? But when Marguerite introduced me…"

"I played along. I've known Marguerite for many years, she's a smart yet mischievous woman, always up to something. I could tell that this…makeover you were given, though quite appealing, didn't necessarily make you comfortable. In fact, you seemed… lost in it. Yet, here you are, as your supposed 'self', and you still seem lost. So, I ask again. Who are you?"

"I'm sorry but I really don't understand. I'm not lost. I know what I want in life, I have a great career, wonderful friends and family who support me. And sure, I hadn't completely adjusted to the makeover, but nothing about that seems lost to me."

"You don't see it because you are not consciously aware of it. If you saw it, you would have never let Marguerite change you.

You wear a mask, Ms. Rivers, and you're uncomfortable in it. Even last week, during your interview, the way you spoke, your eye contact, your very body language revealed that discomfort."

"Did it dawn on you that maybe it was just *you* making me uncomfortable?"

He tilts his head to the side slightly. "Was it?"

I'm not sure what to say. Honestly, this whole conversation makes me uncomfortable. Who is he to be so presumptuous of my character anyway?

He responds to my silence. "You don't know, do you? You don't know because you don't know who you are."

"You're wrong."

"Furthermore, when you came to interview me last week, you had every opportunity to press me about my life, yet you did not. Why?"

I'm growing mighty pissed off and cross my arms over my chest. A snarky reply rolls off my tongue. "Let me guess, because I don't know myself?"

He's unphased by it and, for some reason, that ticks me off more. "I can wait," he says.

I roll my eyes, which only now triggers a hint of dissatisfaction on his face. "It may surprise you to know that I was taking your feelings into consideration. I'm sure every reporter approaches you trying to find out about the fascinating mystery that is your life. I didn't want my approach to be that intrusive." I'm, of course, lying through my teeth but, at this point, I'm ready to say anything that will get him to loosen the reigns on this interrogation.

"Tell me, Ms. Rivers, how else do you plan on figuring out the 'deep mystery that is my life' without being intrusive?" If only he knew. I wonder if he'll ever suspect the lengths I'd go, the lengths I'm going, to uncover his story.

As much as I want to defend myself against his brazen assumptions of me, I hold my tongue. "I think you are an incredible man, Mr. Marc. I admire you a lot. What you do… it's inspiring to many people, including myself. A man who does such significant work deserves some respect. Deserves to be treated like a human being like everyone else.

"I took this job knowing that all I may get from you is a tidbit of information about your event. If that's all I get, I'll take it. If I'm lucky enough to be provided with more, I'll take that too."

It's not entirely a lie. I admire him quite a bit. It takes a highly intelligent man to build his kind of empire while keeping out of the limelight, and a great man to still make time to focus on helping those who may not be able to afford the help themselves. Still, I can't help but feel incredibly guilty talking about respect considering the deceitful plan I'm carrying out.

"Well, you certainly have a way with words."

"You don't believe me."

"I don't believe a lot of people. There's something about having a lot of money and privacy that causes many individuals to present to me the farthest thing from their authentic nature." Well, I can't exactly argue with that.

"I'm not sure what I can do to gain your trust."

"It's quite simple really. Be genuine."

This is proving difficult. I'm experiencing an internal struggle because I want him to be wrong, and in certain instances, like his insistence that even as myself I lack authenticity, it's bogus. However, I'm not being genuine with him at all. He smells the bullshit and my mind is racing trying to grasp the best way to throw off his scent.

"Allow me to ask you something else," he continues. "How can you expect me to tell my life story to a journalist who lacks security in herself? The person who writes the truth about who I am needs to understand depth, and listen with intuition and empathy, in order to ensure the effectiveness and impact of my story. To do that requires harnessing a certain level of self-awareness that I don't believe you've yet to achieve. But, with a little help, you could." Did I hear him correctly or is my severe lack of sleep this week finally catching up to me? I allow my brain to push past the security talk and zoom straight to the part where it sounds likes he's considering letting me write about his life!

As he continues, I do my best not to show how desperately I want this to go my way. "I took it upon myself to do my research on you. I've spoken to some of my peers who you've interviewed before, and I've read a few of your articles. You're quite good at what you do. But you could be great.

"Now, I'm no fool Ms. Rivers, I know what it is you and Ritter want, and it goes well beyond a small article on charity. Although I despise the attention of the media and paparazzi with a passion, I am a businessman and I understand the value of connecting with my audience. The world wishes to know more about who I am, huh? Get a peek behind the curtain? Very well. I suppose I've made them wait long enough." He chuckles softly to himself. "The right person has to write it though," he says, pausing momentarily to gauge my reaction. "It could be you, although I'm not fully convinced. You're lucky though, I love a challenge. Getting you to the point where you are equipped to write about my life… that's a challenge I'm willing to accept, believe it or not.

"I believe I can help you be the very best you can be. So, I'm prepared to teach and show you some valuable things that will change the way you approach your career and positively increase the impact and effect your work has from here on out."

"Do you have a degree in psychology that I don't know about, Mr. Marc?"

"Not at all, but I'm highly experienced in what you are lacking." What, arrogance? It's just like a man to think he can tell me about myself and "educate" me. However, this offer he's presenting seems a little too good to pass up. The irritation caused by his judgement still looms over me, but I'm going to do all I can to play along.

"You really think you have something to teach me?"

"I know I do." A half smile slides up the side of his face. "I'd like to offer you the guest room at my home for the next few weeks leading up to the banquet. It might help you with your research to see how I go about my life, and it will be easier for me to challenge you in the ways I'd like."

"This is all sounding a little too unreal and perfect. What's the catch?"

"No catch. You need my story. I am giving you the opportunity to prove you are capable of being the one to write it. Will you toss it away simply because you are not willing to at least explore whether there is truth to what I am claiming?"

"That I lack self awareness and the ability to be authentic?"

"Precisely."

I match his gaze full force. It truly is interesting to hear that he sees me as a woman with insecurity issues. He was putting it nicely, but I know that's what he means. I'm used to being underestimated by men, so I'm not incredibly phased. I'm more so finding it hard to compute that he's making it this simple. All I have to do is allow him to believe he's some prince charming know-it-all who can "teach" me to be more efficient in an industry he really knows jack shit about, "prove myself", and in return I get the story that's been sought after for almost a decade.

"I still think you're wrong about me, but I'm not opposed to the idea that you could be right. So, okay. I'm in."

"I consider myself an open minded individual and I do take accountability for my mistakes. There's always the possibility that I've erred in my assessment of you. That remains to be seen. If we go through with this experiment, at the very least, you will prove me wrong and show me that you already have what it takes to do my story justice. At most, you'll learn a bit more about yourself and gain the necessary skills to not only write an excellent story, but also stand more firmly in your power. In any case, you could win, Ms. Rivers. But, you should also know going into this that I'm not convinced you're innocent in your intentions either.

"I know enough about Dante Ritter to know the man is all about riveting drama. I'm sure he's told you to do whatever it takes to find some with me, so I am aware that I'm taking a risk here bringing you into my life like this. Don't expect that I'll be rolling out everything in one main course. But there's something about you that I find intriguing, and I really do sense that you have the potential to write something honest, real and profound in its own way. Something that you will deliver confidently, regardless of what Ritter may want."

Again, interesting. So, he's doing all this in the hope that I will write the story he wants me to write. He certainly is taking a huge risk because he's right, Ritter is asking me to do whatever it takes. I have a heart, I'll always do my best to consider the person I interview, but I can't promise he'll like everything I write. In the end, Ritter gets the final say. "I understand."

"I have a meeting to keep so I must go. But instead of interviewing today and meeting for brunch tomorrow, you can accompany me to a picnic at the botanical gardens with some colleagues early tomorrow evening. Afterwards, you'll come back to the house and we'll get you set up in a room. The picnic will give us an opportunity to talk more about what I can do for your article and your personal and professional growth, Ms. Rivers." He grins. "Carmyn will email you the details. Good day."

He swiftly makes his way past me. "Wait! You assume I'm free tomorrow evening."

Still smiling, he smugly replies, "I assume no such thing. See you tomorrow." Well, he certainly has more than enough confidence to spare! More like an enormous ego.

I make my way back to the exit feeling incredibly relieved. This has turned out better than I could have hoped! Alexander Marc has just given me access into his life! I don't even care about his crazy assumptions of me, I'M IN!

No sooner than I hop in my car, my phone chimes with an email from Carmyn. I'm to meet them at Alexander's home tomorrow evening at four sharp. She asks that I wear something suitable, whatever that means. What exactly does one wear to a picnic with a multi-billionaire? Maybe I should see if I can utilize Aralyn's wardrobe fairies, Marie and Jovana.

Damn! I still have to tell Aralyn about the sudden diversion of our plan. Ugh, that should be fun. Just as I'm pulling off, I receive a call.

Well, speak of the devil.

9

waited until I arrived at my flat to call Aralyn back and tell her the news. As expected, she wasn't happy, but there wasn't much she could do about it and I reveled in that knowledge, thrilled about the opportunity to show her that I'm not her puppet and she need not think she can control me. I'm more than capable of making some calls on my own. I didn't tell her about my invitation to stay at Alexander's home, however. I don't believe she needs to know everything, and the more she thinks I'm struggling, the bigger my upper hand. She'll keep assisting me however possible while not knowing how far along I'm getting. The control, for the most part, will remain my own.

Despite her frustration about my diversion, Aralyn agreed to send Jovana to my place to provide me with some adequate attire for tonight's event. Jovana arrived at noon with a whole two racks of garment bags, filled with enough outfit choices to last me all the days leading up to Alexander's banquet. In my mind, I questioned the quantity. There's no way I'm going to wear even half of them. My plan is to play dress up only when absolutely necessary. Although it hasn't been that long since my transformation, every day I've secretly wanted to shield myself in my normal, less flattering wear. It's been years since I've worn anything even remotely close to the trendy and fashionable garments Jovana brought over.

"Do you need assistance with your makeup, Mademoiselle? I brought my kit just in case." Jovana looked at me with concern. I probably would too if I were her. I'm sure it was clear, by the evident shock on my face upon seeing the outfits, that I have no clue what I'm doing. I graciously accepted all the help I could get.

By the time we finished picking the perfect dress, finalizing my makeup look for the evening, and getting my suitcases packed with everything I'll need during my stay at the mansion, I only had about twenty minutes to make it to the estate, thirty minutes away! I couldn't be late! That would weigh heavily on Alexander's trust in me. If anything, I had hoped to make it early. In the professional world, on time is late, and rude.

Alas, here I am pulling up one minute before four. I spot Alexander and Carmyn descending the front steps as I jump out of the car. "Mr. Marc!" They look my way. "I'm sorry I'm late! I should have called. I thought I'd make it earlier than this."

His face doesn't give much away as to how he feels about my tardiness. "As did I. But you're here. Hop in." I question whether he wondered if I'd actually show, and if the thought of my absence was the least bit concerning. Especially considering his bold assumption that I'd drop anything I was doing to be here.

Carmyn gives me a questioning look over before following her boss into the car, as if she's still trying to wrap her head around the new and improved Jess Rivers. Not to mention she must be asking herself how this new Jess Rivers, a journalist, ended up being asked to accompany said boss to a picnic with his business colleagues. The driver holds the door open for me, and I slide in, relieved. I made it. Right now, that's the most important thing.

My seat is directly across from the pair. I spend the first fifteen minutes of the drive invisible, watching as Alexander speaks to his assistant about plans for the week as Carmyn intently jots down, arranges, and re-arranges everything on her digital notepad. They work poetically together. It's easy to see why he keeps the gorgeous, dedicated woman around; she doesn't miss a beat.

And Alexander is… utterly alluring. I shake my head in an attempt to expel the images flooding my mind. I don't want to think these things about him. Afterall, he basically insulted the hell out of me yesterday. But damn, it's hard for me, as I'm sure it is for any woman, to deny the magnitude of his attractiveness. Ambitious, young, charming in a way, radiant sun kissed skin, perfect jawline and well put together with a sort of ruggedness you can sense hiding beneath it all. Mmm, beneath it all… my eyes travel the length of his relaxed, seated frame, imagining what beneath it all might look like in reality. I'm thrust into a vision of him slowly unbuttoning his white shirt while he's gazing at me in that way he did for a moment the other night.

"A few things to note, Jess." His words jilt me from my naughty imagination. Guess I'm no longer invisible. "You'll be keeping your alias persona for this picnic. My colleagues have never seen me with anyone besides my assistant. They'll be curious about you. Considering you are a journalist, and I know the type of individuals my colleagues are, I'm sure a few of them will be looking you up as soon as they have the opportunity and I'd rather not have rumors possibly spread about my personal affairs with the media. So, for today only, you will remain Isabella Evans… erotic author."

Carmyn slides her black rimmed reading glasses down her nose and peers up at me, one eyebrow cocked to a full raise though she says nothing. She doesn't need to. I understand her perfectly and I can feel the blush rising to my cheeks. "Uh, perhaps I should have a different occupation? Something more professional sounding, like a lawyer?"

"That occupation seemed to suit you just fine when you were at the art exhibition."

"Trust me, that occupation was not my idea."

A playful look glints across his features. "Erotic author will do just fine."

"You know, the simple title of novelist would sound much better. More professional, don't you think?"

He shrugs one shoulder. "I think that depends on who you ask."

I give a nervous laugh. "Mr. Marc I–"

"Alexander. Or Alex if you wish. No need for such formalities at this point, Jess."

"Alexander. I'm sorry, but I just don't see the necessity for such a title at an event like this. Even though it's just a social gathering, it's a social gathering with people you work with."

"Jess, do you recall when I said we'd work on your self-assuredness?" Much to my annoyance, of course I do. "This is the perfect opportunity. Why should you care what a group of people you don't know think about who you are or what you do? You should be able to walk into this function and proudly utilize this title with no shame."

I'm in total disbelief. Is this really his reasoning? To test my level of confidence? He was actually serious about what he said. He truly thinks I'm this lost, insecure little girl! My response comes out a bit snappy. "I'm thinking about you and your reputation."

"Is that so? Well, you'll be happy to hear that my reputation will be just fine. So, you should have no problem being Isabella Evans, the incredible erotic novelist from the states."

I want so badly to prove him wrong, throw my hands up and say, "You know what, fuck it, let's do this"! But it's difficult to ignore the pang of fear ripping through my gut. It's bad enough having to show up in clothes that are completely out of my element, now I have to keep up with this façade I started in front of a whole group of strangers who will be heavily interested in who I am. And it has nothing to do with my confidence and everything to do with my distaste for being ogled over. "But, what about when your colleagues look up this name and can't find anything on me?"

"No need to worry. Everything has already been prepared for this day, every single detail. Including that one." Is there anything this man doesn't have covered?

We arrive at the Botanical Gardens, and I try my best to mentally prepare for whatever will come from this. The driver opens Carmyn's door first and she steps out. As Alexander waits for the driver to come around and let us out, he asks, "Now, any further questions before we go in?"

I'm still quaking inside but, I can't deny that Alex is right about one thing. Why should I give a hot damn about what anyone at this function has to say about who I am? Besides, what am I so worried about? I'm not Isabella Evans. I'm not even an erotic author. Who gives a shit? I shake my head in response to his inquiry.

"Good girl." He steps out of the car. I'm taken aback by his words. Those two little words he said in a fairly seductive tone has me feeling... pride? I shake off the thought and tell my inner self to focus on the task at hand, then I slide out of the car and take my first step into the world of Marc.

I had wondered how we were expected to have a picnic in the frosty January weather, but I receive my answer when we are ushered inside and enter the butterfly pavilion. Apparently, this is where the picnic is, and the pavilion is breathtaking! There are trees, foliage and flowers everywhere. Butterflies flutter about, adding magic to the already enchanting environment. Classical tunes, from a band playing in the back, drift through the air. Fancy blankets and baskets are laid out across various grassy mounds that have surely been added for aesthetic. I'm not certain whether it was Alexander or one of his colleagues that orchestrated the closing off of the pavilion specifically for this, but I'm highly impressed!

Alexander extends an arm for me to take. As I do, a blue butterfly lands on our linked arms. He chuckles. "Well, would you look at that? It matches your dress." Jovana helped me pick out this form-fitting, electric blue number with a large bow crossing my left shoulder. I thought it would be entirely too much, but she insisted it would be perfect. I figured she probably knew best so here I am.

I gently hold my hand out to the butterfly hoping it might climb on a finger, but it flies away in a magnificent display of beauty. I watch it fly, mesmerized. "Wow, it's stunning."

"Indeed. The butterfly is too." I look at him, caught off guard by his compliment.

"Shall we, Ms. Evans?" He winks and proceeds forward. I follow in tow, allowing him to guide me as we make our way through the pavilion, greeting people as we go. I put on my best smile and give a warm hello to everyone who stops to clamor for Alexander's attention. Many people have a flabbergasted look on their face upon noticing me. There's a multitude of questions apparent in their gaze. Alexander did warn me that this would be the case but being in the spotlight now has me wishing I was anywhere but here. When I look behind me, I am met with a bunch of peering eyes staring at me up and down. They all whisper amongst themselves.

In order to calm my nerves, I opt to turn my attention to the trees filled with butterflies, fluttering, floating and gliding. I wonder if they, too, detest being gawked at. I wonder if they know their pretty little lives merely serve the purpose of entertaining people like us today. Most everyone here will have their picnics, get their fill of dopamine, and go about their merry way forgetting all about these creatures. But I won't forget. I won't forget because I know what it's like to be the butterfly, trapped because you're beautiful, enjoyed because you're beautiful, forgotten because beauty is fleeting. I know.

"Isabella."

"Hmm?" Alex pulls me from my drifting thoughts once again. "Oh, sorry. I was distracted."

"I see. I've been calling your name for at least thirty seconds."

I flash a large, amused smile. "Yeah? Which one."

"Mm, cheeky, aren't you?"

"I'm just saying, if you consistently called me Isabella for those thirty seconds, you can hardly blame me for not responding to a name that isn't my own Mr. Marc."

"Yeah? And what is my name?"

"That's an odd question."

"Well, I recall requesting that you call me by my first name instead."

"Well, I recall not wanting to go by Isabella Evans anymore. We can't always get what we want, Mr. Marc." I grin and walk ahead leaving him speechless. He thinks he's so clever. Little does he know; he's met his match in me.

I approach Carmyn who's standing next to a blanketed area with a plaque posted next to it displaying Alexander's name. "This is us, darling," she addresses me, rummaging through the basket as I take a seat. She kneels down and pulls out a wonderfully arranged charcuterie board and other delectable bite sized treats. It's such a French setup. Alex is still back where I left him, chatting away with a few gentlemen I've yet to meet.

"Carmyn, how come Mr. Marc doesn't take anyone else to these functions?" She appears irritated that I'm asking.

"I wouldn't know. I imagine he has his reasons." Honestly, I don't know why I even try to get anything out of her. "It appears I've left something. I'll be back." She gets up and walks off toward the entrance.

I spend some time alone, enjoying the sights, sounds and delicious hors d'oeuvres. "Do you have the right area, Mademoiselle?" A man seated on the blanket nearby ours directs his question at me.

"Pardon?"

"That blanket is reserved for the CEO."

"Yes. I'm aware." I'd place the man in his late fifties. Either that or his outrageous mustache and Shakespearian pointed beard is aging him a few years.

"Pardon. I did not expect him to bring anyone other than Mademoiselle Calloway." Geez, he really doesn't step out with anyone. "Ah, Alex! Bonsoir."

Alexander takes a seat beside me. "Bonsoir, Laurent. I see you've met my friend, Isabella Evans."

"Oui, though I had not yet had the pleasure of introducing myself properly. Enchanté, Mademoiselle Isabella."

"Enchantée Monsieur."

"Isabella, this is Laurent Coultier. He is the president of my management branch here in Paris."

"Oh! How lovely." A waiter comes by with a tray full of flutes of champagne just in time.

"What is it you do, Mademoiselle?"

"Um, well I'm, uh, I'm a novelist." I don't care what Alex wants me to say, there's no way I'm saying–

"Izzy here is being quite modest, Laurent. She's an erotic novelist." I choke on my champagne. Dear God, say it's not so!

"Littérature érotique? How interesting! My wife would love to speak with you. She adores such work." I give a coy laugh in response and go back to sipping my drink, hoping no one will notice the embarrassment plastered on my face. This is absolutely mortifying. "She said she would meet me here soon. She was meeting with a friend of hers that she's bringing."

My mind wanders briefly as Laurent and Alex transition into conversation that loses my interest as quickly as it begins. Something business related with numbers. Carmyn finally comes back with a bag she didn't have with her earlier. Looks like a small pocketbook.

The whole pavilion is a buzz with conversation while basking in the ambiance of what is now a lantern lit picnic since the sun has almost disappeared below the horizon. Of all the places I thought my career would take me, I never imagined this adventure, and to think it's only just begun. It's grand, thrilling, nerve-wrecking and wildly overwhelming all at once.

"Ah! There they are. Claire, my love, over this way!" Laurent waves over to a pair, a woman and a man, standing at the entrance and scanning their surroundings. They spot us and the woman waves back, excitedly making her way toward us with the gentleman in tow. As they get closer and my eyes adjust to the sight of them in the dim light of the room, I am gripped by utter disbelief. No way I'm seeing who I think I'm seeing. Claire's friend is Charles Deflour?

This is bad. Oh, this is very bad! What the hell is he doing here? If he notices me, my cover is at huge risk of being blown! My heart is pounding in my throat. I have to act fast. "Uh, please excuse me for a moment."

"Oh, won't you stay? Claire is almost here," Laurent asks, confused by my urgent need to flee.

"It really can't wait. Excuse me."

Alexander grabs a hold of my wrist as I spring to my feet and softly whispers, "What's wrong?"

"Just trust me. I'll explain later." I shake loose his hold and swiftly take the roundabout way to the entrance in order to avoid the two incoming guests. I'm so thankful for the low lighting, hoping it's enough to keep me obscured from their sight while I make a beeline out of here.

My head is spinning. This doesn't make sense. What is Charles doing with Claire Coultier? How friendly are they really? This has to be a set up! Once again, Charles is forcefully inserting his ego into my work! I bet anything he wormed the intel about the function out of one of his connections and found a way to gain access. What better way than to befriend the wife of the president of Alexander's company branch here in France? He knew this would be his best chance to sit face to face with him and covertly gather intel, not just from Alex, but from one of his head employees. I'm fuming! I should have known he would pull this crap, again!

I make it outside and pace back and forth, trying to calm down. Snowflakes are falling but I'm so heated, they melt as soon as they hit me. Ugh, why now? Can't I just get a break? This was my opportunity to really sit with Alex and gain some insight from not just him, but potentially Laurent as well and he just had to come in and make a mess of things!

"Jess!" Alexander hurriedly approaches me. "What's happening? I could tell something's wrong." He actually seems concerned about me and it's odd to discover that it's that realization causing my heart rate to settle.

"I'm sorry if I embarrassed you in there, but I had to go. If he would have recognized me–"

"Wait, woah, if who would have recognized you?"

Before replying, I do my best to regain control of my breath. "That man with Laurent's wife, he's another freelance journalist that Ritter employs from time to time, like me. My guess is he somehow found a way to get close to Claire in order to be here tonight."

"In order to find out more about me."

"Yes, exactly."

Alexander starts laughing and for the life of me I don't understand what's so funny. "I'm glad it's a joke to you! Besides snooping around for information, he could have totally blown my cover! Then you'd be looking crazy right along with me."

"It's not that. Jess, where on earth is your coat? I swear woman, hypothermia will be the way you exit this world." My confusion turns to amusement, and I, too, laugh at how silly I, once again, appear.

"At least I'm wearing my shoes this time."

"At least." His smile remains and I melt along with the snowflakes that kiss our skin. He really should smile more often. The world is missing out. Though there's this greedy part of me that loves the fact that I'm one of the few who get to see it. "Come inside. I can't take you seriously out here."

He leads the way back into the building. "I'm honestly amazed that there's anything you don't take seriously."

"Prepare to be amazed a lot then. I'm far from predictable." So, it appears. Layers. Alexander, I'm beginning to sense, is a man of many layers. Huh, not a shabby way to start off my article. I'll have to remember that.

We make our way into the main hall, and he requests my coat from the coat attendant. "Wait, what are you doing? We're inside, I don't need my coat anymore."

"Are you planning on going back in there to say hello to your friend?"

"I'd say he's more like my mortal enemy, but no."

"Well then, put on your coat so we can leave your mortal enemy thoroughly disappointed. Carmyn can fill in for me. Let's go home, Ms. Rivers." His words are music to my ears.

10

I'm woken by the sound of icy rain hitting my windows. Groggily, I peek at the clock on the nightstand. Four in the morning. Ugh, how annoying, I turn over, trying to slip back into sleep, but it's a struggle, as I'm distracted by how dry my mouth feels. Definitely in need of some water! I crawl out of bed and throw on a navy-blue, satin robe I had discovered hanging neatly in the master bathroom earlier. I don't care much for sleeping in pj's so it's the perfect cover up, and it feels wonderful against my skin.

Somehow, I'll have to find my way to the kitchen. When Alexander and I got back to the house, there wasn't much time for the grand tour. As soon as we made it in, Carmyn called letting him know that there were some pressing matters to attend to regarding some sector of their facility back in Britain. He apologized for how short the evening had to be cut and had his doorman assist me with my luggage and show me to my room.

I had fallen asleep pretty disappointed with how the night shaped out, knowing I wasted an opportunity to get more information for my story. There wasn't much I could take away from the evening other than the knowledge that Charles DeFlour is officially out for my job. And that bit of information does nothing for my stress levels. I have to figure out some way to make this article a success. Alexander says that he'll give me his story, and he did have me basically move into his home for the next couple weeks, but I have my doubts. For all I know, his intentions could be to give me the run around, making it look like he wants to do this, but plans to do the same thing he did day one of our journey and find a way to avoid all the deep, personal questions.

I walk out of the room, ready for my kitchen hunting escapade. For the most part, I'm able to keep my footsteps light as I descend the large staircase, stopping abruptly when I hear the sound of music softly humming through the air. It grows louder as I reach the first floor. I listen for the direction it might be coming from and follow it to a familiar room, the parlor where I first met Alexander.

The door is slightly ajar. I peer through, trying my best to catch a glimpse of the music's origin without having to open the door any wider. On a slightly raised platform in the corner of the room near the trickling fall, I spy Alexander seated, playing a cello. It looks as if he's on a throne. The strings are like his subjects; he orders them around and they, ever so loyal, do as his bow and fingers command. The melody is haunting, moving, utterly beautiful, and I find myself enthralled by the manner in which he plays, such passion.

The room is candle lit— the perfect mood for his grand performance. He's still in black slacks and a white formal shirt, though his tie is missing, and the top three buttons of his shirt are undone, displaying a peek of his chest. Everything about this scene, I find incredibly hypnotic. Before I know it, I've stepped fully inside the room, gazing upon him in awe.

Suddenly aware of my presence after several moments, he stops. "Jess, I apologize. I do hope my playing didn't disturb you."

"No, not at all. I had just come down for some water."

He smirks. "Trouble finding the kitchen I take it?"

"I admit, I have no idea how to find it. But I forgot all about the kitchen when I heard you. You play beautifully."

He looks down at his instrument, studying it intently. "I feel close to my father when I play. My very first cello was his. He was one of the finest musicians I knew. He played many instruments, but this was his favorite. Sadly, he gave up on a career in music prior to my entrance into this world. Took up entrepreneurship instead. But every so often, he'd dust off his cello and play it, usually just on special occasions." He takes a pause, reliving memories in his mind no doubt. "I loved listening to his music. There were a few birthdays where all I really wanted was for him to teach me, just for a couple hours."

"Did he?"

"He did once. But then he ended up passing his down to me and hiring someone to teach me instead. I think it was too painful for him to constantly be reminded of what he left behind. I often wish he would have stuck with it. I really believe he could have been one of the greats."

"But then you wouldn't have such an empire to run."

He's silent a long moment before answering. "Perhaps. However, I'm not sure I would have minded."

It's intriguing to hear him say that. Is Alex content with being where he is? It's something I hadn't pondered before. What else, I wonder, would he have preferred to do than to carry on his father's legacy? How many of his own dreams did he pack away to keep the business alive?

"I can tell you really admired him."

He glances up at me, a small smile on his lips. "Looks like you just got your first bit of exclusive information."

"It would appear so. Thank you for sharing that with me. It's very insightful."

"Yes, I'm sure the readers will thoroughly enjoy it." He places the cello to the side on a stand.

"I meant it was insightful for me." It would certainly pull views but, for once, I'm not concerned with the article. In the short time I've known him, I've begun to see Alex as a giant jigsaw puzzle. So many pieces that I'm eager to put together simply because I find it thrilling to do so.

"Let's get you that water." He clears his throat and steps off the platform, walking over to the bar area. He then grabs a glass bottle out of the mini fridge. "Is spring alright?"

"Perfect." I walk over and take a seat, observing closely as he pops the top and pours two glasses. "So, I know why I'm up but why are you? Don't you have another busy day tomorrow, well, er, today I mean?"

"I have off." My eyebrows raise in astonishment, and he slides over a glass. "I know, shocking. I'm not a complete work addict. I do take breaks, Jess."

He's right, I do find that shocking, though I'm not sure why. I suppose I had assumed he was all-work-no-pleasure. "I take it you got your business back in England all squared away then?"

"I'd probably be on a jet right now on my way to take care of it personally if I didn't have such a thorough team. Thanks to them, I can breathe a little easier."

"What do you do on your days off?"

"Whatever I bloody want." He raises his glass to mine, and they chime with a clink. "Cheers."

I chuckle. "You really are a conundrum. The way you can be so forthcoming with information one minute and entirely covert the next is baffling."

"Always keep them guessing."

"To be honest, I'm not sure if the readers will understand the enigmatic character you are."

"I'd be entirely shocked if they did." Ahh, I see. He likes this, being a misunderstood mystery– a foreign concept to me. I've spent more time and energy than I'd like to admit trying to convince people of who I am and what I'm made of, and yet, remain overlooked or misunderstood more often than not. So much energy spent trying to get people to see me for me! Yet here he is, totally content with the knowledge that many people may never truly see him.

"You know, Jess, I'm not the only enigma in this room."

"Me? What, you think I'm hard to read?" He smiles, seemingly amused by the question.

"No, I personally don't find you hard to read at all, but you are hiding parts of yourself from others, and that tends to add an element of mystery to you." What does he keep thinking I'm hiding? "I'm willing to bet you've been misunderstood a great deal, haven't you?"

Okay, well, he isn't wrong about that. "I suppose. Though it hasn't always been that way."

"So, when did things change?"

My brow furrows and I chortle. "Um, when did we suddenly go from talking about you to talking about me? I sense some deflection."

"Or you sense genuine interest."

"Perhaps… but it's hard to tell with you." Is Alexander Marc really that interested in me? And why? I represent the very thing he dislikes, the media. And yet here I am, staying in his home, drinking from his glass in the early hours of the morning, being told by him that he's interested in who I am. I'm not sure what to make of this besides questioning whether or not I'm in the twilight zone.

"How about this, I promise to tell you something deeply personal about me, in exchange for your truth."

Hmm. "I'm curious to see what truth you're looking to hear, but okay. Is this on or off the record?"

"Mm, good question." He clears his throat. "As you know, I don't trust journalists, I'm sure that's been made very clear over the past several years but, I'm trying hard to trust you. Don't ask me why. I'm still figuring that out myself. I won't give away too much, but yes, whatever I tell you here tonight, you may use in your article if you wish." My stomach ties itself in knots as the guilt creeps up, settling into my throat. I don't believe I'm deserving of what little trust he's willing to give. "So, shall we begin?" he asks.

"Sure. What's your question?"

"Same as before. When did things change and you started becoming misunderstood?"

My thoughts open up the closet of my mind that I've tried hard to keep shut. "When I moved to Paris, I was so naive. I came here quite confident that I could have it all– the happiness, a highly successful career, maybe meet a great man. I even envisioned growing a family in this city someday. I think I was so immersed in the dream that I didn't take into consideration that things may not go according to plan. My first job out here was with my dream company. Like, since my freshman year of college, this was the company I was gunning to get a position at. So, when I got hired by them not long after my graduation, I was absolutely thrilled!

"During the first month, I was full of excitement and passion, life seemed great. But overtime as the months passed by, I started noticing certain behaviors from some of my coworkers that made me question a lot about myself, my career choice and my decision to leave home and come to the land of my dreams. I truly thought the biggest issue I'd face was judgement because I'm American, but that was the least of the problems. Men in the work environment would make uncomfortable, sexual remarks about my body. Some women too… though most of the women I had issue with would pretend to be kind but spread ugly rumors behind my back.

"They made it hard to feel accepted, hard to feel sane in some cases, and hard to feel safe. I'd never experienced that before. And it wasn't just not being accepted for who I am in general, but also the unfair disadvantages I was subjected to when it came to my work. I'd have to beg my boss to give me assignments that were actually good and not just some trivial assignments you throw off on interns.

"I thought that perhaps I had to prove myself worthy of getting the hard-hitting stories because I was the fresh meat from overseas, so I busted my ass at that company for two years. All I got in return was repeated harassment. It was as if my boss was purposefully making it difficult for me to be there because I wasn't giving in to his advances!" My breathing becomes shaky as flashes of memories I've ignored for so long flood back into my mind. "The last straw was when he had… um… he had, um–" I choke on my words, trying to keep the well of tears from surfacing. I've never spoken about this to anyone before, not even to Arthur.

"Don't. You don't have to continue." One lone tear manages to escape down my cheek. I move to wipe it, but Alexander's thumb beats me to it, gently sweeping it away with the knuckle of his index finger. I'm astounded by such a caring act.

"I'm sorry. I didn't expect–"

"Don't ever apologize for expressing yourself. Ever." His hand, still lingering on my face, is warm and comforting. I stare into his eyes and then avert my gaze, shy and a bit embarrassed, thinking that in an instant he may have caught the hint of longing my heart stirs up within me. Longing for more of his touch on my skin, especially as he draws his hand away.

"I appreciate you sharing that. When and if you're ready to share more, I'm more than willing to listen. But it needn't be tonight." He grabs a napkin, handing it to me while chuckling.

"Looks like it's my turn to be a little vulnerable. What would you like to know?"

"I really enjoyed hearing about your father's love of music. I'd love to know a bit about your upbringing."

"I was born in Florence, Italy, to an Italian mother and a British father. When I was two, we moved to the UK and I primarily grew up in a flat in an urban area of Manchester, where I experienced a fairly normal childhood. My father's company took off around the time I entered secondary school, and it was then that we moved to a home in the suburbs. My father wanted me to be well rounded and have the best chance at getting into an Ivy League university. So, I was enrolled in everything I could manage to make that happen. Became class valedictorian, was captain of the rugby team, attended every popular societal function you could think of."

"Wow! You were quite popular. I'm sure you were a real catch with the ladies."

"I did receive a lot of attention but I didn't have time for relationships. I barely had time for casual encounters. Even still, I tried dating this great girl right before graduation. We'd both been accepted into the same university so we figured we might actually be able to make it work. But everything changed after my father's passing." His father's death was no secret. I had thoroughly combed through the articles about the tragedy that befell his family. His father, murdered at the hand of his own brother–Alex's uncle– out of greed. It's enough to make my stomach turn.

"He passed after your graduation?"

"Before." He gazes off into the distance. "It was rough. You always have this vision about how these important moments in your life will go. I pictured my father being the one to drop me off on my first day of uni and looked forward to seeing him at my graduation ceremony, so proud of my achievements. But it's like you said last night, we can't always have what we want. I never made it to uni; I had a business to run." My heart breaks for him. Alexander had spent years building up dreams that fell apart because of the actions of one heartless person. His own blood at that! I knew he took over the business at quite a young age, but I had thought someone else had helped him run it for a year or two till he could get his life in order again.

"So, you don't have a degree?"

"No. My father started teaching me the ins and outs of the business when I was twelve, so I acquired an in-depth understanding of the company and how it was run. I saw firsthand what worked and what didn't. He prepared me to take over eventually. Of course, neither of us thought 'eventually' would ever come so soon.

"When you are thrust out into the world, life becomes your greatest teacher, you have no choice but to sink or swim. I felt I owed it to my father to swim. So, I did everything I could to keep his legacy afloat." He was just a boy. The amount of growing up he had to do in such a short time frame boggles my mind. At eighteen, he inherited a multi-million-dollar company that was declining and, within three years, that company's net worth grew to be in the billions! The amount of dedication, intellect and skill required to pull that off at any age is astounding.

"I'm really sorry. I had no idea that you had such a jarring introduction into your role like that."

"Well, how could you? Most people don't know." I catch the bits of pain that subtly cross his features as he stares at his now empty glass. His Adam's apple moves in a curious way, as if he's swallowed the emotion that comes with the memories.

"You're amazing." He looks at me, bewildered by my compliment. "Seriously! Do you realize what you've accomplished? It's unheard of!"

He smiles coyly. "Will that do for now then?"

I beam. "It's a great start."

We sit in silence for a few moments, looking at one another. His stormy gaze is penetrating as he runs a thumb along his lower lip. "I think I'd quite like to take you somewhere tomorrow night. This may be incredibly reckless on my part, but there's something about me and my…taste, that you might find rather surprising, and it may just provide you with some solid content for your article."

After the past few days I've had, I'm not sure anything can startle me too much anymore. "So, to be clear, wherever you're taking me is going to reveal something eye opening about you?"

"Precisely. But there's a dress code. I'll have Carmyn pick you up something to wear."

"If you tell me what the dress code is I may already have suitable attire." Lord knows Aralyn supplied me with a lifetime worth.

"That's quite alright. I need to make sure it's perfect." Geez, control freak much? "I should warn you that what you will see may be a bit shocking. So, if a shocking adventure doesn't sound like something you'd be into, please let me know and we won't go."

"And you can't just tell me where we are going?"

"No."

I'm incredibly intrigued. No way I'm backing out of this opportunity. I mean, after all, what's a bit more shock and awe? "Count me in."

"Okay then." He stands erect. "Well, I do believe if I'm to have any semblance of a day off, I should make my way to bed. After I escort you to yours, of course."

I cock an eyebrow. "Escort me to bed? I think I'm capable of finding my own way back, thank you."

He snickers. "Are you sure about that? You seemed to have trouble finding your way to the kitchen."

"Funny. Real funny." I cheese. "Goodnight, Mr. Marc."

"Must you insist on the formalities, Ms. Rivers?"

"Must you insist on treating me as though I'm incapable of taking care of myself?"

"Cheeky girl. That mouth is trouble." There's that fluttering in my nether regions again. I don't think I'll ever get over the way he looks at me like he does right now. It's both incredibly confusing and arousing. I'm getting the sense that the line between business and personal has been gradually blurring, and I have no idea how we got here, or if I'm just imagining it all.

"Welp! Me and my trouble making mouth are just gonna scurry off to bed. Thanks for the water!"

I hop off the bar stool and hurriedly walk to the door. Suddenly, I notice an odd breeze and look down to see my robe wide open. My bra and panties are on full display! Thank God

I'm not facing him! I suck in a sharp breath, immediately closing the fabric around myself and frantically scanning the floor for my robe tie, only to discover that it's looped around a hook on the bar. I can feel myself turning pale.

Alexander chuckles, walks around the bar, and collects it. "Come here." Hesitantly, I do as he commands. He fondles the fabric in his hands and meets me halfway.

"May I?" He asks.

I take it back– perhaps there are still some things that can startle me. It takes a moment to process the fact that this man is asking for my consent. It's literally dumbfounding. I don't even remember the last time I've been asked my consent for anything. This is sexy as hell, and I can't control my trouble-making mouth from saying, "Uh, yeah…okay."

He smiles softly. "Turn."

I turn with my arms still hugged around my chest to keep the fabric from falling open again. He comes up behind me, gently wrapping the sash around my torso. I can feel his body heat on my back, but his body doesn't touch me. It's such a tease to have him this close, yet so far, when I want him as bad as I'm finding I do. I'd drop my hands right now and let the robe fall where I stand if I wasn't so unsure whether I've been misreading his body language. Briefly, I wonder if he can hear my heart beating out of my chest, fluttering a mile a minute.

When he finishes tying me up, his hands gently cup the sides of my arms and he leans in close to my ear, whispering, "Perfect." I melt. I may need help to my room after all.

I pull myself together and turn to face him once more. "Good night, Alex."

With a divine smirk he replies, "Pleasant dreams, Jess."

11

pon returning to my room, I fling myself onto the bed and bury my face into a pillow, screaming at the top of my lungs in hopes for some type of release other than the one my body begs for but my mind is insistent on rejecting. How I could have allowed Alexander to trigger this need raging within is beyond me. Somehow, he has me tied up into a billion knots that I'm now left to undo myself.

I curl up under the comforter, creating a cocoon. The cozy warmth only makes the aching worse and does absolutely nothing to stop the imagery running through my mind. Thoughts of Alexander behind me, his breath raising the hairs on my neck, his fingers trailing down my abdomen causing my muscles to constrict from the tingly sensation his touch ignites. No, the warmth of my bed does nothing at all to stop this fantasy. Nothing to stop my pussy from throbbing, nor my own fingers from traveling south to do the job I wish he would have.

My back arches as I revel in this mixture of imagination and self-gratification. Flashes of wanton indulgence dance in my head the way I envision his tongue dancing across my clit, flicking and twirling and making me lose my mind. I picture the seductive curl of his lips upon witnessing my awe as he slowly lowers the zipper of his jeans. I imagine the sensation of him inside me, stirring the lustful desire that holds me hostage. So, it has come to this; this moment of ecstasy building to an intoxicating level that's certain to spin my world out of orbit.

Incredible how he's managed to achieve this small victory, and he doesn't even need to be here to know it. The look he gave downstairs as he bid me sweet dreams said he knew all too well; that glint in his eye that showed his satisfaction in the knowledge. I'm confident that he sensed it would be his face I'd envision as my fingers finish what he started. He knew that it would be his name that would breathlessly escape my lips as I finally, finally, found sweet release.

I was getting ready to head over to Eiffel when Arthur called to let me know that Ritter had postponed my progress meeting with him, which was relieving to hear. Alexander was beginning to open up to me, proven by our conversation in the wee hours of the morning yesterday. And though I'm certain Ritter would be pleased to find that I've managed to gather something of interest, I know he wants more. He wants the juicy tidbits, the jaw dropping details. If he could get a whole damn memoir on Alexander Marc's life he'd be thrilled, but he'll take it summarized in an article instead. That's a lot of pressure.

While he had me on the phone, Art took the opportunity to let me know how much he's looking forward to our date tonight at seven and I almost freaked out. I totally forgot he had made the reservations for tonight! I accidentally double booked! Alexander is also taking me out tonight to that mysterious location he mentioned. He left a note with the doorman this morning saying that we'd be leaving at nine, so I have two hours to somehow make this dinner with Art and make it back in time to get ready for my outing with Alex. Two men, two outings, one eventful evening. Holy hell, and I thought my life before had been hectic.

I stand in the entryway of my new bedroom's rather large walk-in closet, gazing at all the outfit selections, searching for something that would be appropriate for dinner with Art. On one side of the closet are all the garments that Aralyn lent me. On the other side is my plain Jane attire. It's weird to see just how different my clothing is from the vibrant, alluring picks that Aralyn hand chose. Like wow! I really turned down the sex appeal over the years. I stare at the mannequin head placed on a shelf at the end of the closet, wearing the long blond wig I was given to change back into in order to look like "myself" again. I had planned on using it today when I was getting ready to go meet with Ritter. I'm once again pondering the possibility of wearing it now that I'm headed to see Art, but I don't know, my new hairdo is starting to grow on me.

I felt sexy this weekend! Really sexy. And though it's been frightening being back in the spotlight, it's somehow been easier this time around. I'm not exactly sure why. Maybe it has something to do with Alexander. I've begun to notice that when I'm with him, I don't feel drooled over. I don't get the sense that I'm being taken advantage of or seen as less than. I'm cared about and respected. All this from a man I still barely know. It's a breath of fresh air that I want to indulge in again and again. Maybe it's okay to step out of my comfort zone and test the limits a little more to allow Art the opportunity to see me too.

So be it! Jess "Isabella" Rivers it is. I trust Art more than anyone so, to me, this is a good step in the right direction. I procure a pretty, peach colored dress with one sleeve that covers the right arm, leaving the other arm and shoulder bare. And I spy some peach pumps that go with it perfectly. I'm pleased with this choice. It feels good to let loose and choose to be bold.

The host ushers me to the table where Art is waiting and I take the seat across from him. "Hey! I hope you haven't been waiting too long. Parking took forever to find. This place is really something isn't it? I just love the–" Arthur's face is overtaken with astonishment. "What? What is it?"

"You…look…"

"Oh, um, yeah, I felt it was time to try something…different. You don't think it's too over-the-top, do you?"

"No! On the contrary. I think you look amazing." He takes a sip of his lemon water and lightly loosens his tie. "Very nice."

A shy smile graces my face. "Well, would you look at that? It's not every day I get a solid compliment from the great Arthur Reed."

"No?"

"No. Usually you make some sarcastic remark about how I look."

He snickers. "It's just a bit of fun. You know how I really feel about you. I think you're absolutely gorgeous. And I think you're far too smart and beautiful to be as lonely as you've been in…well, forever. Which leads us to why we're here."

"Uh oh, do I hear a proposal in the works?"

"Maybe."

I laugh until I notice his expression never relinquishes its seriousness. My phone chimes loudly, disturbing the consequential silence that's developed between us. Another chime follows.

"Uh, are you gonna get that?" My eyes blink a few times as I break myself from the strange hold of the moment. Picking up my phone, I look at the text notification and my eyes widen. It's from Aralyn.

We need to talk!
Now!

"Everything okay?"

"Not sure. I'm sorry Art, I need to make a call." He nods. I rise from my seat and make my way outside.

Aralyn picks up on the very first ring and I'm met with a tone of near panic. "Where is Alexander taking you tonight?"

"Hello to you too. And how did you know he was taking me anywhere?"

"I heard from a source." Oh God, whatever. Here we go again with the concealed information.

"Look, I have no idea where he's taking me. He just said there's someplace he wants to show me and to be ready by nine. I didn't ask any further questions, I'm sure that's something you can understand." I made sure to put a spicy emphasis on that last part.

"Jess, listen to me very carefully. I believe I know where he's taking you and if it's where I think, you are going to see some things that may…alarm you."

"What do you mean alarm me? Where is he taking me?"

"Just be open minded and try not to jump to any conclusions. We can talk about whatever you discover later and I'll answer any of the questions you have." Wow! Aralyn, willing to answer questions? That's the shock of the century. She hangs up before I can get a word in. My mouth opens releasing only a small squeak where words should have escaped instead.

Per usual, after a conversation with her, my mind is swarmed with questions. The intrigue I had about tonight's affair turns to that of concern. I compare it to how I felt merely a week before in Madame Chérot's Salon, about to step through the doorway into the secret room, not knowing if I should, worried that my life could take a dramatic turn if I did, and it certainly has! I know Alex warned me that what I witness tonight could be shocking, but alarming? Can I even handle another bout of drama at this point? Do I have the mental capacity?

After fixing my dress and collecting myself, I head back to the table where Art still sits, ever so patiently. I hesitate before entering his line of sight, taking the opportunity to reflect on what to tell the most important friend I have on this side of the world, should he discuss with me what I think he might. I have had suspicion for a while that at some point he's going to ask me to take things to the next level and I am nervous that that point might be tonight.

As I have a seat, I say nothing. The magnitude of everything said to me since I first walked into this restaurant still shuffles through my head. I know I'm not doing myself any justice by dwelling, but I can't seem to help myself.

"Got a hot date tonight?"

I almost choke on my Merlot. "Excuse me?"

Art chuckles. "I'm messing with you. I mean, unless you really do." Well, he's not too far off. I give my best passive laugh and it suddenly feels as though a spotlight is beaming in my direction and every eye in here is on me. Small beads of sweat start to form across my brow thankfully covered by my bangs, for the most part.

There's a growing, unspoken pressure building that's getting hard to avoid. Am I going to have to tell my best friend that I'm not ready to provide him with his ultimate happiness in being his woman? It isn't that I never considered it. It isn't even that I don't want to be because, in truth, the past two of the four years we've known each other, I saw myself potentially sharing a life with him.

Art's an amazing man, especially to me. He's supportive, caring, attentive, always there to lend an ear or a shoulder to cry on and he knows when to put me in my place. With him, it's easy, fluid, and yet, there's something preventing me from taking that next step to the place where he's already standing, waiting for me. I've yet to put my finger on what that something is.

"Art…"

"Anyway, what's going on with Marc? You've been M.I.A for almost a week. Anything new on him?"

I'm relieved by his decision to change the topic but now I have a whole new dilemma. How much do I tell him about the events that have taken place over the past several days? How do I explain the real reason for my makeover or being invited to stay in Alexander's home? How do I explain how fascinating, deep and utterly intoxicating I find the man? Simple. I won't. He'll just have to get the basics.

"There's been a reasonable amount of progress, I think. I was able to get a bit of a backstory from him which is good. For the most part though, he still seems very cautious about answering questions. On top of that, everyone I've asked who's somewhat close to him gives very little away. From what I've seen, he keeps no journals, no physical records or pieces of mail laying around that even remotely reflect anything regarding his life outside of business."

"Wait, you went through his mail? How did you pull that off?"

"Well, I wouldn't say I checked his mail, more like I checked around to see if there was any mail. He left me alone for a bit, so I took the opportunity." No way on God's beautiful, lush earth am I telling him how I ended up spending an entire day by myself in Alexander's home that I now conveniently have a room in.

Yesterday, while he had been doing heavens knows what on his day off, I took it upon myself to take that house tour I never got. I didn't exactly rummage through his belongings as Art may think. I just inconspicuously took a thorough look around for anything that could stand out as newsworthy information.

Art leans back in his seat. "Huh. How did you manage that?"

"Manage what?"

"One of the most private businessmen in the world leaves a journalist alone in his space. You really expect me to believe THE Alexander James Marc took that risk?" The waitress arrives just in time to save my ass! She sets a piping hot bowl of stew in front of me. "Oh, I hope you don't mind. You were making that call. I figured you'd want your favorite anyway, so I went ahead and ordered it."

"You know me so well." I stare at the dish. Normally I would have dug in instantly, but I'm almost disappointed with the selection, which stupefies me. Beef bourguignon is my absolute favorite meal in the entire world. Usually, if you give me this and a bottle of red wine, I'm in heaven. So why do I feel so unsatisfied?

"Do I really? In all my years of knowing you I've never seen you gaze so unpleasantly at a dish as you are now."

"Am I?" I pick up my spoon and take it to the stew, pushing the beef and vegetables around and around before lifting it to take a bite.

"Is everything okay with you?"

"I'm fine. There's just been a lot of pressure lately, you know? A lot of expectation and a growing list of people I don't want to let down…including you." Art's hand reaches across the table and envelops mine.

"Jess, no matter what happens with this article, you won't let me down. Know that and take some comfort in it. Please." That's the thing, I am most certainly not able to take comfort in it at all. He doesn't realize that it's not about the article. There are so many things that are rapidly evolving with my feelings that have the potential to impact Art harder than he'd ever suspect. It's obvious he wants me to share the weight and burden of my world with him because he truly believes that there's nothing I can do to disappoint him. How could he ever imagine that the weight of my world can potentially lead to the obliteration of the one he's dreamed of with me?

I want to hang on tight to every last fiber that keeps us tethered as just friends, but I know sooner or later, just friends will no longer be enough for him, and I'll be given an ultimatum. Of course, Arthur would never fully cast me aside for denying him, but I know he wouldn't be able to be there for me the same way he's always been. With each hangout, I become increasingly aware that our clock is ticking, and the sound annoys me to no end. I'm not ready to choose.

"You'll be fine. You just said you were already able to get some backstory on him which is big! That's a lot more than others have been able to achieve."

I let out a deep sigh. "True."

"Ay, I know just what is needed to lift your spirits. How about we take a nice stroll along the Seine after we're done here? I'll get us a bottle of red on the way and you can hear me crack jokes for an hour or two." I burst out in a fit of giggles. "Ah, see? The perfect cure."

"You're unbearable Arthur Reed. I, um, I'd like to-"

"Uh-oh. Why do I hear a 'but' coming?"

"I told someone I'd attend an event with them tonight." His face playfully calls bullshit. "I'm a woman of my word, Art. Trust me, it would have been incredible hearing jokes for an hour, especially your jokes." I reach across the table and give him a playful punch on his arm.

"Ow, Jess! You're kinda strong! Only kinda though." He's got the cheesiest grin on his face. I shake my head amused. What a cheese ball.

"Hey, uh, by the way, I'm not really sure if this is the best time to mention it, but early today when I was at the office, Ritter told me that Charles came to him on Friday pushing his proposal to work on the Marc interview instead of you."

"WHAT?! That fucking asshole of a, ugh! Who does he think he is?"

"A short man with a large ego to stroke. You should have expected that to happen. I did."

"Whether it's expected or not, the fact that he actually tried is infuriating. Did you know I caught him trying to get an audience with Alexander a couple nights ago?"

"Again, not surprising. He's always been a sneaky bastard."

"But it doesn't make it acceptable, Art." Charles had gone behind my back many times in the past attempting to get a particular story out before I did. I'm not sure what he has against me, if anything, but the past year had been free of his sneaky thievery and I'd hoped that it was mostly behind us. Apparently not.

"Hate to say it, but Ritter is actually considering it."

"No way. No fucking way!"

"Now, before you go all postal, he's only considering it as a backup option."

"Oh, in case I fail." I throw my hands up in a surge of frustration. "Nice to know Ritter has so much faith in me. I mean honestly, why even give me the assignment?"

"Please don't hate me, but I sided with him."

I'm in such disbelief. No way I heard what I think I just heard. "You *what*?"

"It makes sense, Jess. I mean don't get me wrong, if anyone can do it, you can. You are! But we need to face facts here. There's a limited amount of time. Very few people on the face of the earth have access to Alexander Marc's personal life. You retrieved a nice bit of information I'm sure, but you and I both know it barely scratches the surface of what Ritter is looking for with this article. If, by weeks end, he doesn't practically spill his guts out to you, there's a good chance Ritter is gonna terminate your contract and let DeFlour take over."

I'm floored. The thought that either of them would think that would be a viable option is well beyond me. "I can't believe you're saying this to me right now. Art, tell me you're joking."

"DeFlour will have his taste of failure for once. He'll have maybe a week to get some dirt before Marc leaves the country. You and I both know he'll never get it."

"So, then what the hell is the point of pulling me if it's clear he's not gonna get it, Art? Are you even hearing yourself right now?"

"You've been a wreck the last few months and you know it. You've been restless, hardly sleeping, stressing out, late to meetings."

"One meeting!"

"Whatever, It's not like you. You're overworking yourself. Believe me, I was happy for you when you were assigned this job. I still am, but I think you're pushing yourself too hard. Why do that for such little odds?"

I sit back in my seat, huffing incredulously. Why push myself? Has he gone insane? Has he completely forgotten how passionate I am about my work? My work is my life! Even if I've been a little more stressed or anxious about meeting demand the past few months and making sure I'm getting enough work to live comfortably, it's the territory that comes with the job. I'm no foreigner to it and neither is he.

"I'm just saying, I think it's for the best. But hey, you still have time to make a good turn out with this."

"For the best? Since when do you get to decide what's best for me? What happened to, 'I'm behind you one hundred percent'? I guess that was just bullshit, right?"

"What? No, look, you're taking this way too seriously Jess, I–"

"Because it *is* serious Arthur! It is! This is my career, which you know is one of the most important things in my life. I have what it takes to do this. I thought you, of all people, saw that too."

"You do have what it takes! I'm not taking that from you. If you had a little more time, I think you'd absolutely pull this off one hundred percent, but time is going to blow by and based on our last conversation, I can tell how much added stress this is putting on you. If you don't make this deadline, you are going to beat yourself up mercilessly for it. I know you will." I'm speechless. I literally have no words left. "Please, just be open minded about what I'm saying. It makes sense, you'll see."

My hand reaches for my pocketbook and I take out some cash, slamming it on the table. All eyes really are on me this time as I forcefully rise from my seat. "You were right to second guess yourself earlier. Maybe you don't know me that well after all. Goodnight."

<h1 style="text-align:center">12</h1>

The drive back to Alexander's estate is a blur. My thoughts and emotions bleed together into a chaotic clusterfuck. I had powered off my phone because Art kept calling every five minutes. There's no way I can speak to him right now. I was completely blindsided back there. Now I'm furious and, above all, hurt. He thinks he knows what's best for me, says he cares about me, blah, blah, blah. If this is his version of care, he can keep it. When I accepted this assignment, I did so fully believing that Ritter, and especially Arthur, had faith in my capability to pull this off. I thought I had so much support, only to find out tonight that the support I thought I had was really just a bit of hope, no true confidence involved.

It's astonishing how easily Ritter has allowed his decision to be swayed. Mind blowing that my best friend basically helped Charles DeFlour's efforts by agreeing to the potential switch without even a fight. And then to have the absolute audacity to try and convince me that it's for my own good? Fuck them. Fuck them all.

I roll into the driveway of the estate an hour earlier than originally planned thanks to my short-lived prior engagement. The doorman, who I've come to know as Luc, lets me in and I hurry to the guest suite to discover two boxes on the bed. Interesting. I don't see a note anywhere, but it has to be from Alex.

Curiously, I open the largest one and find it holds a neatly folded dress. I take it out to examine the detail in more depth. It's a pretty cocktail dress with a halter neck design. The torso of the dress is made of black lace and an open V neck extends down to the waist, where the lace transitions into a gorgeous black satin, knee length skirt.

Quickly, I strip down and slip it on, smoothing the fine fabric around my curves as I admire my image in the mirror, smiling softly. Wearing so much fine clothing in such a short span of time is another first for me. It's wild to think that just a week ago I would have never agreed to wear something this revealing and eye-catching. But circumstances are changing and changing rapidly. To say it feels like I'm living a double life seems like an understatement and this causes some conflict within me.

When the curtain closes, and all of this is said and done, can I go back to my life the way it was, when I'm gradually falling in love with the life I'm living now, even knowing it's supposed to be temporary? Can I return to simply being the smart, passionate, ambitious, work obsessed woman who deeply lacks any real social life and prefers hiding in oversized shirts? Or will I return to my world as Isabella Evans who is adventurous, bold, headstrong, adaptable and not afraid to show a bit of cleavage?

There's a soft rap at the door and I grant permission for whoever is there to enter. I expected the maid or, potentially, even Luc to tell me that my precious, but finicky car stalled on its way to the garage. I didn't expect to see Alexander. Once again, the way his eyes sweep my body upon sight of me sends electric waves rippling through my core, the aftershock of which pools between my thighs. I'm not sure if he realizes how much his presence has affected me lately. I hope not. I've made it a point to do the best I can to hide how turned on he makes me. But something tells me he very much has his suspicions.

"Alex, you're home! I expected you would be out till at least eight-thirty."

"Work ended up being light this evening."

I take notice of his attire. He's wearing a black T-shirt that accentuates his muscular frame and gray sweatpants that hang deliciously low on his waist, showing off a print that's hard to ignore. Dear God, the man is blessed! His dark hair is slightly damp and wavy, his feet bare, and his stance…well…dominant, but that, itself, is not unusual. This is a rare sight. I have never seen him in anything but business attire. Not in pictures or on tv and certainly not in person. I do my best to keep my gaze from lingering too long, though it's oh so hard to do. "You showered."

"You noticed." There's a sarcastic tone in his voice and a playful spark in his eyes. "I was in the gym earlier. Just freshened up when I was told you had arrived."

I look down at the beautiful dress adorning my body just to make sure I'm not naked because the way he keeps looking at me makes me feel so damn exposed.

"I have great taste. The dress looks impeccable on you." Oh! So, he was the one who picked it out, or at least made the final decision. I'd expected that had been assigned to Carmyn.

I bite my lip, slightly coy but flattered. "Thank you. I suppose you do."

"Your dress at the exhibit… it was my inspiration for tonight's look. The satin was quite flattering to your physique."

Woo, I'm a bit flushed. "It really is very lovely." I turn, once again looking at my reflection. "You don't think I'm too overdressed?"

"Does it matter?"

My eyes roll in playful annoyance and I choose not to answer, knowing the direction the conversation would lead– insistences that I need to be more comfortable in my skin, so on and so forth. I walk over to the bed, take a seat next to the last box and pull off the top. A pair of black stilettos lay inside. The heels must be a good six inches. It's been a long minute since I've worn heels that high. The five inches I wore the other day was already pushing it.

"Allow me." Before I know it, he's on bended knee at my feet with one of the heels in his hand. His swift action combined with the touch of his fingers on my skin as he lifts my leg onto his lap sends my heart racing. Who the fuck is this guy? The more time goes by, the more I desperately want to know and not for the world, for my damn self.

He slides the first shoe on. "Fits like a glove. Like I said, great taste." A brilliant, captivating smile plasters his face, showing off his dimples. He winks, then moves to the next foot and I can't contain my need to ask. "You really are quite confident in yourself, aren't you?"

"I am."

"You're not afraid it can be interpreted as cocky?"

"Not at all. People can think what they'd like."

"So basically, you don't care about anyone's opinion."

He finishes slipping on the other heel before answering. "I'm not careless about the opinions of others, Jess. In fact, I hold a lot of value in opinions and take many into consideration. I am, however, comfortable enough in who I am as a person to not let what someone may think or say about me affect my confidence, especially in such a way that it keeps me from being true to myself. You should try it sometime. It's invigorating."

"Well, maybe I don't feel very true to myself in this dress. This is what *you* want. Your requirement, remember? Sooo, you're not setting a very good example."

"Firstly, it's not *my* requirement, it's the requirement of the function we are attending. There's a dress code. Even I have one. Second, I asked you a question earlier about why it mattered if you're overdressed and you rolled your eyes at me– I absolutely detest that by the way. Third, you should know that I was trying to get you to see how much concern you were investing into whether people care about how you present yourself. You, yourself, said it looked lovely on you. If you are happy with what you are wearing, should that not be enough?"

"It's not that simple."

"Isn't it?" He stands and I cross my arms like a teen with an attitude.

"You aren't being very fair. I asked if I was overdressed because you still haven't told me where we are going. I'm blindly trusting you right now. For all I know, you could be whisking me away to a casual family friendly restaurant!"

"And? If I am, would it matter?"

"You could be taking me to a funeral!"

He gives me the most beguiled look and chuckles. "A bloody funeral. Really?"

"Well, I am wearing black!" I know it sounds ridiculous. But this stupid debate is ridiculous and, well, screw him for trying to be right all the time!

I roll my eyes and huff. Next thing I know Alex yanks me off the bed and pulls me to him. One of his hands cups the area under my chin and around my neck as his face draws incredibly close to mine. His breath warms my skin as he speaks; his tone stern, yet, controlled. "I believe I did mention how much I detest you rolling your eyes at me." Woah, so this is a new side of him! One that's intimidating, yet, incredibly sexy. Dear God…all I keep thinking is, *Don't let him see you cave*.

"What are you gonna do about it?" I flirtatiously giggle. I'm impressed by my sudden display of boldness. I can see in his eyes that he wasn't expecting that.

"Not sure you're ready to find out, Ms. Rivers."

"Is that so? I thought you liked a challenge, Mr. Marc."

A guttural growl reverberates from his diaphragm as he smirks ever so slightly. "Mm, don't test me." The grip on my neck tightens a tad more, not hard enough to hurt, but enough to make a statement. His other hand thrusts to the back of my head as he pulls me flush against his body. There's no denying the subtle twitch of his hardened cock against my abdomen. Alexander Marc is, undoubtedly, turned on… by me. It hasn't all been some act. I hadn't imagined it!

His face continues to hover close to mine. "You are maddening woman. If you could only know how much I–" Abruptly, he doesn't finish his statement. A large part of me wishes to the heavens he would. Instead, he drops his hands and steps back several feet, eyes wild with an unrecognizable emotion. He closes them and we both stand here, panting and longing. Why did he pull away?

Another few seconds' pass before he opens his eyes again, drawing in a deep breath before nonchalantly speaking. "I'll meet you in the lobby in thirty minutes." And just like that, he walks out, leaving me breathless in a buildup of desire. In all my life, this has by far been the most exhilarating and mind-boggling interaction I'd experienced with a man! I have no earthly idea what the appropriate response is to what just occurred.

The whole entire week has tested my very being in every way imaginable. I feel like I'm on the verge of combustion when it comes to trying to process it all. And now, *NOW,* I still have a task ahead of me tonight. A task that, according to Aralyn, may alarm the hell out of me. I'm not sure how much more shock my system can take before I'm too overwhelmed to function properly.

I don't feel ready nor prepared for anything that's about to happen next, but one thing is for certain: ready or not, it's happening. Here I come.

13

The ride to the undisclosed location isn't very social and we've been driving for quite a while. Alexander's busy taking a few calls while I'm busy trying not to fume reading through the texts Arthur has been sending all night.

Jess, let's talk about this please.

I don't understand why you're so upset.

I'm thinking about you here, give me a break!

Please just call me.

Arthur can try and twist it as much as he wants, but he's made it clear that both him and Ritter have their doubts about my success in this endeavor. They aren't thinking of sending Charles in to have his shot at failure, they are sending him as plan B. For Art to pull this crap is low, especially for him!

The car turns down a dirt road and I peer out the window, examining our surroundings. We are somewhere in the countryside. Certainly no longer in Paris. There isn't a single city light in sight but certainly a grand overhead of stars. We move along gravel through acres of lush, grassy fields. I look over at Alexander just as he abruptly stops mid conversation. He looks at the screen of his cell and tucks it in the inside pocket of his coat, then turns to meet my questioning gaze. "I always forget the service cuts off out here."

"And where is here exactly?"

"Not yet. Soon. Patience, Jess." I've been more than patient ever since this whirlwind of an adventure began.

Alex clears his throat. "I, uh, I'd like to apologize for what happened back at the house. It was highly unprofessional and inconsiderate of me to intrude on your personal space like that. It won't happen again." What? No, no, no. It must happen again! I *need* it to happen again. He can't just tease me like that and then call it off! I don't get it. Why the sudden resistance? Is it because of what I do?

"There's nothing to apologize for. I'm just as guilty, if not more, for egging you on."

He smirks, his finger gliding along the bottom of his lower lip. Dear God, I want to kiss that lip. "Yes, you are quite a cheeky little tease." He clears his throat once more and straightens his tie. "All the same, better to keep things professional."

I don't like the sound of that, even though I know that's exactly what we should be doing. Ugh, what am I thinking, getting caught up in such a fantasy world? How did I think I'd actually have a chance with him? I'm frustrated that he's backed away, but in truth, he's only doing what I should have done days ago. I have a job to do. It's about time I realign my focus back to that and only that.

Within a few minutes, we roll into the driveway of what appears to be a château and get in line behind a few other cars preparing to be valeted. "Before we go in, I have one more thing for you to wear."

He grabs a small rectangular box from out of the car's safe and hands it to me. My fingers run along the soft navy-blue velvet and lift the lid. Inside is a simple, yet elegant, black, lace mask. I look up at Alex. "Another requirement of this place?"

"This one is my requirement. Trust me, you will want this on, at least for tonight. It will let everyone in there know that you are not to be approached or touched."

"Touched?"

"Yes. You'll see what I mean. Would you like help tying it?" I'd actually like help understanding what the hell is going on. There are so many questions I want to ask, but I opt to say nothing as I know how much Alexander enjoys the element of surprise.

I permit him to help me tie on the mask. "What you will see inside will seem quite unusual to you. All I ask is that you keep an open mind and I will be happy to answer any questions about it later. Deal?"

Huh. Same thing Aralyn said. After he finishes the tying, I turn back to face him. "Deal."

He gives the window a firm knock, and the driver opens his door. We both slide out and he holds his arm out for me to take as we begin our walk toward the entrance of the residence. The château is massive. Vast, white pillars stretch far above the doorway where two men stand guarding. One of the men opens the door for us and greets Alexander as Mr. Marc as we proceed through the entryway.

I had no real expectations coming here, but what I'm witnessing walking into the foyer is far beyond anything I could have even imagined. Before us is a large, elegant staircase and on that staircase is a pudgy, middle-aged man, completely nude, on all fours with a muzzle over his face, being led on a leash by a gorgeous woman in a tight red latex bodysuit. My mouth falls agape.

After handing off our coats and phones, Alex leans in close. "Remember Jess, an open mind." I close my mouth, and avert my gaze, especially after the man makes eye contact with me.

Alex steers us in the direction of the laughter and loud conversation echoing from a nearby room. It looks like a large ballroom draped in white cloth with purple lights streaming through them from the ceiling. There are people everywhere and an incredible amount to take in. I have no clue where to focus my gaze. Men and women both seated and standing, conversating. Like us, many are dressed in formal wear. Some are scantily clothed, if not completely nude.

"Alexi! Alexi, my love!" A woman, seemingly in her thirties, with her black hair in a high ponytail, power walks over to us. "Alexi, you're back! It's been so long! How wonderful to see you again!" She exchanges cheek kisses with Alex.

"Angelique, good to see you too. I'm not in Paris for long I'm afraid, but I wanted to stop in and see how the club is doing."

"Ah, oui! We are doing very well Alexi. You came on the perfect night. Collette is here and will be so excited to see you!" I can't ignore the pang of jealousy that suddenly comes over me. Who is this girl? And who the hell is Collette?

"Angelique, allow me to introduce you to my guest this evening. This is Jess." Oh! So, we are on a real name basis now

I see. Thank God. "Jess, this is Angelique, a longtime companion of mine." Companion, huh? To what extent, I wonder.

I force my sweetest smile. "Pleasure to meet you."

"Ahhh, American! Pleasure indeed. Alexi, I did not know you were into the American girls. Always the mystery you are. Come! Let's get you both a drink." We follow the eccentric bombshell across the room. The uneasiness I'm feeling grows stronger as my body is scanned by almost every man and woman we pass. I'm literally the only one in here, that I can see, with a mask. Just another thing that makes me stick out like a sore thumb. Fantastic.

Angelique orders us drinks that have bizarre names I haven't heard of as soon as we approach the bar. "Lucien will take your order. I will be right back!" She walks off and I frantically turn to Alex. I want an explanation!

"Where the hell are we?"

"This is 'La Tanière du Plaisir. It is a fetish den, or what's also considered a kink club."

Mind literally blown. "And how, exactly, is bringing me here supposed to help me write my article?"

"You wanted the inside scoop on my life? Well, you're in. Welcome." I look around confused, completely lost. Of all the places I'd imagined in his hidden world, this was never one of them. "Why don't you take a seat for a moment while you aim to compose yourself?" He pulls out a bar stool and I take the seat without hesitation. I'm starting to feel incredibly warm.

The bartender, a beautifully crafted man with skin the color of midnight, wearing nothing but tight gold pleather shorts, finishes our order and Alex hands me a drink. I quickly sip it and am immediately thrown off by the taste. My face must give away my sheer disappointment because Alex snickers. "I suppose I should have told you that the drinks here are non-alcoholic."

"I suppose you should have told me a lot of things," I say under my breath.

"There's no alcohol because of what takes place here. Safety is top priority. Alcohol can distort judgment, so alcohol is banned." This was all so wild. I'm still not sure what to say. I'm not even sure how I'm feeling right now other than completely flabbergasted.

I notice Angelique walking across the room to speak to yet another member and it's the first time I allow myself to get a good look at what she's wearing, which isn't much. Only some black pasties, a black thong and what must be ten-inch stilettos. I could never, I'd just die or, at very least, break both ankles.

Something on her shoes catches my eye. On the back of each heel rests a three-dimensional sparkling butterfly. Her heels are almost identical to the ones Aralyn wears, they're just missing red soles! My astonished gaze shifts to another woman walking by with a similar pair. Then another woman. There are multiple women in these heels!

"Alex, what's the story with the heels Angelique and some of the other women are wearing?"

"Those women are called Papillons Diamantés, Diamond Butterflies. They provide certain, special services to elite members of the club."

"You mean, they're prostitutes?"

"Haha, no, I wouldn't say that. They do get paid for their services, but they are paid legally through the club. There are many high paying clients here, men and women alike. All of the members in attendance come to mingle and consensually have kinky sex or intimate encounters with whomever they choose to, but there are particular fetishes that the Butterflies indulge in that certain members will pay big money for, especially if they cannot find a partner here to fulfill those naughty fantasies. For legal reasons, they can bring a client to orgasm but sex with clients is forbidden."

If what I'm deducing is correct, and Aralyn is a Butterfly, this means there's a huge chance she knows Alexander. She hasn't confirmed nor denied that she knows him, but I'm beginning to see this as highly plausible confirmation. I need to find out from Alex without giving Aralyn away. "Have you ever, you know, acquired their services?"

"No. My kinks are interesting, but not to the extent that I've needed the Butterflies to fulfill them. There's usually always another member here who's perfectly suited and willing."

Alexander Marc has kinks! This certainly was not the headline I was picturing. "You're not ever afraid someone in here would go to the media and blab about your membership at a place like this?"

"I don't just go to any fetish club. The reason I come here is because they are highly strict and confidential. Everyone in this room has had to sign a non-disclosure agreement in order to be here. Even you."

"What? I didn't sign anything."

"You did, you just don't realize it." I give him a puzzled look to which he responds, "You recall the signatures Luc collected from you so he could park your car in the garage?" He told me it was a liability form. Which, I'll admit, I thought was odd at the time, but it made sense too. I thought perhaps a rich man didn't want strangers claiming his employee dented their vehicle so they could sue. So, that was a scam. Sneaky!

"I don't even know what to say."

"I had to get you in without you realizing where we were going. I figured you wouldn't mind, you know, since you really want strong content for your story." He winks and out of habit, I roll my eyes. His jaw tenses and the vein at the side of his neck protrudes as he swallows. Oops.

I quickly change the subject. "So, what exactly is your kink?" Just as soon as I ask, Angelique walks up to us.

"Alexi, I found Collette engaged in a play session. But you're welcome to go watch. Room eight."

"Thank you, Angel." The Butterfly blushes and walks off with a little too much pep in her step.

"Alexi? Angel? I see you two have pet names for each other. Cute," I say sarcastically.

"Feeling left out? I'm sure I could come up with a good one for you."

"Yeah, don't bother. I'm good."

A salacious grin plasters his face. "You ready?"

"Ummm, ready for what?"

"To find out what my kink is."

"Let me guess. Voyeurism?" I don't know much about kinks, but I believe voyeurism involves gaining pleasure from watching others engage in sexual activity.

He laughs. "Come. You'll see." Taking my hand in his, he leads me through the bustling room and out into a long and narrow hallway, lit up in purple, with what looks like ten doors, maybe more. Each room has a decent sized viewing window and, as we make our way past the rooms, I catch glimpses of the heavily kinky action taking place. In one room, a woman is strapped to some sort of tall board. A man, in a business shirt and slacks, holds what looks like a vibrator to her clit as she convulses with pleasure.

In another room, a man is bent over a table while an individual in head-to-toe skintight latex whips him with a long, frayed whip I've never seen before. It looks like it has chains and strips of leather. The man yelps as the whip kisses his bare ass, creating a snapping sound. He cries out, thanking his "Mistress".

In yet another room, a woman has been expertly suspended by ropes. Two men, one of whom wears a full, black mask in the shape of a skull, are on each side of the woman. One of them eats her out while the masked man receives oral from her. Everything I witness on this walk makes me very nervous, but also incredibly intrigued.

We stop before the viewing window at room eight and my eyes grow wide. A dark-haired woman lays on a bed, completely nude, eyes covered with a blindfold. Her hands and feet are bound in cuffs and tied to each bed post. A tall man of Asian descent, bare chested with broad shoulders and six-pack for days, hovers over her, dripping the wax of a candle along the woman's abdomen. I cringe but am stunned to find that she doesn't gasp in pain, but in ecstasy.

Alexander answers the question I haven't yet brought myself to ask. "It's called wax play, a form of sensation play. The wax is hot when it first hits the skin, but it cools quickly, which can be quite an exhilarating feeling."

"Sooo, is your kink dripping hot wax on women?"

"I like toying with a woman's senses, and I enjoy control in the bedroom, but in a way that's gentler and more sensual than aggressive. Though, make no mistake, I will be firm and rough where it counts. To answer your question simply, my kink is Domination. I'm what one might consider a sensual dominant.

"Now, as I mentioned, wax play is one of a few ways sensation play can be achieved. Another example would be taking a cube of ice and gliding it slowly across the skin. The experience can be even more enticing when you're blindfolded. A blindfold would restrict sight so that you'd have no idea where on your body you'd be touched with the ice. All you'd have to go off of is the sound of my voice, perhaps my footsteps or the rustling of my clothing and, even then, you won't know where or when the ice will touch you." Huh, so the ultimate tease.

"But why Domination?"

"It comes natural to me. I've always had a dominant persona. And there's something about a woman making the choice to submit that I find beautiful. It takes a decent amount of trust; trusting me to lead the way, to provide the perfect tease, to fuck her just right. Trusting me to care for her and keep her safe, understand what she wants and give her what she needs, how I see fit. Only when she's burning with uncontrollable desire will I give her what she yearns for." He peers down at my entranced face. "I hope you're taking mental notes, Jess. For the article, of course."

Holy fuck. Can this even go in the article? I have no idea how I'm going to sit down and summarize what he's just told me. And the only way I can summarize my response to this right now is with one word: wet.

His smirk tells me he knows I'm tongue tied. He doesn't wait for a reply. "The gentleman you see in there is Collette. He's a good friend of mine. We actually met back in the UK. He moved to Paris some years ago." Collette finally notices us through the window and grins wide as he lowers himself onto the bed, crawling on top of the woman who's squirming with anticipation.

"Collette is a sensual dominant too?"

"Yes, when he wants to be." What's that supposed to mean?

I watch as Collette slides his hand over the woman's bare mound and inserts his fingers inside her. She gasps. His pace, slow at first, eventually quickens as she bucks against him, squirming until her legs quiver. It feels so taboo to watch, yet I find myself unable to avert my gaze. Alex, takes notice. "Enjoying what you see?"

I keep my eyes on the scene before me, afraid that if I look at him, he'll see the fantasy I've formed in my mind of him on top of me in a similar fashion; of him making me scream his name, making my legs spasm and the muscles in my body constrict. "Just, you know, taking notes."

A woman's voice calls out from behind us. "Alexi, why don't we go in? We can join in the fun like old times." Angelique walks up and runs her fingers across Alexander's shoulders, then leans against the door. "Your sweet American pet can join too if she likes. Though, it does appear you have her off limits. Such a shame." Wait, like old times? Angelique and Alexander slept together? Have they *all* slept together?

"Yes, she's off limits."

"Ah, but you are not, oui?" Her finger slides along his jaw and trails down to his chest, stopping to undo the buttons of his shirt. He's not stopping her. Why isn't he stopping her?

His hand finally grabs her wrist when she reaches the third button. "Perhaps another time." *Another time*? I can't. I can't stomach this. I'm actually appalled that he'd be willing to have this conversation right in front of me! My mind has officially reached overload and I want off this ride. *Now*!

"Fuck this." I spin on my heels and make a swift exit, convinced I'm living some sort of freaky, chaotic dream at this point. Maybe Arthur was right. Maybe I am pushing myself too hard because I definitely sense a mental breakdown on the horizon. I rip off my mask as I rush through the large château and outside.

I make it as far as the driveway when Alexander catches up to me. "Jess, stop." My swollen feet are pleading with me to listen to him, but I don't dare surrender.

"Jess!" His tone is louder and more demanding. Look at Mr. Dominant thinking he owns the world. Owns *ME*. Yeah right! I whirl around and give him a taste of my rage.

"What the fuck was that? Did you bring me here to watch you take part in some, some orgy? Is there a big sign across my chest that says slut?"

He chokes out a laugh. "There's nothing wrong with being a slut… at least my definition of it anyhow."

"Ugh! You are infuriating! Take me home at once! Actually, you know what, no. Why don't you stay here with your buddy and your Demon Butterflies–"

"Diamond Butterflies."

"Whatever! Just stay here! I'll find my own way home!" I storm off once again, not making it far before one of my heels catches a decent sized crack in the stone pavement and I come crashing to the ground. Alexander is at my side within seconds trying to help me up. I attempt to shake off his grip, but he isn't that shakable. "Just let me go! I'm fine, Alex!"

"Really? So, your leg isn't bleeding then?"

"What? No, it's fine. It's–" I look down and, sure enough, my knee is running blood. My stomach turns and my equilibrium goes off kilter. I've never been good with the sight of blood, especially my own. "Oh God..." My body begins to sway and Alexander's arm on my shoulders is the last thing I feel before everything goes black.

14

I vaguely recall bits and pieces of the journey to the car in Alexander's arms. I don't quite come too until we reach the house. Alex helps me to my room and I take a seat on the bed. He leaves for a short time then returns, holding out the French equivalent of Aspirin and a glass of water. I take it without argument, happy for something to ease the pain radiating throughout my body. I must have landed harder than I thought.

After he collects a first aid kit from the bathroom, he addresses me. "I'm going to clean you up a bit." He smiles softly, taking a seat at my side. "Don't look."

"Trust me, I wasn't planning on it." I turn my head toward a nearby wall and wince as he pours what smells like rubbing alcohol over my wound. I need something to get my mind off of this and the sheer embarrassment looming over me.

"I don't get you Alex. You come across as the picture of class, professionalism and intellect, the perfect gentleman. Yet, on the low, you're this lustful, domineering kinkster."

He laughs. "Is it completely implausible for me to be all of those things?"

"Suppose not. I don't know. I don't know much of anything anymore. My brain's all scrambled. Help me understand something, is this the story you want told? The story of a man who gets his rocks off going to underground kink clubs with people who procure the services of sex workers to fulfil their every, dirty desire? I can't imagine that could possibly be the case."

"I'm not ashamed of that part of my life."

I turn my head back to face him. "Obviously. But that can't be it. That can't be the riveting, in-depth knowledge you want the world to know about you."

"Not yet. Not done." His hand guides my face back towards the wall. "What you saw was a mere glimpse into my life, Jess. And to be honest, I don't think you really understood what it is I was showing, nor what I was explaining to you."

"You were explaining to me that you like sensation play, making women plead for you to fuck them and all that other stuff. I'm actually really baffled that you showed me this side of you knowing I'd most likely write about it."

"In the gardens, back at center where the banquet is being held, I told you that the person who writes about my truth, my life, needs to be confident in the effectiveness and impact it will have. I meant every word. This is not child's play, Jess. It's true, I can be a complicated man. In order to write about my life, you have to understand it, dive deep, figure out my inner workings. The question you truly need to ask yourself, is how far are you willing to go to gain that understanding?

"My kink does not define me, it's merely an extension of who I am and much of who I am plays out in my role as a Dom.

Everything I do as a Dom reflects a piece of my story, a chapter on how I go about life, how I see things, my likes, dislikes, etc. The relationship between a dominant and his submissive is not just about intimacy, it's about mutual trust, safety, vulnerability, communication and respect. All of those things are crucial in a healthy dynamic."

He wraps my knee up in a bandage. "I didn't bring you to the club so you could write about my love of kink or my sexual escapades. I brought you so that you could open your mind and begin to see the values I uphold from a more in-depth perspective, so that when you write about me, you know how to make it impactful. So that you'll write in a way that speaks honestly about who I am, not just as a businessman, but as a human being, as a man who isn't much different than anyone else." I mull over his words.

Fuck, this man is deep. All this time I thought he was bullshitting me about what he could teach me, but this is honestly incredible insight. I'm still unsure exactly how the dynamic he's referencing will yield such promising results but, then again, I hadn't really been as open as I could be to understanding.

He reclaims the hold on my chin and draws my face back to his, then gently rests his hand on my thigh, rubbing the side of it with his thumb. "All done."

"Thank you." I almost whisper it, my mind still busy processing his small speech. I look down at my nicely wrapped up knee, admiring his handiwork. I'm grateful. I wouldn't have been able to stomach cleaning it on my own.

"Well, thank you for being such a legend. I could tell you were uncomfortable back there. And I do apologize. I did suspect my methods would be a bit reckless, but I see I probably should have educated you a bit first instead of springing it all on you."

"You think?" I smirk.

His face lights up. "Are you being cheeky again?"

"I'm just agreeing with you!" He rises, collecting the first aid items. "I'm sorry too. I shouldn't have been so weird bolting the way I did, I just– well, I don't know, I guess I wasn't sure how to feel about everything."

"Yes, jealousy can be quite the conversation killer… among other things." Ugh, I wish I hadn't been so obvious. "To answer some of the questions I know are swimming around in that wild journalist mind of yours, yes, Angelique and I have played before in the past. There were quite a few women in that club I've had play sessions with. And yes, she, Collette and I did have a joint session once a few years ago, along with another woman. I remember Collette had utilized his skills as a rigger. He's experienced in the use of Shibari, a type of Japanese rope bondage."

"In one of the playrooms, I saw someone suspended from ropes that were tied to a hook on the ceiling. Like that?"

"Precisely. Of course, not all rope bondage deals with suspension via rope, but it is enjoyed by quite a few individuals who practice the art. Now, rigging isn't my go-to thing, but I am fairly well versed in it. At the time, Angelique had suggested that we do a joint session and, well, I'll spare you the rest of the details. But yes, it happened." While the ever so curious part of me wants all the juicy information, the other part of me– the one that sent me flying out of that building– would rather not know a single thing more.

He's right. I was jealous, very jealous, which is so unlike me. I can't explain why seeing that woman touch him like that and try to persuade him to join her irked me. I mean, it shouldn't matter, right? Alexander and I aren't together. There's a likely chance we'll never be. Why can't I just pull my head and heart out of the clouds and focus on getting the job I came to do finished? It shouldn't be this difficult!

A trio of buzzes comes from the nightstand where I see my phone had been placed. "Arthur must be worried sick about you."

My eyes bulge! How does he know about Arthur? Oh God, please no. "Wait, what did you say?"

"Arthur… the man who's been ringing your phone non-stop since we reached service again." It's indescribable the speed at which my stomach ties itself in knots. I'm sensing my face grow pale or maybe flushed with red, either would be equally explanatory for how I'm feeling.

"Um, wh-what did you say to him?"

"Oh, come now Jess, you don't honestly think I was snooping through your phone and answering your calls, do you?"

"But you just said Arthur had been calling me."

"Yes, well there's this incredibly brilliant thing these days called Caller ID." Ugh, I feel like such an idiot! But at the same time, I've never felt more relieved to have misunderstood a situation.

"Oh. Right. We're just friends." Seriously? He didn't ask what Art was to me! I'm mentally kicking myself. I could use one of those muzzles I saw at the club right about now.

"Interesting…"

"I mean, he wants to be. More than just friends, that is. But…" But what? What's there to say? That I've been betrayed by him so now, even if there was a chance, it's gone? "But it's not going to happen."

"And why not?" He stares at me quizzically and I'm not sure if he's testing me or genuinely interested in why I wouldn't be.

I shrug my shoulders. "He's just a friend. I'm pretty sure that's all he will be."

"Uh huh. Pretty sure, not certain. So, there's a chance he could be more?"

"No? I mean, no." I sigh, feeling a bit defeated. There's so much left to sort through when it comes to Arthur. Despite what's happened, it doesn't erase the connection that's built up between us for years. Guilt looms over me. Guilt because I still have feelings for Art. Guilt because I can't tell Alexander that I don't. There's a battle raging within and it started long before Alexander Marc entered the picture. There are things I still haven't dealt with. Things that laugh at the future I've allowed myself to fantasize about, a future with this intriguing and beautiful man standing before me. I'm finding it hard to separate what I want from what I need, dreams from reality, who I was and who I see myself becoming. Everything is a blur.

"Well, it isn't my business. I can answer any other questions you may have about tonight's outing later. You should get some rest. I'll be out most of the day tomorrow, so there's a chance I won't see you. I'll have Carmyn provide you with my number in the morning. Should you need anything, feel free to call. Goodnight, Jess."

"Goodnight." He exits and I flop back in the bed, run my hands through my hair and let out a groan of frustration. I've got to get my shit together. I need to figure out my life. I need to figure out this article. I need to not be so foolish.

I sit up and grab my phone off the nightstand. Five missed calls and eight texts from Arthur. I don't read them. Instead, I start a new text to Aralyn. I've got to talk to her about what I saw tonight and I have to get more answers out of this woman. Aralyn is clearly a Butterfly which, to me, appears to be an immediate connection to Alexander. Could she be one of the many women at the club that he mentioned he's played with? If so, that's a piece of information that, if I connect some dots, may help me get the name of Alexander's supposed love interest. Because as far as I can tell, he's doing a very good job of hiding who she is, if she actually exists.

I've figured out what you do. When's a good time to talk? I definitely have questions.

Send.

Since Alexander is out and busy with business for a second day in a row, my main mission is to have a discussion with Aralyn. She never responded to my text the other night, but I have a pretty good idea where she might be. I'm going to head over to La Chérot Salon. Even if she isn't there, perhaps someone can point me in the right direction.

I make my way to the kitchen to grab a piece of fruit for the road but come to a slow stop, just shy of the entrance, when I hear a woman's voice coming from inside. "I know, I know. I really wish I was there, but we just have so much work to get done before this event that I can't afford to be behind, you know that. I know you'll do great without me." Is that Carmyn? I thought she was out with Alex. She squeals and giggles, excited by whoever is on the other end of the line. "I love you too! I'll see you when you get in tonight, okay? Okay, cheers darling. Bye-bye."

Carmyn has a boyfriend? Maybe a girlfriend. I shouldn't make assumptions. I would have thought she could have been speaking to anyone before I heard her giggle so flirtatiously. She definitely has a lover. And I'm pretty sure she's not married because she doesn't have a ring on her finger. I round the corner and Carmyn looks up, stunned. "Ms. Rivers! I didn't expect you to be here."

"Oh, I thought Alexander would have told you that I'm staying in the guest suite for a bit."

Her lips purse and a hint of annoyance crosses her features which is odd. "Yes, he did mention that. I meant that I didn't expect you to be in. I thought you'd be out handling business or something."

"I'm on my way out actually. Just stopped to get some fruit." I grab an apple from the island where she stands. In front of her is a rather large bouquet of red roses in a vase. Must be at least thirty of them. "Wow, those are beautiful!"

"Aren't they?" She admires them, smiling to herself. "I was so amazed when they arrived. He's so sweet."

Okay, so there *is* a 'he'. "Boyfriend?"

Her smile fades as she looks up at me. "Um, something like that. It's complicated." Complicated? What could be so complicated? She received a beautiful bouquet from the man who I'm assuming I overheard her saying 'I love you' to on the phone. Carmyn doesn't strike me as the sneaking-around-with-another-person type of woman; she doesn't have the time for that. I'm surprised she even has the time to the establish a love life, so I don't get it. Unless…what are the odd's it's complicated because of a restricted type of love? A love that's frowned upon. Perhaps a love for her boss? Aralyn's request for a name rings out like an alarm in my head.

"You're not with Alex today?"

"Mr. Marc had a private meeting. My attendance wasn't necessary." Could it be? When Carmyn was on the phone, she said, "I'll see you when you get in tonight". Could she have been talking to Alexander? He said himself he wouldn't be back till late.

My mind races. I wouldn't have considered Carmyn as a candidate for Alexander's love interest, seeing as they were always so professional with each other, but that was in the public eye. What about behind closed doors? This woman might just be one of the luckiest women on Earth, and I try to hold back the rising pang of jealousy that possibility brings forth to my consciousness. Could it be possible that Alexander is secretly in love with his assistant? I have to figure this out.

"You know, I've had the pleasure of observing you and Alexander in action lately and I must say the two of you have incredible chemistry." Her brow furrows, trying to grasp my meaning. "Professionally, of course."

I can see that she's suspicious of my statement. Her eyes squint. "Of course."

"Is it hard to have certain freedoms with this kind of job? I imagine a dating life might actually be difficult when you are at Alexander's side a majority of the time. Something like that could certainly make love life complicated."

"Ms. Rivers, I'm not sure what you're trying to do but I think you should quit while you're ahead. Lest you forget, you're not here to interview me so I'd kindly ask that you mind your own bloody business." Before I can get a word in, she grabs her roses and strides past me, fast and furious.

I didn't mean to upset her. For the most part, Carmyn has been nothing but kind to me. But it's hard to ignore that she's acting strange this morning. It seems like she's irritated that I'm here and even more irritated that I'm trying to get to the bottom of what the hell is going on, which is what I desperately need to do. Is there anyone in all of Paris who doesn't have some sort of life secret they are trying to keep under wraps?

The receptionist at the salon greets me with the same sunny smile that she had the first time I was here. "Bonjour. I'm looking to speak with Aralyn. Is she in?" And the same look of disappointment she had the last time I asked for Aralyn too.

"She is unavailable. Perhaps you can try again tomorrow." No way I'm trying again tomorrow! Time is up.

"Unavailable, but here, yes?"

"Really, it's not a good time." Fuck that! I'm sick of running on everyone else's time. It's time for people to start respecting mine! I walk past the reception desk into the salon, heading for the door to the secret back room.

"S'il vous plaît, madame! You cannot go in!" Oh, I'm going in. Aralyn has been avoiding my questions for long enough. It's time for answers!

I do think it peculiar that the receptionist isn't chasing after me but, as I enter the room, I immediately see why. I've just walked in on an argument between Aralyn and a woman with short, blonde hair who's back is turned to me. They are speaking French, and I, unfortunately, understand every word. "She's a journalist! Do you know the risk you are putting yourself in? The risk you are putting me and my establishment in? How could you do this?"

"Madame, I assure you..." Aralyn's eyes shift to me standing in the doorway like a deer in headlights. "Jess!"

The blonde spins around and I realize who she is right away. Madame Chérot. A bombshell of a fifty-three-year-old woman. She looks impeccable, even as she eyes me with a look of immense irritation and disapproval. Her cheeks are sucked in and her lips pursed like she's taken a bite out of the world's most sour lemon, as Art would say.

Now I see why the receptionist was so insistent on me coming back another day. Clearly the wrong damn time for me to be stubborn. "Um, should I come back some other time?" Cause I could leave, oh, I could definitely leave. I see that I'm not, and most likely never was, invited by this woman to be in her facility, let alone her presence. How incredibly oblivious I've been to forget about her and what she might think of me being here.

"No, no. I'm so sorry." Aralyn gives a nervous glance at the Madame before continuing. "Please, come in. I'd like to introduce you to Madame Chérot."

"Madame! Quel plaisir." I extend a hand to her which she does not take but, instead, glares at as though it's diseased. I drop my hand back to my side. "I'm sure this must all be a bit questionable to you. I apologize for any intrusion or trouble I may have made. I had hoped Aralyn would have informed you of my presence here."

She glances back at Aralyn shrewdly. "Oui. It has most certainly been an intrusion." She takes a couple extra steps forward until she's mere inches in front of me, staring me dead in the eyes. "Whether or not you are trouble has yet to be revealed, but it will no longer be risked. Aralyn has been informed that you are not to meet with her here again. Other than a no-good journalist, I don't know who you are or how she has somehow convinced you to go through with this plan of hers, and I don't care. Don't come back." She pushes past me and proceeds to exit but not before saying her last few parting words. "Mademoiselle, if you write a single word about this place, if you even breathe a single word about this place, to anyone, you will answer to me in a most unpleasant fashion." And with that, she walks out.

I look Aralyn's direction, wide eyed and astounded. "Well, I certainly wouldn't want to be on the other end of her sheers."

She gives a weary smile. "Madame Chérot is a good woman, but she's like a lioness with cubs when it comes to protecting this place, her reputation, and me."

"You?"

"She is like a mother to me. I have great respect and love for her."

I frown. For someone who claims to have so much respect for her, she certainly was fine with sneaking behind her back. "Then why on earth did you not tell her about me being here? You had to know she would find out."

"Oui. I knew at some point she would. I did not tell her because I felt she would not understand. As you can see, I was right."

I did see. And I also see before me a young woman who's visibly upset that she disappointed the older woman she looks up to so much. I see crushed hope within her, as though despite knowing the Madame's reaction would be a disapproving one, she had greatly hoped for a brighter outcome. I see a moment of conflict as she struggles to figure out what to say to me next as we stand in silence for what feels like an eternity. And even with all that, I see the unyielding commitment in her eyes. Nothing, not even one of the people she cares about most in this world, is going to stop her from getting what she wants.

"Is a name really worth the sacrifice you're making, Aralyn? Is it truly worth disappointing her?"

"That name means my peace of mind Jess. It means my freedom. Honestly, there isn't much I won't sacrifice for that." It's killing me, the impenetrable wall she has built around herself. She's worse than Alex. I have done much over the few years in my career to chase down a story and get to the root of what's taking place. Yet, it's as though I'm trapped in a maze when it comes to chasing down her truth. At this point, even if I manage to get the name she seeks so feverishly, I'm not sure I'll get any closer to figuring out who she is, where she's come from– the story I've wanted to know since the moment I first saw her.

And this name. This damn name I'm not even sure exists. This name that has yet to be produced by the lips of a man who, too, is so… guarded. Alexander has, indeed, opened up in some surprising ways, but I still sense the hesitancy he has with me. I may intrigue him to a degree but to him I am still a journalist who, with a few paragraphs, could put him in the very media firestorm he's been avoiding for so long. There's a huge chance he will never tell me about this woman who has his heart.

My mind drifts to my curiosity about Carmyn. "I'm wondering if it could be his assistant."

She raises an eyebrow in suspicion. "His assistant? Highly doubtful."

"Why? It's not a ridiculous notion. Relationships like that do happen. I mean Carmyn is at Alexander's every beck and call. They sure as hell spend enough time together for something like that to develop. When I first met her, I recall her telling me that she is the only personal assistant he's had in the past five years who has stuck around for longer than four months. Much longer in fact! She's been his assistant for three years now."

To me, the possibility of it being Carmyn makes sense. She's dependable, brilliant, headstrong, not to mention loyal as hell. She'll avoid bringing up Alexander's business at all costs. I even spotted her tagging along with him on his day off. She's gorgeous too! Certainly, one of the most naturally beautiful women I've seen. All that, coupled with how she acted towards me being at the house this morning, makes her a very plausible candidate. "I'm just saying, we shouldn't rule it out."

Aralyn sighs and takes a seat. "I suppose." She stares at the fire crackling in the fireplace, deep in thought.

I walk over and take the seat across from her. "I'll figure it out, but I honestly came here to talk to you about last night." I look down at her heels. "Alexander told me about the Diamond Butterflies."

"What did he say?" Her ocean eyes look deep into mine, like she's searching for something, perhaps judgment.

"Just that they provide certain fetish services to elite members that may have difficulty obtaining such services elsewhere. You're one of them, aren't you? They all wear shoes similar to yours, with the butterflies on the back."

"Mm, yes and no. I am a Papillon Diamanté, but I don't provide the services, not anymore."

"What do you mean?" She gives me a knowing look. Oh shit! I see. Aralyn is the Head Bitch In Charge. "Oh...oh! You manage these girls?"

"Oui." It makes so much sense now. The way the receptionist, Jovana and Marie always look so serious around her, almost like they either hate her or are intimidated by her. The way Aralyn carries herself like she knows she's the boss; even the way she sits there in that chair like she owns the world. She is a woman who is sure of herself. She does not question her place.

Wait, a moment, "So, Madame Chérot is letting you operate out of her salon?"

"I'm Madame Chérot's protégé." I would have never guessed any of this! This whole time, the most famous hairdresser in all of France was the head of an underground fetish society?

Aralyn continues to explain to me that Madame Chérot does not own the kink den I attended but is in partnership with the owner. Apparently, that club isn't the only one in Paris they partner with. Their business is primarily in France, but extends to multiple dens across Europe. She mentions that the Madame took her in as Butterfly at one of her lowest points. Early on, she saw something in the young beauty that compelled her to teach Aralyn the business and prepare her to eventually take over one day.

After some inquisitive questioning, she also reveals that the reason they all wear red and black is because those are the uniform colors all the Butterflies are required to wear to stand out at the clubs and social gatherings they attend. The Butterflies don't need to stick to the dress code when they aren't working, but for Aralyn, wearing the colors consistently is like wearing a badge of honor and pride. Strutting around in the colors, adoring the fact that most people will never understand their significance, is a secret indulgence. The Diamond Butterflies are her life, and she sits at the helm of their operation, proudly declaring who she is in both a non-verbal and fashionable manner. I find this all so fascinating!

"How did you all meet? What did she see in you? What kind of fetish services did you provide?"

She chuckles. "I've said too much already. Madame would kill me if she knew what I'd just told you."

"I'm pretty she'd kill me first if I said anything." I remember her ice-cold stare mere moments ago. "Also, I agreed to your request to be confidential, remember?"

Her smile is soft but weak. "I trust you. I shouldn't, but I do. We both have a lot to lose. Without trust in each other we might fail." She keeps saying "we".

"I promise, when this is all over and we are successful, I will tell you my story, Jess. You will know everything." She keeps saying that, too. All this talk of trust, yet I can't say the feeling is mutual. I don't believe her. I want to, but I don't. Aralyn may be mysterious, but it's not because it's who she is, it's a choice. She's hiding information for a reason and that's reason enough for me to be highly suspicious of "her promise".

"Will you, at least, tell me how you met Alexander? Was it at the club?" She hasn't admitted to knowing him yet, which I can't understand. What's the big deal?

She gazes at me, expressionless. "I've never stepped foot in 'La Tanière du Plaisir. As far as I know, that's the only fetish den in France that Alexander joins. Honestly Jess, you should spend more time finding out about the man than asking me silly questions that don't matter. I thought you wanted to know about his personal life."

My voice is laced with irritation. "Well, you aren't exactly helping me get any leads."

"Why not ask your boss?"

Her question throws me for a loop. "My boss?"

"The older man with short hair, works at Eiffel."

"Are you talking about Dante Ritter? He doesn't know that much about Alexander."

"Are you sure about that?" What is she on about? There's no way Ritter knows Alex enough to give me the scoop on him. He'd be writing the damn article himself if that were the case.

"Aralyn, please, I really don't have the mental capacity for your games."

"Ask your boss what he knows about Alexander. I did."

No fucking way!

15

*A*ralyn spoke to Ritter. Aralyn asked Ritter about Alexander. Ritter knows something about Alexander that I don't. I'm floored by this information. How? How did any of this come to be?

"Back up. When did you speak to Ritter?"

"When I first approached you at the café, I noticed the name of the company you are working for printed on one of the papers laying on your table. A couple days later, after I hadn't seen you come in at all, I went into Eiffel to see if I could talk with you and get you to meet me here at the salon. All I had to go on was the bit of information about yourself that you had given me at the café, so I asked the woman at the front desk if she knew any of the female freelance journalists who worked there specializing in entertainment journalism. I tried describing what you looked like but she looked at me like I was insane for even asking her.

"It just so happened that your boss walked by and overheard my inquiry. He told me he thought it was you and I asked if he could get me in touch." So, that's how she knew who I was and got all my information. Why didn't she ever just say that? What was the point of holding out for so long?

I observe her grab a cigarette from her pocketbook and light it. "I thought you didn't smoke anymore."

"I didn't. But I don't really care any longer. C'est la vie. Life is short. Might as well enjoy doing things that bring you pleasure. In my case, pleasure and comfort." Her smile doesn't reach her eyes as she takes a drag. "That boss of yours, Ritter, he's very… undesirable. He told me he would give me your information if I slept with him." The shock on my face is surely evident. I'm befuddled to hear that he would be so blunt. I knew he was a sleaze bag, there were several times his gaze would give me the creeps, but I didn't think he'd ever push the boundaries of inappropriateness that far.

"Did you?"

"I'm not a whore. Of course I didn't. But I did manage to get him to provide me with your information. I could have just kept going to the café in hopes I'd see you there, but I wasn't sure when that next opportunity would be and besides, I've dealt with men like him before. Men like him are desperate. They will settle for any little attention they can get from a woman if they think it will increase his chance to fuck her. He settled for drinks. We went to a spot around the corner, and I endured his endless rambling until he finally wrote down your number, as well as your address. I found it interesting that he had that committed to memory." Same. Interesting indeed.

"Anyway, then he mentioned that you were writing an article on Alexander Marc. This also piqued my interest, for reasons you know, and without even needing to ask, he slurred something about how Alexander had to do the interview because he had information on him that he knew Alexander would hate to have publicized."

"So, Ritter's blackmailing him?" Looks like that "favor" wasn't a favor after all. Is this why, despite not trusting journalists, Alexander started opening up to me? Not because he wanted to, but because he felt he didn't have a choice? That's also possibly why he's trying to get me to understand him authentically, in hopes that whatever I do write will at least make him feel comfortable. Yet, the truth is he most likely doesn't feel comfortable with any of this.

"Oui, it appears that way."

"You said you asked him what he knows. What did he say?"

She taps the ash of her cigarette in a nearby ashtray and takes another drag before responding, smoke wisping from her red lips. "Nothing. He avoided my question. I even tried to coax it out of him. I put on my best act, slid my hand up his leg and grabbed his balls. He liked that, of course, but unfortunately it wasn't enough. If you ever wondered, your boss has a small cock." Okay, I could have gone without that image.

There is a lot to unpack here. Whatever information that Ritter has is significant enough to make Alexander do his bidding. I have to dig into this more. I didn't sign up to be a part of a blackmail scandal and I don't want Alexander opening up to me out of a feeling of obligation. That doesn't sit right with me at all.

This must be why Ritter was so easily swayed by Charles to consider allowing him a shot at this assignment. He knows that either way, he's getting his story. But, if he doesn't see the progress he wants in the time frame he wants it, why wouldn't he send someone else in? Ritter has nothing to lose. I wonder, could Arthur have known about this too?

I spring up and gather my belongings. "Where are you going?" Aralyn asks.

"I have to get to the bottom of this. I need to go talk to Ritter."

"Perhaps you should think of a strategy first. He may not take too kindly to being confronted."

"Aralyn, I respect that you are a woman of strategy, truly. But I don't have time for strategy. I need answers. I need results. And now, I need to go. I'll reach out to you soon." I bid the auburn haired beauty goodbye and quickly make my way out of the salon, briefly comprehending that it would be my last time doing so.

*M*y heels bound across the pavement as I march towards the front door of Eiffel Inc. I'm livid. I can't believe these men have me caught up in a blackmail scheme! My phone dings and I take a look at my screen and the text that comes from a number I don't recognize.

Jess, it's Alex. Where are you?

Oh, yeah, I forgot to get his number from Carmyn this morning. Though, to be fair, it's more like she forgot to give it to me. I respond that I've stopped at Eiffel to handle a matter, then continue my stride through the building, onto the elevator and toward Ritter's office.

I'm on a mission. I've quite had it with the secrets. I've had it with the games. I've had it with men thinking they can use me as a pawn to make themselves feel better. I have some frustration left for Alex too, but I can't even bring myself to dwell upon that yet.

"Jess!" Oh God, Arthur. "Jess! Hey!" He takes a short sprint to me, cutting me off.

"Arthur, I don't have time for this. I need to talk to Ritter." I skirt around him but he continues to follow.

"Ritter isn't here. He took off about an hour ago."

"I whirl around. "Did you know? Did you know that this article was a part of Ritters fucked up blackmail plot?"

"Blackmail? What are you talking about?"

I huff out a breath of agitation and walk into an empty office room, slamming the door shut when we enter. "I am so sick of being kept in the dark! I know that Ritter has dirt on Alexander. I know that he's convinced Alexander to go through with being interviewed in exchange for not having his dirty laundry aired. What I don't know is if you've been in on this all along."

"Jess, I swear I had no knowledge of any of that. What reason would I have to hide that from you?"

"Well, it wouldn't be the first time you took it upon yourself to decide for me. Maybe you decided it was best that I didn't know. Is this why you agreed with Ritter about pulling me from the assignment? Felt guilty about allowing me to get entangled in this, perhaps?"

He chortles in astonishment and disbelief. "Honestly, have I wronged you so much that after four solid years of friendship you'd suspect me of setting you up in a scheme?" It's at this moment that I realize how much I've lost trust in him. What he did wasn't the worst thing in the world, but it came as such a shock, and the sting of it is intensified by his mere presence. "I don't know why you just can't understand that what I did, I did out of love and consideration for *you*!"

His words trigger the flood gates to open and everything I had built up within me over the last several days comes rushing out. "I don't need a savior, Arthur! I never have! I don't need anyone making decisions on my behalf, trying to mold me or shield me! You have been a great comfort to me over the years, a magnificent friend, and you have helped me thrive in many ways. But, I have clearly made the mistake of allowing you to become too comfortable with me if you actually feel entitled to have the final say on what I do and do not do with *my* life!"

His incredulous gaze intensifies. "So, I suppose I'm the bad guy in your eyes now, huh? I'm wrong to care about you, wrong to want what's best for you, to consider your needs, right? I've given you my all! Many times, I've cared about your needs more than my own!" The pain in his eyes that I've tried to avoid witnessing for years becomes present now and it shatters my heart even more. Even in my moment of anger, I don't wish to see him hurting. But I know I can't enable his actions any longer.

"I need a partner not a father, Arthur! A partner supports, a partner suggests. They don't push their wants onto the other! A partner gives of themself without giving all of themself! If you were so worried about me being overwhelmed, you should have communicated that and provided recommendations on how I could ease the stress, but you didn't, you chose for me. And to be completely honest, you've been choosing for me for years! This isn't the first time, it's just the worst time."

This is it. This is the real reason I couldn't take that extra step towards a relationship with him. This was the thing I couldn't put my finger on. Now, I finally have, and it feels so damn freeing to not only realize it, but say it. It's as if my voice has been begging me to express these words for such a long time and my tongue is more than happy to sync with the truth my spirit has been yearning to bring forth.

Arthur stares at me, stupefied, and I stare back, my eyes pleading for him to understand. Perhaps, there is still hope yet. Perhaps, he can learn from this, understand and respect my boundaries. Perhaps there's a chance for us to make things right and have that future we had both fantasized about. "Wow. You sound so fucking selfish. Do you realize that?" His words stab like knives to the heart, deep and deadly. In one sentence, he has set a match to all the hope I had left for us.

Tears begin to well up. I'm struggling to choke them back, but manage the best I can, my voice wavering as I say, "If explaining my needs is selfish, I'd rather be selfish all my days than choose to be with a man who sees those needs as a flaw. Take a look in the mirror, Arthur. Maybe one day you'll see your words reflected back to you." I brush past him out the door, still holding on to what little strength I have keeping me from falling apart. All eyes in the office follow me to the elevator. No one is sure what to say. And I'm glad no one says a thing, because I'm such a wreck inside, I might crumble at any second.

Any chance of a relationship with Arthur is officially over in my mind. Potentially our friendship, too. I'm not sure how we will rebound from this. Our connection with each other has completely shifted. Arthur needs someone he can coddle, I need someone who will let me breathe and allow me the freedom to be the independent woman I am; a man who truly sees me and believes in me and my capabilities.

It isn't until I walk outside that I notice it's pouring rain. I don't even care. I tilt my head back and let everything go– all the tears that need to be released, all the pain. Arthur was one of the closest people to me. The weight of this falling out hits harder than I could have imagined.

"Jess?"

I turn my head to see a figure approaching under a large black umbrella. My eyes, bleary with water, finally focus on the sight of Alexander, now feet away from me. "Alex? What are you doing here?" I quickly try to hide how choked up I am as he hurries over to shield me from the downpour.

"You told me you'd be here, so I came to get you. Didn't you get my text back? And where the bloody hell is your umbrella, woman?" He laughs in disbelief, and I laugh with him, sniffling and now much more aware of the bone cold chill from the freezing rain and air enveloping my body.

His hand cups the side of my face and his thumb wipes away some of the water from my cheeks. As he stares intently at me, his face takes on a more serious look. "You've been crying. What happened?"

"It's nothing."

His lips curl into a soft smirk. "Liar." He hands me the handle of the umbrella, asking me to hold it, and goes to work removing his trench coat.

"No, Alex, you don't need to do that. I still haven't given you back the last coat you lent me now that I think about it."

"Hush darling. It's a coat, not my kidney. Come, put this on." I do as he wishes, reveling in the body heat left behind on the fabric. His intoxicating scent ignites my senses and immediately calms my restless soul. My heart swells at the sight of him. It's so hard to believe he has a secret worth being blackmailed over. A secret I may never know, and that shouldn't sit well with me. I should probably find it unsettling right now. But I can't overlook how at ease I always feel around him, even in the strangest of scenarios. No matter how many times I attempt to draw away from the thought of him, something rooted within my being draws me back, like a magnet that can't resist the pull of the other.

"What do you say we stop somewhere and get you some dry clothes, yeah?"

"Oh, it's fine, I can wait till we get home."

"We aren't going home. That's actually why I came to get you. I had planned to be out all day today handling business, but it appears that duty calls elsewhere. I'm needed in Monte Carlo for a last-minute conference tomorrow afternoon. So, I'm on my way now. Since I'm going all the way out there, I figured I'd stay for the weekend, enjoy myself for a bit before all the festivities next week. You're welcome to stay here, of course. It's not required that you come. I just thought you'd like to take the opportunity during my free time to ask me some of those questions I'm sure you've been dying to get answers to." Oh, he has no idea the questions I've been dying to ask.

"And you'll answer them?"

"Within reason." I give him the side eye and his eyes soften with understanding. "I promise you, I'll do my best, Jess." I'll take it.

It's true, I have a long list of questions to ask him for the article, but honestly, I couldn't give a flying fuck about the article right now. I need to understand what's going on. Who is Alexander, really? Does he actually care about me or is it all part of his own personal scheme to butter me up and get me to write a story that puts him in the best light? Who is this woman he's supposedly in love with? And where, if anywhere, do I fit into his world? Do I even want an in or should I be running for the hills?

I didn't think I'd prioritize anything over this article when I first started, but now it seems mundane compared to the truth I need to know for my own peace of mind. I'm not even sure how comfortable I am with going through with this anymore. But I do know that if I miss out on this opportunity to go with him, this may all end with me never knowing a thing at all. There's only one week left until the banquet. Ritter could choose to pull the plug on my involvement with the assignment any day now. There isn't much time remaining. At some point this weekend, I need to come up with a plan of action. I need to figure out my next move.

"I'll go. But don't I need clothes, toiletries, the basics?"

"We can get you anything you may need in Monte Carlo. Come, let's hurry and get out of this cold, you're soaked."

I follow him to a parked black SUV. "No, not there. That's for security and staff." We walk past the car to a beautiful black Bugatti parked in front of them and walk up to the passenger side. My eyes widen as he opens the door. "Wait. This is yours? Are you driving?"

"You think I want to be chauffeured all day, every day? Not a chance." He grins. "Hop in." Okay new note, Alexander adores luxury cars. I suppose I shouldn't have expected anything less. I mean, if you have the money, you might as well, right? I get in. He already had the car on which allowed the fine leather seats to remain heated. I don't believe I've ever sat in anything cozier and so expensive in my life.

Alex closes the door and, as he moves around to the driver's side, I spy Arthur out my window, standing by the door of the building, watching us. His face is marked with anger. My breath catches and emotion rises in my chest. I face forward, closing my eyes for a moment, trying hard to gather myself and not give him the satisfaction of seeing my distress.

Alexander is attentive to the shift in my energy as he gets in the car. "Are you okay?"

"I'll be alright," I say with unease. "Just please, take me away from here." Far, far away.

16

Although we had to take a flight to Monte Carlo, Monaco, Alexander hired someone to drive his car the whole nine plus hours so he could have it for the weekend. It was my first time on a private jet of any kind so it was quite a thrilling experience, though I didn't immerse myself in it as much as I could have. The exhaustion from such an emotional day crept up and overtook me. I had faded into slumber almost as soon as we took off.

I've been to plenty of places across Europe, but Monte Carlo was one I hadn't yet had the pleasure of visiting. We passed by the main city on our way to where we'd be staying and it was stunning. Such a picturesque town overlooking the French Riviera, like something straight out of a traveler's magazine! I'm happy to be here. Happy to have a moment to be away from Aralyn and her secrets, Arthur and his despair, Ritter and his scheming. This weekend, it's just me and the one man I fully intend to place my sole focus on.

We are driven up to a gorgeous white, modern villa, framed by tall trees with a few palm trees out front. The exterior screams wealth, as does the interior. We walk in and I can't help but gawk in awe at how sleek it all looks. Alexander's manor in Paris is a marvel for sure, with its historic meets modern appeal, but this? Oh, this is a classy dream. There's an open foyer that stretches all the way to the back of the house, which is nothing but a wall of glass windowpanes reaching at least three stories high. Loft style rooms protrude out over the first floor living area where there are plush black leather couches with hunter green pillows. They color coordinate perfectly with the earthy tones of the surrounding furniture. A fireplace crackles, adding to the overall ambiance.

Alexander walks up behind me and collects my coat when I remove it. "Not bad for the weekend, huh?"

"Don't tell me you own this place too." My face is still stuck in awe.

His smile is warm. "No. Though, if I like it enough, perhaps I'll consider it."

"Mr. Marc." Carmyn approaches. It's the first time I've seen her since our strange interaction at the house. She wasn't with us on the flight. Must have taken one down before we did. Interesting. When I overheard her on the phone earlier today, she mentioned to whoever the man was on the other line that she was so excited to see him tonight. That probably won't be able to happen if she's here now, that is unless her admirer is here too. And perhaps that admirer is standing here at this very moment. I'm still highly suspicious of her connection with Alex. "I've made the proper arrangements for the meeting. Would you like to go over them tonight?"

"No, that's quite alright, Carmyn. I trust that you did well. You can brief me in the morning if you wish. Is Tommy here?"

"No, sir. He mentioned he'd come down tomorrow, possibly sometime in the afternoon."

"Good, it will be nice to see him."

"I will turn in for the night then. Good evening, Mr. Marc." Alex bids her goodnight, and she heads towards a nearby staircase. It would appear she has a room here.

I call out to her. "Goodnight, Carmyn." She peers back at me, her eyes are squinted ever so slightly, hinting at the irritation she still has with me it seems.

"Good evening, Ms. Rivers." Her tone is a touch cold. She continues her ascent up the staircase.

I turn to Alexander. "Tommy?"

"Yes. A very good friend of mine. He and Carmyn have had a thing for a little while now, so he flies out every so often to visit her when we're away from London." Oh God, I can't believe I put her in such an awkward position earlier! I feel awful, but I feel even more awful for feeling relieved more than regretful. Seriously, what is wrong with me?

And now I'm realizing that I'm, once again, back at square one. Alex hasn't mentioned anything to me since our first meeting that suggests he has a love interest at all. However, I'm trying to keep in mind that there is a lot about the bachelor that remains unknown.

"How about a nightcap before bed?" I nod in response and follow him to a bar opposite the living area, taking a seat while he grabs two glasses and a bottle of red wine. He clears his throat. "I know it's none of my business. But I do want to make sure you're truly alright. You were quite emotional earlier. Didn't seem like 'nothing' to me."

"I'm fine, really, I just... had a bit of a falling out with someone."

"Mm. Let me add a little extra wine in your glass then. Sounds like it's needed." His comment makes me giggle. I'm enjoying how he has this way of bringing such subtle and charming humor to a moment in much need of it.

He beams, "Ah, there we go. That's the sound I was searching for." His soft yet sultry smile melts my heart as he slides a healthy glass my way.

"You're too charming for your own good Alexander Marc."

"Cheers." Sipping from his own glass, he peers at me, eyes filled with so much that I find myself attempting to decipher.

I'm compelled to take advantage of the ease of the moment and gain clarity. "Is now a good time to ask you one of those questions I've been dying to ask you?"

His chuckle is light. "If you wish."

"You told me you want to trust me with your story. Is that actually the case *or* are you really just opening up to me because you feel you have to?" Confusion pulls at his brow. "I found out Ritter has been blackmailing you. Just so you're aware, I have no idea what he has on you, but I know now that there's a scheme I've been thrust in the middle of."

Alex sets his glass down. He rolls up the sleeves of his white dress shirt and places both hands on the edge of the counter, leaning in. The veins in his arms flex under the pressure of his grip. He lowers his head, processing what I've said. "Alex, I'm honestly second-guessing taking part in any of this. This feels dirty, possibly even dangerous. And I want you to open up to me because you want to, not because you're being threatened to somehow be outed if you don't."

He's quiet for a few moments longer, then draws in a long breath before responding. "I suppose I did mention it would be a conversation for another time." He glances up at me, gauging my reaction. "I um, all I will say is that yes, Ritter contacted me weeks ago with a threat to headline information he discovered. But it's not myself I was trying to protect when I agreed to his demands. It's someone I care about."

My ears perk. Could this someone he cares about be the woman whose name I'm looking to obtain? The revelation moves me and upsets me all at once. On one hand, I find it touching that he's willing to accept being blackmailed in order to protect someone he deeply cares for. On the other hand, I'm pissed because it was bad enough learning that Ritter was holding damaging information over Alexander's head, but to now learn that he's using someone Alexander loves to get what he wants is a low I never fathomed Ritter capable of.

"That bastard."

"It's okay, Jess." He smirks. "One of the advantages of having a lot of money is that problems like this can be resolved. I agreed to the article merely to stall for time. I hired a team to do some exploration into Dante Ritter. As it turns out, your boss is the definition of scum. He harbors a few secrets of his own. So, I've been organizing what you could consider reverse blackmail." Holy shit!

"So, wait, I mean, that's totally genius, but if you already got it handled and don't need to be interviewed for an article anymore, what am I doing here?"

"I meant what I said when I told you that I think you could be the person to write my story, Jess. I truly believe you're capable of making it impactful in the best way. Again, it's just a question of whether you have it within you to be empathetic and dig deep into the understanding of who I am; if you feel confident enough in the execution." I soak in his words as he rounds the bar and steps close to me. "So, tell me, do you?"

I gulp. Him being this close makes my breath hitch and my knees feel weak. Thank God I'm not standing. "Do I what?"

"Do you feel confident in the execution?" I do. I want to understand Alexander more than I've ever wanted to understand anyone, even Aralyn who I'd been so enthralled by for weeks. This man's layers have become a safe I greatly desire to crack. I just hope he'll give me the key.

"I believe so."

His eyes sparkle. "Good. And I'm not opening up to you because I have to. I'm doing it because I genuinely want to." Wow. All this time he's been choosing this; choosing to try his best to let his walls down with me, as challenging as it is for him.

"It's funny, I went into this thinking I had so much to bring out of you, but you've really brought it out of yourself. You've inspired me, Jess. You may not see it yet, or maybe you do now, but you aren't the same woman that walked in to interview me three weeks ago. That woman was a mask. You hid behind that woman. You were afraid to show the world who you are because the world had hurt you, backed you into yourself. And when I thought about it more, I realized we aren't too different in that. I, too, have hidden behind a mask. I may have confidence, but I possess little desire to be vulnerable. I've shielded myself from expression for so long."

He stares off into the distance again. "I was always raised to be strong, but when my father passed, I had to be stronger; strong for my mum, strong for the thousands of employees that were rocked by the tragedy of his departure, and strong in front of the media. I don't think I've even grieved his passing to be honest, I just carried on, business as usual. In my eyes, vulnerability became weakness and weakness was a looming enemy that could destroy everything." My heart hurts for him. I can see the hidden trauma trying to break through his distant gaze.

He shakes his head as if he were trying to shake away the memories and releases a heavy breath. "There are very few people who have ever seen the vulnerable side of me. For the longest time, I preferred it that way. Part of me still does; gutted that I've agreed to do this article, and yet I'm also relieved. I've kept a wall up for quite some time now and I fear I've imprisoned myself. But it's time I set myself free."

His eyes shift back to my dismayed face, and he gives a half smile. "Don't look so sad, Jess. I'll be quite alright." I want to hug him. I want to comfort him and let the little boy within him know that it's going to be okay. Let him know that he doesn't have to be strong, not with me.

He leans closer, lightly pressing his forehead to mine and speaks in a hushed tone. "You're so adorable when you're concerned. But please, don't be. Everything will be fine." I reach a hand towards him, placing it on his chest, half expecting him to flinch and pull away from me, but instead, he brings his hand to rest over mine. We stay here like this for a length of time unknown to me. His beating heart pulses against my palm and his warm breath tickles the fine hairs on my skin. He shifts his head position ever so slightly so that his temple touches my own, his mouth now close to my ear. His words cut through the hold, "What are you doing to me?" I'm still rendered speechless.

He draws back and takes my hand from his chest, bringing it up to his lips, and plants a sweet kiss in my palm. I slide my palm from his mouth up the side of his face, cupping his cheek. His gray eyes bore into mine, shining in the dim light. "You're making it very hard to keep things professional." He says softly.

I croak out a breathless reply. "Then don't."

We are no strangers to this place, the border between casual interaction and deep desire. We've teetered on it, brushed against it, resisted it, but sweet heavens am I ready to cross it. I don't care about professionalism. Fuck business. The deep seated need I've developed for this man is overwhelming and surpasses the priority that I had placed on business for so long. I want pleasure, blissful, indulgent, unyielding pleasure, with him.

Alexander steps away from my hand and straightens up. He looks heavenward and sighs, running a hand down his mouth. "I'm sorry. I…I really shouldn't. I just can't let myself go there."

An ache of disappointment radiates within my chest. "I um, I understand." But I really don't. Why won't he give in? It's obvious he wants me too. What is holding him back so much that he's fighting this hard?

He picks up his glass and in one gulp finishes off the rest of the wine before setting it back down. The echoing clink it makes against the counter pierces the silence between us. I lower my head and twiddle my thumbs as I try to wrap my mind around the disconnect. He once again clears his throat before speaking. "I was told that the guest room is on the second floor, at the end of the hall to the right."

I can't bring myself to meet his eyes. "Yeah. Okay, thanks."

He shoves a hand in his pocket and rubs the back of his neck with the other. "Alright then. Goodnight, Jess."

"Goodnight, Alexander." He breezes past me, and I'm soon left alone in the large room with nothing but my thoughts to consume me.

I'm not sure what to make of his refusal to have me. I don't want to take it personally but it's difficult not to. Maybe I need to give him more grace here, this could be a part of the vulnerability and fear he still needs time to overcome.

Sighing, I rise from my seat and walk out one of the glass doors leading onto the oversized balcony with an infinity pool overlooking the glistening moonlit water of the Mediterranean. Fresh air is just what I need to help me find clarity. Every emotion I've experienced over the last twenty-four hours sits tight in the back of my throat, ready for me to crack, preparing for me to surrender and fall to pieces, which would be so easy to do right now. And why not? Why hold it together? Perhaps I need a good breakdown for a second time today, a good cry, a good scream.

I watch my breath dance across the cold night air, reminding me of the very life filling this vessel that threatens to collapse under the weight of everything that's been thrust upon me. The voice of my consciousness whispers to me that all is not lost. Yes, everything has, indeed, transformed rapidly. Yes, nothing has gone according to plan. Yes, I've been severely disappointed more times than I could ever care to be. But I have an opportunity still; an opportunity to write one of the most impactful stories of my career so far. And the opportunity to grow closer to the man my mind won't let me turn away from and my heart refuses to let go, if he'll let me. This has become greater than a desire to impress Ritter, appease Arthur or prove myself worthy to anyone else. I'm proving myself to me.

I ponder what Alexander had said about me no longer being the woman hiding behind a mask and he's right. As strange as it's been, I've never felt more pushed to growth as I have these past couple weeks. I've stood up for my truth and stepped out of my comfort zone, especially in the ways I present myself, wearing things I once loved but shoved away in order to be less desirable. I did it to keep others from hurting me, but I only ended up being the one to do the hurting by convincing myself that I had to be small in order to get big. Existing behind a shield of illusion for so many years has held me back from doing all I can and being all I can be. I truly had been lost. And now, I'm tired. Tired of living in the shadows of fear that keeps me stifled from all I hope for in this life. It's like Alex said, the time has come to be set free.

I sit at the edge of my bed, still swimming in my thoughts. Normally I'd call up Arthur to talk through my worries and calm my soul but, that's obviously no longer an option. There is one person I can call though– my best friend from back home, Genevieve. We don't talk as much as we used to. Mostly my fault. I've gotten so caught up with work and making Paris feel like home over the past few years, I isolated myself a lot from people I had once been very connected to. I barely even call my parents. Come to think of it, I only spoke to them three times last year. A record low.

I came to a new land seeking opportunity, success, and an improved quality of life. And though I suppose I've received that in different ways… at what cost? I allowed my world to solely revolve around work, hiding in the shadows of the least authentic version of myself. The only real friend I bothered to make and keep was Arthur. And now look at me. Peeling away the layers of my cocoon, alone.

I decide to call the friend I have so unfortunately neglected. She picks up on the second ring. "Jess!" Her peppy greeting brings a sense of nostalgia that tugs at my heart.

"Haha, hi Gen!"

"God, I miss your voice! How long has it been?"

I sigh. "Way too long. I'm sorry it's taken me forever to reach out to you."

"Don't even worry about it! Life happens. BUT now that I do have you on the phone finally, I need a total run down. You're literally saving me from the clutches of a reality show marathon at present. I'm sure your life will be far more entertaining. Catch me up to speed babes!"

"Wow, um, I honestly don't even know where to begin."

"Last time we spoke you were telling me about that handsome journalist you were seeing. Please tell me you two finally made it official!"

"Arthur? Um, well we were never actually seeing each other."

"Oh? Interesting. I remember you were telling me he was some sort of dreamy Adonis who was totally head over heels for you." Wow, I did say that didn't I?

"Yeah… haha, uh, well it just wasn't meant to be. Anyway, how have you been? How's the business?"

"Jess?"

"Hm?"

"I've known you practically my whole life. I can tell when you need to get something off your chest. So, spill it. What's got you in your head?"

It's as if my entire being was simply waiting for permission to spill my guts! And I do. I don't think I even tell her everything in chronological order, I just let it all out. Every word spoken feels like an ounce of weight off my shoulders. I feel lighter.

Per usual, Gen listens attentively, gives her two cents where necessary, laughs with me, and gives me words of empowerment and affirmation. I don't know how I allowed myself to go so long without her warm energy. This conversation is everything I've needed and more.

The only thing I tell her about my connection with Alexander is that I've been assigned to write an article on him. I choose to leave out all the juicy bits. I'd like to keep this, large, yet personal bit of information to myself for a while longer. Especially because I have no idea where things are headed. Until it's clearer,

I'd rather not indulge in fantasy or drag anyone into the hectic chaos that has been this journey so far.

After all is said and done, there really isn't any going back for me. I am a woman reborn unto herself. Resurfacing from years of living under a sea of emotion begging to be expressed.

17

My eyes flutter open, my senses ignited by the smell of bacon. Sunlight streams through my window, bouncing off a tableside statue made of glass which creates a prism effect throughout the room. What a beautiful way to wake up to a new day. I stretch out in my royal blue satin sheets and contemplate the surge of hope I feel, especially after my period of reflection last night and my conversation with Genevieve. No matter what, today will be a good day. Today I plan to fully embrace whatever comes my way, take it in stride if I need to, but embrace it and own who I am in the process. No matter what.

As I get myself prepared, I pause at the bathroom mirror, stare at the woman who'd been hiding for so long, and say hello. It's a strange feeling, to be confronted with oneself this way, not doing my hair or makeup or checking to see if what I'm wearing looks decent, just full-on gazing at myself. I say a silent apology to the image reflected back to me. It's been too long. Gone are the days where I choose to shield myself from stares. Where I worry about how I will be viewed or who I impress with my skills.

I'm grateful for Isabella Evans. She reminded me of who I always had been but was scared to let out of the cage I locked myself in. She was fearless, bold, confident and free. Becoming her for a short time empowered me to push against the limitations I needlessly placed upon myself. She coaxed me out of hiding and prompted me to step into my authenticity. She led me to the promise land of my truth. And now, I can fully be Jess Rivers.

I follow the smell of bacon to the kitchen. No one is down here but there is a lovely breakfast display spread out across the island, accompanied by a note with my name next to a jug of orange juice. I pick it up and open it. It's from Carmyn.

*Mr. Marc will be out until four this evening. He would like you to know that, should you desire, you can request a car to take you wherever you'd like to go. There is a phone in the front parlor. Dial *96 to connect to the chauffeur.*

Mr. Marc has also left a card for you to utilize should you wish to purchase a new outfit for the banquet and to cover the expenses of anything else you may like to engage in.

Good day, Ms. Rivers.

Hmm. I'm not too sure how I feel about this. For one, I'm shocked. For a man who says he wants to keep things professional, he sure is shelling out some serious cash for me. From my understanding, Monte Carlo isn't called the city of millionaires for nothing. It's rich. Very rich. Upscale isn't even the word to describe the luxuriousness of the city. Doing anything here, including shopping, isn't going to be cheap.

I pick up the black card that was sitting under the note and twirl it in my fingers, taking notice of Alexander's name on the back. Holy shit, this is an actual personal card of his! I set it down, staring at it for a time and pondering what to do about this oh so generous gesture. It says a lot that he trusts me to use this but it, once again, stirs up some confusion within me. What if this is a test? Perhaps it's not that he trusts me but that he's trying to gauge whether he can. But if it isn't, and he really does trust me with this, why make connecting on a greater level so complicated? He's offering the gift of money, but I don't want his money, I want him. I huff in frustration and leave the card on the countertop. I'll be perfectly fine staying at the house. Besides, it will be nice to finally have a moment to relax and enjoy time away. A refreshing break from the hustle and bustle, chaos and stress.

Plate now full, I make my way to the deck that hangs over a portion of the backyard balcony. It's clear skies today. The sun is shining bright and it's the perfect temperature, much preferable to the dreary chill of Paris. I have a seat at the patio table, take a bite of the bacon I've been craving since I awoke, and begin scrolling through a news app on my phone to catch up on all the happenings in entertainment since my disappearance into the world of Marc the last couple weeks.

A notification pops up on my screen– an email from Ritter. I reluctantly open it and read his message. He's asking me to come into the office ASAP. Yeah, I don't think I'll be doing that. In fact, I may not walk into Eiffel ever again. Thankfully, there was nothing in the contract I signed that says Eiffel owns any of my research, only that they own the article I write for them. If he releases me from the contract, there's nothing he can do to keep me from using the information I've gathered to create an article that gets published elsewhere. I can do what I wish with this story and I'll soak up the opportunity for everything it's worth.

Ritter has yet to realize just how much he's fucked up. Let him get tired of my lack of response and put Charles on the assignment. Like Arthur said, there's a little under a week left now, leaving Charles a very small window of opportunity to secure a solid story. Not to mention, I know there's no way Alexander will give him even a millimeter of his time. Shouldn't play dirty.

With pleasure, I block Ritters emails and his number and power down my phone for the day. I'm taking the reins now. It's time to play by my own rules.

*T*he heated water of the infinity pool, the breathtaking view of the sea and the city in the distance is absolutely perfect. There's been nothing but peace and quiet for hours and it's been heavenly. I could get used to this!

"Hey! How's the water?"

I let out a startled scream as I whirl around. I remove my hand from my chest and use it as a visor to get a clearer view. In the doorway stands a tall, handsome man dressed in a white shirt and black shorts. His dark brown skin glows in the sun, his smile radiant.

"Sorry to scare you." He comes closer. "I'm Thomas. You can call me Tommy though." Ah, so this is the rose man. Carmyn sure has excellent taste.

"I'm Jess. Nice to meet you."

"You as well. I must say, I'm surprised to see a journalist in Alexander's space." Tommy takes off his sandals and sits down at the edge of the pool, extending his legs into the water.

"How do you know I'm a journalist?"

"Carmyn mentioned it, said you'd been staying with Alex for a spell."

"Haha, gotcha. Yeah, it doesn't seem like she's been too thrilled about it."

"Eh, I'd say she doesn't understand it. And I get that, I don't quite understand it myself honestly. But if there's one thing I know about my mate, it's that he's full of surprises that one. You never quite know what he'll do until he does it. And even then, you might not get why he's done it. Far from predictable." So I've come to learn.

"But anyway, it's not my business. If you're here, he must be comfortable with you and that's enough for me." Tommy's energy is refreshing. He might be the most direct person I've encountered as of late. No beating around the bush or concealing, he simply says what's on his mind. I think we'll get along great.

I soon learn that he is not just Alexander's close friend, he's his best friend. They met each other at a young age, shortly after Alex and his family moved to the suburbs of London. They've done a lot together over the years. It's pleasant hearing stories about their adventures, some of which detail a trouble making phase I would have never guessed Alexander experienced. I had taken him for the proper, follow the rules, no-time-for-mischief type of teenager.

Tommy cackles. "So, there was this one time yeah, swear to God this man convinced me to break into the neighbor's house with him. Not to take anything, just for the hell of it. 'It will be fun' he said. It was something alright. Mans broke through a bedroom window and had us walking straight into the scene of his neighbor shagging her stepson. I'll never forget it a day in my life." The images his story brings to mind has me cracking up. "We never got in trouble for it either. She let it slide in return for our silence." He winks.

"Are you telling lies about me, Tommy?" We both look over to see Alexander and Carmyn walking toward us. Alexander's face beams at the sight of his friend.

"Ay, look at this bloody wanker here!" Tommy jumps up. His locs, pulled back into a ponytail, bounce and swing as he bounds over to meet his friend, bringing him in for a hug. It's heartwarming to see the two of them so excited to be in each other's presence. There's genuine brotherly care there that I've yet to see Alexander express and it's a joy to witness.

Tommy goes from Alex to embracing Carmyn in a deep and passionate hug as Alex walks toward me. I blush upon realizing that I'm still here in the pool in nothing but a bright white bikini. I shouldn't feel shy about it, but I do. Alexander comes and squats down at the edge in front of me. He looks so damn good in dress shirt and slacks. His tie is missing, and the top three buttons are undone, providing a tantalizing peak of his chest. This man is beyond gorgeous.

His mouth curves up into the smile I adore so much. "Good evening, Brown Eyes. Did you have a good day?" Is that a pet name I'm hearing? It should make me thrilled but I'm growing tired of this back-and-forth, flirting and lusting one minute and then serious and distant the next.

I titter, narrowing my eyes. "It was pleasantly relaxing, Mr. Marc."

His brows raise, taken aback by my use of his formal name. "Oh, we're back to Mr. Marc now?"

A mischievous half smile slides up my face as I glide towards the pool entrance keeping my eyes on him. I rise and walk out, no longer nervous that he'll see my sopping wet body or embarrassed by my injured knee tightly wrapped in a fresh bandage. It's time he gets a taste of what he's been dishing out. I watch as his eyes blaze with curiosity and awe, and I challenge them playfully. "Just keeping it professional."

I stick out my chest and hold my head up high as I stride away, leaving him speechless. My conscience cheers me on, and I swell with pride. I pick up a towel and walk past the two love birds holding each other, giggling as they speak. Then I take one last glance back at Alexander who's now standing, glaring at me with the most puzzled, yet focused, expression.

Got him.

*M*y fingers type away at the keyboard as I lay in bed. I've been able to write a decent start to the article based on the information I've gathered so far. There are still plenty of questions that I have for Alexander, but one of my primary interests is trying to understand his fascination with sensual domination.

I took it upon myself to do research the past couple of hours, discovering various videos and articles thoroughly explaining the different types of power dynamics in the BDSM world. I've learned that there are even different types of Dominant and Submissive partnerships. I've also been learning about the norms and the importance of practices like conversations about safe words or the effectiveness of after care, all new concepts to me, but intriguing to say the least. Alex told me he wanted me to understand his role in the kink world so that I may better understand who he is in general. I'm hoping he will expound more on that intent.

A knock on the door jilts me from my focus. "Yes?"

"It's Carmyn." I give her permission to enter and my jaw hits the ground upon sight of her. She wears a beautiful, form fitting olive green dress that touches the floor and appears to be made of velvet. The color is perfect against her skin and brings out the hazel in her eyes. "Ms. Rivers, Tommy and I are headed out for the evening. Mr. Marc asked me to let you know that he will be downstairs in the living area should you wish to interview him."

I'm elated that I'll finally have the opportunity to interview Alex properly! A good sit down is what I'd been hoping for since we met. "Thank you."

I stop her right as she's about to head out. "Carmyn, wait." Her attention darts back to me. "I want to apologize for yesterday. It wasn't fair of me to grill you the way I did. I didn't mean to make you feel uncomfortable. I know you're just looking out for Alexander and yourself. I hope you can forgive me."

A sweet smile plays on her lips. "You're forgiven." She steps further into the room, closing the door behind her. "You know something, Ms. Rivers, I may not understand what's going on between you and Mr. Marc, and it's truly none of my concern, but I will say that he does seem more relaxed around you than I've seen him around anyone in quite some time. And I am happy to see it. You're right, I do my best to look out for him. I may be out of place to say it, but even though he's my boss, he's become like family to me. I've witnessed him endure heartbreak and I've watched him scrape up the pieces alone. I don't wish to see that again."

"Carmyn, I–" She raises her palm to silence me.

"Again, what is going on between you both isn't my concern. Just, tread lightly, please." I nod my head in understanding of her request. "Well then, I should be off. Have a good evening, Ms. Rivers."

As she exits, I stop her once more. "Wait, Carmyn! You look really lovely. Tommy is a lucky man."

Her eyes soften and she lets out a light laugh. "Don't I know it." With that she closes the door behind her.

How interesting that even she couldn't deny the attraction between Alex and I. Now that I think about it, I hadn't even considered how other people might perceive us. For the most part, whenever I've been around him lately everything and everyone gets blocked out. It's strange to think that there's actually people paying attention to how we move and interact with one another.

After gathering myself, I head downstairs and find Alex exactly where Carmyn mentioned– in the living area sitting back in a chair, peering into the fireplace, a glass of whiskey in his hand. The glow of the fire flickers across his divine features with such perfection.

"Penny for your thoughts?" He snaps out of his trance and looks my way. His smile is warm and endearing as I take a seat across from him, tucking my blue maxi dress comfortably beneath me. I hold up a pen and the pad of paper in my hands. "I've actually come prepared to take notes this time."

"So you have." His voice is a low hum, tickling me in areas that cause incredible distraction. He sits up straight and I take him in, barefoot with dark denim jeans and a black long-sleeved shirt with a V-neck that cuts down in that teasing way, sending me in a tizzy. I'm going to have to work extra hard to focus.

He sets his glass on a side table and clears his throat. "Okay. What would you like to know?"

"I'll start with a question that I don't feel you fully answered in our first interview. What about your family inspires your humanitarian endeavors?"

He takes a moment, possibly pondering whether this is something he's willing to discuss. To my relief, he does. "My mum is an angel. Since I can remember, she was always invested in work that improves humanity and the environment, volunteering at shelters, orphanages, and getting involved in numerous pursuits regarding environmental activism. She always told me, 'Alexander, whatever you do in this world, do your part to leave it better than it was when you came in'. That's stuck with me since the first time she said it. Now I have a large platform in which I have plenty of opportunity to do my part, so I'm doing what I can."

"That's beautiful." I chuckle. "Would it have been so hard to just say that the first time?"

He smirks but his eyes are stoic. "I try not to bring her up much. She's been through a lot. I've been careful not to put too much of a spotlight on her."

"Oh, I see. I understand." I look down at my list of questions. "What would you like readers to know most about your rise to success?"

"Well, success is the hardest mountain one will ever climb. You will be met with failure after failure on the way to the top. You will be left breathless, exhausted. You will question yourself over and over, your mind will tell you to quit, even your body will want to give in. But, if your soul wants it, and I mean really yearns for it, success is not out of reach."

I'm entranced by his words. The man should switch to a career in motivational speaking. I have an epiphany, realizing just how alluring I find his mind. His tongue speaks poetry, and now I find myself wondering what else his tongue can do. The very thought causes a delicious ache between my legs. I give myself away when I squirm in my seat and briefly draw my lower lip between my teeth. He gives me a once over, eyes gleaming with knowing.

I do my best to quickly transition to the next subject. "Um, okay great. Well, besides business and humanitarian projects, what are some other things you're passionate about?"

He rubs the base of his index finger along his lower lip. "Sex."

My eyes grow wide. "I'm sorry, what?"

"You asked me what else I'm passionate about." He grins mischievously. "My answer is sex."

"Okay." I gulp. "I was thinking you'd say something more, PG rated. You know, like hiking or martial arts… something like that. I'm not sure I should list your passion for sex in the article."

"What a shame."

"Is that so?

He sighs and rolls up his sleeves. Leaning forward, he places his forearms on his knees, his stormy eyes glare into mine with seductively scorching intensity. "Respectfully darling, I really don't give a fuck about the article right now." Gesturing with a finger, he points down at the floor in front of him. "Come here."

What the..."But I–"

"Jess, for the love of God, bring your ass over here." I've never been a fan of being ordered around, but this man is making it too damn hot to resist obedience. I hesitate for a mere second, questioning if this is some ridiculous prank, then inevitably do as I'm told, taking a stand in front of him.

His eyes trace up the length of my body nice and slow. Though the light of the fire gives them a certain glow, they have become dark and lustful. There's no containing myself from reaching out my hand to lightly brush aside the few loose curls that hang delicately over his hairline. Then my fingers slide down the side of his face tracing all those fine features. I'm in total awe of his beauty.

"Kneel." I obey his command, spoken in a gentle tone, and he reaches a firm hand outward, lightly griping the back of my neck to pull me to him. "Why am I so drawn to you?" He presses his forehead to mine, his nose brushing my own. "If you only knew the things I want to do to you, the things I want to teach you." He exhales a deep quivering breath. "I'm trying so very hard to resist you."

My reply comes in an almost breathless whisper, "Why?"

He draws back just a bit, his face mere inches from my own. "If we keep going like this, you'll have my heart. I can sense it. And I'm not ready to give that up. Not again." I remember Carmyn's brief mention of witnessing him go through heartbreak, as well as Aralyn's request to find out the name of the woman he loves. Could it be that the woman he loves is the same one who broke his heart? An unfamiliar feeling bubbles up to the surface; it might be hate. I hate that he was left heartbroken, so heartbroken that he's afraid to love again. And that, in turn, makes me feel hateful toward the unknown woman responsible.

How do we conquer this? What can I do to show him that his heart is safe with me? "Alex, I've no intention of hurting you."

"Many people don't intend to hurt others, darling. But it doesn't always keep it from happening."

"I'd be putting my heart on the line right along with you. I know you could hurt me too, and that scares me. But honestly Alex, I'm more afraid of losing you. I'm terrified of what will happen once the charity event comes to a close. I'm terrified that there will be no more you in my life." It's this bit of truth that spills from my lips that sends my emotions into overdrive. It's the first time it dawns on me that I'm petrified this will all be short lived.

"So, what do you suggest we do about this fear of ours?"

"We face it."

He lightly sweeps his knuckles across my cheek then tucks my hair behind my ear. "And how do you suppose we do that?"

I say the first thing that's on my heart. "We take a leap of faith. Together."

I can see the heavy calculation through the windows of his soul, trying to determine if the risk is one he's willing to take. Then, his face drops down to my ear and in a low tone he says, "I truly don't know whether to walk away or strip you down and have my way with you."

The ache between my legs becomes unbearable. I whisper, "I'm yours, Alex. I'm all yours."

His head moves to the base of my neck. His groan is deep as he plants a tantalizing kiss there that causes a surge of pleasure to ripple through my body. My head falls back, indulging in this moment of bliss. With each kiss, his tongue grazes across my skin, hot and wet, setting my nerves on fire. Then his lips run a slow and passionate trail up and over my jaw stopping just shy of my mouth where he hovers. I want him so damn bad.

I make a move to kiss him, and he pulls back ever so slightly, causing me to miss. "Mm, greedy girl." God, I can hardly take this teasing.

My plea is breathless, "Please." I've never begged for anything, but damn, I'll beg for this with everything in me.

He cups my chin and runs a thumb across my bottom lip, studying it. "You might just be the end of me, Ms. Rivers."

"There doesn't have to be an end, Mr. Marc." We could share moments like this forever if he'd only let me in.

"Fuck it." In an instant his mouth claims mine. We dive into the vast pool of desire that's tempted us both for what seems like an eternity. His aroma, his tongue overtaking my own, the warmth of his breath against my skin, everything is beyond intoxicating. A moan escapes my lips and I thrust my hands up grasping his neck, pulling him so close that there's no room for breath.

One of my hands falls to his lap and I move it up his thigh, eager to feel him, to please him. But he clutches it, halting me, and smiles, mouth touching mine with the weight of a feather. "Not here my love." He stands, causing my eyes to be level with the bulging erection fighting the fabric of his jeans. Sweet mercy, the way I desire to peel down that zipper and set his cock free feels beyond sinful.

His fingers grasp my chin, tilting my head up to meet his burning gaze. "Do you trust me?"

"Completely." He holds his hand out, gesturing for me to take it.

I do.

18

Alexander's hand runs through my hair as he towers over me. My breathing is as heavy as the anticipation of his next move. "Stand."

I do so and he bends down and scoops me up over his shoulder. I giggle with surprise. "Alex! I'm perfectly capable of walking."

"And as you can see, I'm perfectly capable of carrying you." We exit the room and I start wiggling in rebellion.

"Honestly, this is ridiculous! Just set me down." A firm smack lands on my ass and I gasp, my mouth falling open in speechless shock.

"Anything else? I can do this all night." My eyes roll and I sigh in surrender. Another firm smack falls on top of where the last one landed, stinging a bit more this time and I yelp. "That one's for the eye roll I can practically hear." This man has come to know me a bit too well.

I can't really tell where he's taking us in this position, but my guess is my bedroom. Though, as we pass the second floor and make our way to the third, that guess goes out the window.

He opens a door at the end of the hall and walks into a room where the only light is the moonlight streaming in through the windows. His bare feet pad across the floor and then he stops, dropping me on a bed… his bed. I try to steal a quick glance around but am lured away from my endeavor by the sight of him peeling off his shirt.

I'm awestruck! His body is every bit as beautiful as I'd imagined, even more! His chest, bare, a vein or two protrudes down his well built biceps. His abdomen shows off the work he's clearly been doing in the gym and his jeans hang deliciously low on his waist, displaying that sweet V pointing the way to an even sweeter spot.

Grabbing my ankle, he yanks me closer to the edge of the bed, then raises the skirt of my dress and gently parts my legs, revealing my soaked panties. I feel so exposed, so shy, and yet I continue to lay here, spread, watching him admire me as he draws his lower lip into his mouth and rolls it back out. I swear I can see every dirty thought he has in his penetrating stare.

"You are beautiful." My heart melts. I've been called beautiful many times in many ways, but not like this, not in the way he says it. There isn't just passion and lust behind the phrase, there's something profound, more genuine, something that comes from a place not easily reached.

Lowering himself onto the bed, he crawls between my legs till he's flush on top of me, holding himself up with a singular forearm. The bulge in his pants is pressed firmly against my throbbing mound, twitching and begging for the release I desire to give it. His free hand clutches the side of my face and his mouth envelops mine. I arch into him, desperate and needy. My hands explore his chest and run down his torso towards his pants but as soon as I reach them, he sits up straight and positions himself in a knelt position over my waist. He collects my wrists and thrusts my arms above my head, pinning them there and leaning over till his face is mere inches from my own. "Patience my love. Keep your arms above you till I say otherwise."

He lets go and repositions his hands at the nape of my neck, then gently rakes his fingers down my body and up again, teasing me once more. Eventually, he brings them to the top of my dress, grips the fabric and cracks a devilish smile, "I do apologize." Before I can inquire as to what for, he rips the fabric down the middle in one sudden and fluid movement, exposing my bare chest to the chilly air and his sizzling admiration. "Then again, not really."

He beams, prideful of his fine work, then cups a breast, rolling my nipple between his thumb and index finger. My body yearns for more. He leans over, taking it into his mouth. The way he sucks while his tongue and teeth take turns flicking and nipping sends the flood gates wide open. I'm so fucking wet!

I moan with pleasure, bucking against him for every tinge of sweet pain that his teeth cause as he bites and pulls with the perfect amount of pressure. I disobey his earlier command and make a move to run my hands through his hair– a futile endeavor. He grabs my wrists again and pins them back where he wanted them. "*Tsk tsk*, Naughty. What did I say?"

I pant. "To keep my hands above my head." Pleased with my answer, his mouth meets mine again. I taste the salt of my sweat on his tongue and it's the hottest damn thing.

"Tell me what you want Jess." I've never been asked, and I don't know where to begin. What don't I want?

"Show me how much you desire me. Please."

He smirks. "You mean how much I crave you." He backs up slowly, leaving hot kisses across my chest and stomach on his way down, all while keeping his eyes on mine.

He reaches my sweet spot. Nothing but thin fabric separates his mouth from my clit. I tilt my head back, anticipating the pleasure I know I'm about to receive. "Look at me, my love. I want you to watch me." Oh, this is simply too much.

I watch as he tucks a finger under my panties and pulls them to the side, taking a moment to observe the ocean of arousal he's created. He sighs in awe and his eyes flicker back up to me. "I see you crave me too."

"More than you know."

"Then let's satiate that, shall we?" He takes the plunge, delving deep and setting my body on fire. His tongue laps over my clit and between my lips with expert skill. This is my fantasy come to life! In fact, it's better than I could have ever imagined. He pauses momentarily, tucking his fingers under the top hem of my underwear and sliding them off. After which, he grabs my legs, thrusting them up to my sides and digs in like a feast he might never experience again. I gasp and moan, my body quivers and I thrust my hands down to his head, disobeying his rules once more, but I can't help myself.

A groan reverberates from his diaphragm and he pins my arms to the bed, denying me again. I am dying to touch him, but I love the fact that I can't, there's something about it I find so frustrating yet titillating. Without warning, he grabs my waist and flips me over onto my stomach. Then he raises my hips, propping me onto my knees, and draws me to the edge of the bed. I feel so fucking desired!

My chest heaves with rapture as he continues to eat me out. After some time, just as I'm reaching the point of a mind-numbing orgasm, he stops. "Not yet, baby." My legs tremble as he stands. I'm almost certain they may give out. "Stay just like this," he commands.

I hear the sound of fabric being fumbled with and I look back, witnessing him slowly drag down the zipper of his jeans, then peeling open the denim to display his engorged package still wrapped in light colored briefs. I watch intently as his jeans drop to his ankles and he steps out of them.

As he pulls down his briefs, his erection springs to life. I'm astonished by the sight of his girthy cock, standing upright like a soldier ready for battle. No, not a soldier, a king. A king prepared to rule over newfound lands and my body is ready to be conquered. He moves in position behind me, and I whimper with need, jutting my hips back so that he has the perfect angle to finally possess what I am all too willing to offer. The head of his cock probes me, gliding up and down between my wet, swollen slit. "Mmm, ask me for it, Jess."

"Please, please, Alex."

"Please what?" He rubs my clit with his thumb and the sensation has me writhing!

"Please, fuck me!" I'd do anything for him right now. Absolutely anything.

"Good girl." My walls expand as he pushes past my opening. I inhale a shivering breath as he exhales a satiated one. He slides back and forth again and again, his rhythm slow and methodical, all while spreading my cheeks to obtain the perfect view. Hearing his low groans of gratification make me feel so pleased with myself.

Eventually, his thrusts become harder and faster. I bury my face in the sheets as I'm taken for the ride of my life, my fingers clasping the fine fabric beneath me as if it's the only thing keeping me tethered to earth. I can feel myself reaching climax again and then everything halts as he intentionally denies me release once more, pulling out and standing there with the most sinful glint in his eyes. Orgasm denial is another first for me. It's strange because it has me feeling like I'll lose my mind if I don't cum, but also as though I never want this to end.

"Turn over my love." I do as I'm told as he crawls on top of me, nuzzling my throat. "God, you're perfect." He penetrates me again and I gasp and grip his arms. "If you could only see yourself the way I see you, you'd understand just how perfect you are." His face hovers and his eyes bore into my soul. Where has this man been all my life?

As he continues making love to me, overwhelming happiness mixes with the intense ecstasy that ripples through me from my head to my toes, and a tear slides down my face. Alexander, gentle, beautiful Alexander, kisses it. "I've got you, baby. Hold on."

Suddenly, he swirls his hips and grinds himself against my clit causing me to descend deeper and deeper into decadent bliss. I strain a whisper. "Alex…"

The sight of his warm smile makes me feel so safe. "You're doing so good, Jess. Go ahead and cum for me." Those words send me over the edge, as if my body was holding out for his permission. My mouth falls open and my entire being shudders underneath him. Blood rushes to my head causing the world to go quiet. The only feeling is that of a thousand bursts rocking throughout my core and Alexander's quaking body over me as he, too, arrives at climax. When I regain my vision and awareness, I feel him planting soft kisses across my jaw and neck and then he plants one on my forehead.

He rolls over, pulling me with him and we lay here, sweaty and entwined, our hearts racing in sync, lost for words, but no words are needed now. I wonder what I've done to deserve such affection, such care. Part of me doesn't feel worthy, but the part of me that's been released from her cage knows that it's about time. She knows that this is what I've yearned for, that *he* is what I've yearned for.

I'm not sure how much time goes by before words come back to us. He strokes my back with his fingers. "Thank you."

I look up at him. "For what?"

"For trusting me."

I beam. "You don't make it hard. I should be the one thanking you."

The look he gives me right now is filled with so much tenderness. "Are you okay?" he asks.

"I'm fine. More than fine. We can go again if you'd like."

He lets out a hearty laugh. "Oh, don't worry, there's plenty more fun I plan to have with you." I snuggle into his side, reveling in his warmth.

Some minutes pass, and he speaks again. "I've expressed to you how hard it's been for me to let my guard down. But I've yet to fully explain the why."

He takes a moment before continuing. "I used to look up to my uncle so much. Besides my father, I saw him as my greatest role model. He played a big role in my upbringing. Helped me become a star rugby player at school and made sure I thrived in my studies. If there was something my father was unable to do because of timing or some urgent business issue, he picked up the slack. So, you can imagine my horror when he murdered my father, right in front of my mum and I. Everyone knows he did it, but since he killed himself, no one outside of our family knew the real reason why. That's the secret Ritter had discovered. The why." My brow creases and my heart flutters.

"Jealousy was the assumed motive and it's true, jealousy was, indeed, a huge factor. When I was a lad, my uncle and my mum had an affair. It was a one-time fling apparently. My mum was wracked with guilt after and put an end to it, but my uncle could never let it go. Overtime he began to secretly loathe witnessing my father's success; loathed him having the life he wanted with the woman he wanted it with and a child he cared for as if I was his own. He had tried many times over to convince my mum that they were meant to be together, but he was unsuccessful in his pursuits. Then one day, jealousy overcame him, and he made one final attempt to get her back at the dinner table in front of me and my father.

"I remember the look on my father's face when he realized what had happened– one of complete shock. However, it was nothing compared to the look he gave when his brother pulled a gun on him. The betrayal, disappointment and fear in his eyes will haunt me all my days. I tried so hard to talk my uncle down. He couldn't even look at me, the coward. My mum begged on her knees, but he did not hear her. He could not hear either of us. Rage had made him deaf. The man I thought I knew was gone, and the stranger I saw in his place, stole my father's life."

My heart shatters and tears rise to the surface. "Your mom. She's the someone you've been trying to protect."

"The world can be quite cruel. My mum was wrong to have an affair, but she is not to blame for his death. Sadly, I know people won't see it that way. It's bad enough that she blames herself so harshly. I don't need the world sending her to an early grave too." He pauses momentarily. "My uncle was one of the people I trusted most in my life and he hurt me more than anyone. That, coupled with the fact that we couldn't be left in peace; all the speculation and rumors, it was a bloody shitshow that I had to gain control of and fast. I didn't know who to trust anymore. So, I chose to trust no one."

"I'm so sorry." I hold him tight, and a few tears fall as I grieve for him. I grieve for the boy whose world had changed forever that day, for the boy who so suddenly had to become a man. He's done everything he can to protect his father's legacy and to protect his mother from the ruthlessness of society. For Ritter to pose such a threat to it all just for the sake of a story is revolting.

He strokes my hair and, with his other hand, grasps my chin, tilting my head up to look at him. "I'm trusting you with this, with everything in me. Please, don't make me regret it." I reach up and grab the back of his head, pulling him in for a deep and loving kiss. It means the world that he's gifted me with such immense trust in the care of such a heavy secret. It's a true honor that I cannot take for granted.

It seems too early to say it, even to feel it, but I know in the depths of my soul that I'm falling for this man. I have discovered a soulmate in him and, with each passing day, I find it harder to envision my life without him by my side. But I will keep my silence on the matter until I know for sure he's on the same page. Afterall, this conversation is already so emotional, and he's made so much of a stride in opening himself to me. He should have time to process before being met with something as challenging as giving his heart again, especially after he spoke about how difficult it would be.

I can be patient. I know he's worth it. So very worth it.

I step out of the shower nice and refreshed. When viewing my reflection earlier, I couldn't help but notice that I looked like a woman who had been thoroughly fucked. And though I personally enjoy the look, it's not going to fly with the other house guests. I change into a white blouse and dark blue jeans that were sitting on the edge of the bed when I awoke. Alexander hadn't been in the room then. I figure he's downstairs getting an early start to the day. Honestly, I would have much preferred us to stay in bed together the whole day, especially because we didn't get around to more fun last night. I would have loved to continue our sexcapade for hours on end, but, alas, we both succumbed to the lure of pleasant sleep in each other's embrace.

I walk out of the bathroom and hear chatter. Alex is on the balcony talking to someone. I step out and see him addressing Tommy who's on the patio doing pushups. "Um haha, what's going on out here?"

Alex turns his sights my way and flashes a bright smile. "Good morning, Brown Eyes." He stands and draws me into his arms. "How are you feeling today?"

"A bit sore and hungry, but great overall."

His muscular frame towers over me as he tucks a few strands of wet hair behind my ear, chuckling. "Well, I can't say when the soreness will pass. If things go my way, it won't pass for some time. But the peckish feeling? That will surely go away after some breakfast. What do you say we get that going?"

"Do you fancy yourself a cook?"

He gleams. "Who said anything about me cooking?"

"So, your chef then?"

"You are a very curious creature. Always so full of questions. Do you ever leave room in your life for surprises, Jess?"

"If you must know, I hate surprises." I chuckle but I'm so serious. I've had more than my fill of surprises as of late.

He steps back and calls down to Tommy who's now doing drills. "Ay, Tommy boy! You gonna stop mucking about and get breakfast started?"

Tommy stops mid set, huffing, and sticks up a middle finger, then goes back to what he was doing. Alex laughs and turns back.

"Tommy is an excellent chef back in London. Owns two Michelin star restaurants."

"Wow! Really? That's impressive! He'll absolutely have to cook for us then."

"You hear that, Tommy? Jess said 'get your ass in the kitchen'!"

Tommy stops again, "Alex, respectfully, you both can go fuck yourselves, yeah?"

Alexander smirks. "That means he'll come in to cook in a couple minutes."

"Uh huh. You two are definitely best friends but you also act like brothers."

"Oh, you haven't seen us at our worst. You probably will when we go out today. Speaking of which," he reaches into his pocket and pulls out a black card, holding it up. It looks like the one I left on the buffet counter yesterday morning. "I see you didn't utilize this."

"I appreciate the gesture Alex, but I can take care of myself."

"I get that, and I respect your need for independence, so how about this: let me take care of you today. You can take care of yourself again tomorrow."

"A negotiation."

"Precisely. We'll both win." He winks.

"Ugh, I don't know Alex, I'm weird about this type of stuff."

"One thing then. Just let me do one thing for you. Final offer."

"Hahaha, you do drive a hard bargain. What's this one thing?"

"It's a surprise. That's part of the agreement. You don't get to know till it's time."

It's so hard to resist his charm. With a surrendered sigh I give in. "Ugh, okay. Deal."

19

*E*very street you turn on in Monte Carlo oozes ritz and glam. It screams lux vintage royalty and I'm both intimidated and impressed. It's definitely a city of wealth catering to the wealthy. It's fascinating and I'm glad to be enjoying it from within the comfort of Alexander's car. We've been taking a short driving tour through the city, which is fine by me, as I don't think my stomach can handle a walk just yet. I'm still full of the delicious breakfast Tommy cooked. I can see why he's a Michelin star chef. I don't think I've eaten anything so divine in ages! He and Carmyn are following behind us.

I've been pretty silent this whole time, taking in all the sights and sifting through the multitude of thoughts and memories they stir. We are headed to Port de Fontvieille. Alex has organized a yacht to take us onto the French Riviera, which should be a lot of fun.

"What's on your mind, love?"

"Hm? Oh, just thinking. I'm excited! The last time I was on a boat of any kind was back in Nebraska when I was a teenager. My dad would always take me sailing during the summer season.

It was one of my fondest memories, so I'm looking forward to the bit of sweet nostalgia this will bring."

"Really? I believe this is the first time you've mentioned anything about your life before Paris."

"Heh heh, yeah, you might be right. The town I'm from was one of those small towns where everyone knows everyone and there's not a whole lot happening. It felt crowded, which I didn't care for. I wanted the big city vibes. Haha, funny how I chose one of the farthest places from home to obtain that lifestyle. But honestly, I can't complain, I had a fairly good upbringing. Had the best parents and some great friends. Did a lot of outdoor activities, enjoyed volleyball, and loved writing, but it wasn't till I got involved in the school newspaper that I truly fell in love with journalism."

"Were either of your parents' writers?"

"No. My dad is an architect, and my mom is an artist, an oil painter to be exact." I chuckle as a memory comes to mind. "When I was a little girl, I used to sit in her studio and watch her for hours while trying to imitate her with my crayons. I was horrible by the way, definitely not artist material. My mom saved some of the pictures I drew and to this day they make me cringe."

He laughs heartily, "I would like to see some of those."

"No! Trust me, you don't. If anything, they are a great reminder that my talent is language, not art."

"I'd still love to see them. You have a story too and I want to know every part of it." I reflect on how much I questioned the authentic nature of his interest in me when we were first getting acquainted. Sometimes people say that they want to know a person just to say it; sometimes it's with an ulterior motive. At least in my experience this is usually the case. Arthur was the only other person I had met in the past few years who expressed genuine interest in my life. Since we aren't on the best of terms right now, it's wonderful to know there is someone else who is invested in me beyond surface level interests.

I respond, "Perhaps you will know every part of my story one day. You already know how much I crave to know every part of yours." A dimple forms in his cheek as he smiles. "Tell me something about yourself that I'd never guess."

"Hm. Well, I might have a slight obsession."

I twist my body toward him. "Oh, yeah? For what?"

"For motorbikes."

Huh, motorcycles. I really wouldn't have guessed it. I raise an eyebrow, intrigued by this information. "And by that do you mean an obsession for riding them or collecting them? Or do you just spend an excessive amount of time gazing at them with intense longing?" We share a laugh.

"Uh, all of the above? When I was in secondary school, I had a few mates that rode, and it wasn't long before they got me on a bike too. We had a bunch of magazines with all these beautiful bikes that we'd dream of owning one day.

"I think my mum hoped it was a phase. She was always going on about how noisy and unsafe they were. But my fascination for them only grew, especially when riding became cathartic for me. To help me cope with the immense anxiety and stress that came along when I took over Ether, I'd go on joy rides. The speed, the adrenaline, the views, especially at night when most people are asleep, and the roads are clear." He takes in a long breath as he indulges in the memory of the experience he loves and the sensations he's hooked on. "It's freeing."

I stare at him with such admiration. "You're really something, you know that?"

He grins. "What?"

"I've never met a man with so many layers. You're like a cake."

The roar of his laughter is pleasant. "Not an onion?"

I squinch my nose. "Meh, I like cake better. Much more delicious."

He reaches over and rests his hand atop my thigh, gives it a quick, firm squeeze and keeps it there. This unexpected move has me feeling so secure, so his. My hand clasps over it, and he rolls his wrist so that his hand holds mine, our fingers linked. We stay like this for a time, perfectly content in the participation of such a simple yet meaningful act.

"Alright, we're here." We roll into the port lot where both small and massive vessels are docked, ready to set sail. While there are a few sailboats, the majority of the vessels are yachts. A couple are some of the largest and flashiest yachts I've ever seen in my life! I'm certainly not in Kansas anymore. Being thrust into Alexander's world has definitely tested my ability to adapt to a foreign environment.

We pull up to the valet and, just as I exit the car, my phone rings. Instantly, my stomach drops when I see Arthur's name on the screen. My thumb hits the ignore call button, but he immediately calls back. As much as I want to power off the phone and forget the calls completely, I choose to face whatever Arthur has to say and, hopefully, put an end to the pestering for good.

"Alex, I'll be just a moment. I need to take this call." He nods and walks over to join Tommy and Carmyn.

I take a deep breath and answer. "Hey Arthur, what is it?"

"You can't ignore me forever, Jess." His voice oozes irritation.

"I'm talking to you, aren't I? Just tell me what you're calling about."

"Ritter is asking about you. Said he's tried reaching you several times the past few days and hasn't heard a thing."

"Uh huh. And did you tell him why that might be?"

"It's not my job to tell him, it's yours. I'm not covering your ass anymore. I'm doing too much, remember? If you want out, tell him yourself. It's the least you can do. He trusted you with this project. Despite how you may feel about what he's done, you at least owe it to him to bow out gracefully. Or is that not you anymore?"

"Fine, Art. Okay? I'll talk to him."

"Oh, great! I'm glad you still have a little dignity left. I never took you for the woman who would screw someone over, especially regarding a job you were hired to complete."

I huff in astonishment. "*I'm* screwing him over? Really? He's the one trying to screw over an innocent man! He should be ashamed of what he's done."

"Please explain to me why the fuck you care so much about this guy! You barely know him. But you do know the business of journalism. We find the truth and we report it. That's what you signed up for."

"No, I didn't sign up for that shit! I didn't sign up to hurt people in the process!" I stop, mulling over what I've just said.

Hadn't I signed up for that though? My mind hurries back to a memory that I seemed to have forgotten in the recent heat of adoration. Words that I exchanged with Aralyn during my first visit to the salon creep back into consciousness.

"...we both know what will happen if this works, he's going to get hurt."

When I started this assignment, I was prepared to get Alexander's story by any means necessary. I followed through with the plan she cooked up to get him to become romantically attracted to me and, thus, more vulnerable. Well, he is certainly into me, and he has definitely opened up. And even though I ended up choosing to go a different direction with our plan by giving him half-truths and reintroducing myself to him as me, it doesn't erase the fact that I went into this initially prepared to get what I needed, even if it meant his pain in the end. My God, what did I do?

"Look whatever, Jess. I don't know what's gotten into you lately, but you need to get a grip. Call Ritter and handle your own business." The call ends and I'm left standing in a storm of thoughts and feelings clashing together.

I glance back at Alex, walking down the pier with the others, and my chest tightens. I get flashbacks of the lies I told him about how I'd come to take on the Isabella Evans persona, about my connection to Marguerite and about the real reason for my initial transformation. Everything that built up between us was based on selfish intention. To my horror, I realize that although I may not have blackmailed him like Ritter, I approached our relationship with the intent to do something just as malicious. To play with his heart and trust in order to obtain his life story.

I don't know where to go from here. I remain frozen in place, not sure whether to run away and remove myself from his life or go catch up to him. This mass sense of unworthiness brews like a dark cloud over my head; unworthy of his time, his energy, his story, him. There's a service car at the entrance and I look between it and the pier trying to make up my mind. If I leave, I risk hurting him without any explanation. If I stay, at least I'll have an opportunity, over the course of the next couple days, to come clean. Either way he'll be devastated. And I do have to come clean; we are in so deep with our connection, it would feel wrong not to. But maybe I shouldn't. At least for his sake.

I opt to do my best to push aside the fear rocking my core and make my way over to the group where they are getting ready to board a yacht. As I approach, I attempt to put on my bravest face but, as usual, Alexander sees past it. "What's wrong?"

"Oh, I'm fine. Just some nonsense call from Eiffel." He frowns. "I'm okay. It's nothing I couldn't handle." He's not convinced, but he doesn't press further and helps me onboard.

The yacht isn't humongous, and it doesn't need to be, especially with just us. I think it suits Alexander's style of maintaining a low-key presence. While it's a decent size, it's not too small that it gets overlooked but not too big that it draws attention. The captain, a brunette woman who appears to be in her forties', introduces herself and the crew of two men. Before long, we set off. All four of us walk out to take a seat on the bow. Alexander hands me a blanket and I take it graciously, my head still spinning and my stomach still a pit of guilt and frustration, mainly with myself. I know the goal is to try to enjoy the day, but how can I when I've just realized the magnitude of my ill choices?

As we sail further out, I peer at the enchanting shoreline. Magic everywhere and yet I feel so dull. Alex and Tommy are chatting away about the good days. The two of them really are like two peas in a pod, but I can hardly hear what they are saying because I'm both here and elsewhere all at once.

"You don't seem as chipper as I assumed you would be, Ms. Rivers." Carmyn takes a seat next to me.

I offer a half smile. "You know, you can just call me Jess, Carmyn. It's your day off after all."

"Ah, there's never really a day off. But I suppose today, due to the current circumstances, I can drop the formalities with you." I chuckle. She's so proper. "I can see you're distant. Anything you'd like to get off your chest?" Oh, she has no idea.

I sigh. "I fucked up. I need to make it right, and my mind is racing a million miles a minute trying to think of the least catastrophic solution to doing that."

"Mm, catastrophic for whom? You? Or is there someone else?"

"Both."

"And does this other person know you fucked up?"

"Not yet." I keep my sights off in the distance, hoping to not give away that it's Alex by peering in his direction.

"Do you think they'll find out?"

"Probably not." Everyone who knows has played a part in it. They'd risk going down too if they told. If I never tell, then there's a good chance he'll never know.

"And are they suffering because of your blunder?"

"No."

"Well then darling, I have no idea what you're worried about. I say keep your mouth shut and do what you can to make things right by doing right by them from here on out." It's not that I haven't spent the past thirty minutes considering that option. But can I really live with it is the question. I care about Alex so much. To keep it from him feels like a betrayal of the trust he's given me. On the other hand, this did happen prior to us desiring one another. But, if I tell him, he will be devastated.

"Yeah, maybe you're right."

"You were fine earlier. So, I'm guessing this has something to do with the phone call you took by the car?" I'm glad she suspects it has to do with someone else.

"Yeah, that phone call really threw me off." I wish I never picked up. Ignorance really is bliss, and I would have carried on in that bliss if my shadows hadn't sprung up to bite me in the form of my own words. "I'm sorry. I know this isn't a great conversation to be having right now. I don't need to rain on anyone's day just because mine has been a bit soured."

"Don't be. I inquired. We all need someone to talk to when things get heavy. You are away from friends and family right now, but that doesn't mean that you have to go without support." I love her for this but it's also making me feel ten times worse. She's consoling a woman who had, in fact, been the intrusive drama thirsty journalist she suspected me to be when we first met. Her heart has only opened because she's seen Alexander's heart open and now, she has become one more person I can hurt with my truth.

Anxiety rises in my chest and panic begins to set in. I don't feel good at all. "Can you excuse me for a moment? I need to use the lavatory."

"Um, sure."

I pop up and speed walk as best I can to the lower deck, blowing past the living and dining area and into the lavatory where I lock myself in. It's a lot more spacious than I thought it would be and I'm grateful. I have the perfect amount of space to pace around and cry my eyes out. I'm trying so hard to breathe and silence my mind, but nothing is helping.

To tell him or not to tell him? Of course, I have to tell him! I can't carry on a relationship with this man knowing my original intent was to deceive him. There's no way I can do that and look at myself the same. The knowledge will always be a heavy burden looming over me and the longer I wait, the harder it will be to seek any sort of forgiveness. But telling him almost certainly ensures the destruction of all that has grown between us. The real question is, can I live with myself if in confessing, I give him one more reason to shield himself from the world; to close himself out; to not let love in again?

There's a pounding at the door. "Jess?" Alexander rattles the handle. "Jess, what's wrong? Open up please." Oh no, I didn't want him to suspect anything was off! I'm beginning to hyperventilate; my body is paralyzed with fear. I can't do this. I can't do this to him. "Jess! Please, you're scaring me. Open up!" My body is overheating, and I sob uncontrollably. My emotions have hit an all-time high, and I'm having trouble coming back down.

In an instant, Alex breaks open the door. Even through blurred vision, I can see the look of terror in his eyes. He rushes to me and holds me in the tightest embrace, and I surrender to exhaustion and distress. My body goes limp. He scoops me up and carries me to a bedroom, sits on the bed and just holds me in his lap, raking his fingers through my hair. "Shhh. It's okay. Breathe. Just breathe, Jess. Nice and slow."

I've only ever had one other panic attack in my life. And that was when I had been locked in a closet during a sleepover in seventh grade. All of us girls had just finished doing a séance after watching a tutorial of how to conduct one online, and my friends thought it would be funny to play a prank on me. They had asked me to grab something in the bedroom closet and pushed me in before I had a chance to turn on the lights. They had placed a chair under the door handle and left me there while they went to the kitchen to make snacks. I freaked out. Besides being scared out of my mind that a ghostly spirit was going to attack me, the closet was incredibly dark and there was hardly any room to breathe, let alone move. I felt much like that in the Lavatory, like the walls of chaos were closing in on me, like the air was being restrained from my lungs.

Alex kisses my forehead and mutters, "Bloody hell, I was so worried about you. I didn't know what was happening." He clasps a hand on my tear-stricken cheek and looks into my eyes. "I still don't know what's happening. You haven't been yourself today, not since we arrived at the marina. What happened during that phone call?"

I can't stomach another lie, but I can't tell him the truth either. Not yet. Not like this. Between sniffling and my wavering breaths, I force a reply. "Ritter wants to talk to me. I'm going to have to tell him that I'm not doing the article anymore, not for him."

"That's what's stressing you?"

"Well, no. I- I think that all the recent, rapid changes have finally caught up with me. My emotions have been so sporadic the past few weeks, and there's also this worry about the uncertainty of what comes next. I've never felt so out of control." I wasn't wrong, everything truly has built up. I think my fear and guilt just triggered the volcano that had already been waiting for the perfect moment to erupt. "I'm so sorry."

"You don't need to apologize to me. I just want you to take care of yourself, Jess." He moves me beside him on the bed. "I'll tell the captain to take us back to shore."

"No! Please, I feel embarrassed enough. Please don't ruin this for yourself or for Tommy and Carmyn on account of me. I'll be fine." His soul-searching eyes bore into my own, calculating, trying to detect a lie hidden in their depths. "I'll be okay." I assure him. "Just give me a moment to collect myself." I give him a gentle kiss, praying that it will be enough to convince him that I will be alright and that he can leave me here in peace for a little while.

When I pull back, his face still displays concern. "Come up whenever you're ready. No rush." He stands and leaves the room.

Even without him saying so, I know he's made up his mind; he's going to have us taken back to shore. I curl up into a fetal position on the bed and close my eyes, hoping that when they open, the past hour will have been a terrible nightmare. But I still feel the rocking of the boat, the hum of the engine still vibrates the bed, and loud intrusive thoughts still echo in my head. It is indeed a nightmare I'm having; a waking one. Somehow, I need to endure it just a few more days. Alexander cannot know until after the charity banquet. There's no way I can ruin that for him too.

Yes, after the banquet, I will tell him everything.

*W*e made it back to Paris in one piece. Not much was spoken on the journey home. I spent most of my time in silent contemplation, over analyzing as I usually do. I felt terrible that I put a damper on what was supposed to be a beautiful and relaxing day. As I suspected, Alexander had the captain turn back to port. From there, we packed up at the house and boarded the jet to return home.

We enter the mansion and I head straight to my room; I just want to retreat for at least a good twelve hours. As I open my bedroom door, I see a large gift box sitting on the bed. It's not marked, and I skim my fingers over the lid, debating if I even want to see what's in it. I know it's from Alex, but I don't feel deserving of anything, especially whatever is in here.

"You should open it." Alex enters the room and takes a seat next to the box.

I really don't want to, but I also don't want to be rude. I hesitate a bit more before making the move to remove the lid. When I do, I softly gasp. My fingers pick up the stunning gown the box contained. It's absolutely breathtaking! It's made of a shear, mesh fabric, adorned with Swarovski crystals from the double strap around the shoulder to the flowering skirt that looks to also have a train. The dress is cut low at the bosom, and the bodice features a gorgeous wrap around to the skirt. This is the type of dress you see but never imagine you'd own. There's a much smaller rectangular box as well. In it, I discover diamond earrings and a diamond necklace. "Oh my God. Alex, I can't accept these gifts."

"Of course you can. It's part of our deal, remember? Today is my day to take care of you how I see fit. Now you have a perfect outfit for the event." I set them back in the box and stare at the dress. It's become clear that part of Alexander's love language is gifts. Unfortunately, not only does it stir my guilt right now, it also reminds me of Arthur. I believe that's also his love language. He enjoyed buying things for me or surprising me with something because he wanted to, and he believed it would make me happy.

I don't like how smothering he became, but I can't deny that he cared about my happiness too. His intentions were good. Perhaps it was unfair of me to be so harsh to him. Though I do still feel he stepped out of line. Ugh, why has today made everything so much more profoundly complicated?

"Hey, come here." Alex pulls me down into a straddling position on his lap. "Why don't you tell me what's really going on in that brilliant mind of yours, hmm? I know you didn't tell me everything back on the yacht. Please." He's so incredibly intuitive, I swear.

Fuck. It looks like I can't keep this up as long as I'd hoped. Might as well get this over with. "Do you recall, back at the garden of the Crescendo, when I told you that Marguerite had me pretend to be Isabella Evans so that I'd feel more comfortable amongst the crowd at the exhibit?"

"I do."

"Well, that wasn't entirely the truth. Marguerite helped me with a plan to get me noticed by you. The goal was that you'd find me alluring enough to bring into your personal life. The hope was that by doing so, I'd be able to gain valuable information on you that I could use for my story without you realizing who I really was." He continues to peer at me in silence, his expression stoic. "I intended to trick you and I feel so damn horrible about it, Alex. I might be just as bad as Ritter." A tear escapes my eye. "I'm so very sorry. You have no idea how much I wish I could take it back."

To my shock, he begins to laugh and my brow furrows in confusion. "What? What is it?"

"That's what you're so upset about?"

"Well, yeah…I wasn't fully honest with you. And you placed your trust in me not realizing that I had intended to deceive you."

He continues to chuckle. "Oh Jess, I wouldn't have expected anything less from a bloody journalist."

"I'm so confused."

"I will say I'm impressed. I suppose you do have more guts than I gave you credit for. But I'm not surprised. You'd be amazed by the things I've seen the media do to get close to me. When you chased me down after I left the exhibition, I knew that it had something to do with what you were seeking. I didn't know exactly what, but I knew there was something more you were after than what you were letting on. Remember, I'd already figured out that it was you before you gave your confession in the garden."

I try to wrap my head around what he's telling me. "So, you're not angry with me?"

"No. I'm not angry with you. If anything, you telling me this has confirmed to me the very reason I've placed my trust in you. I can tell that your feelings for me are genuine Jess, even if that's not how it started. When you told me you wouldn't hurt me intentionally, as fearful as I was, I saw the truth in your eyes." His hands grasp my face, and he brings me in for a sweet kiss. "You may be a mischievous little minx, but you are not Ritter."

"But I could have hurt you, Alex. What if the plan had worked? What if I didn't have genuine feelings for you?"

"Your plan wouldn't have worked Jess. I'm not gullible. And I'm highly cautious, as you've gathered. I originally told you I wanted you to stay in my home because I felt it would allow me the opportunity to better teach you how to be more comfortable in your own skin, and that was the truth, but there was a far greater reason as well.

"Ritter sent you to achieve what he wanted, and I felt there may be a need to keep my enemy close. You were the closest thing to Ritter when it came to this situation. So, when you chased me down at the exhibit, I realized I had a fairly decent window of opportunity to draw you in so I could keep tabs on you. I knew that as a journalist, particularly one hired on by

Ritter, you most likely wouldn't pass up the chance to be close to me."

I raise an eyebrow. This is blowing my mind. I mean, he did explain that he was biding his time so he could collect enough intel on Ritter to blackmail him instead, but I didn't know the extent of his plan. It makes sense that, in the meantime, he'd do everything in his power to control the situation as best he could, including keeping the very journalist Ritter sent to do his dirty work on his radar constantly. It appears I wasn't the only one with ulterior motives.

"Oh." I'm not sure what else to say. I'm happy that he doesn't hate my guts but I'm still in disbelief.

Wrapping his arms around my torso, he pulls me into him and I tuck my head under his chin. His pulse thrums in his throat, calm, rhythmic, beautiful. His fingers stroke my back, and in a hushed tone he says, "Don't be sad, Brown Eyes. The past is behind us, and our future has yet to be written. All I know is that in this present moment, there is no ill intent between us, just true care and consideration." And love. I know he won't say it, not yet anyway. But perhaps he's thinking that too.

I wish we could stay here like this forever. I wish for a great many things. But I'm terrified of what will happen once the clock strikes midnight and the charity banquet everyone has been anticipating comes to an end. I'm terrified that there will be no more moments like this, because after the event, then what? Alexander must return to his life in London, and I'll be left here, picking up the pieces of everything that's crumbled, and rebuilding a life that fits the woman I've transformed into. Will we be able to make things work? Will he forget me? Am I still a fool to believe in a happy ending for us? I live for a good story, but even I know that happy endings don't always exist.

I push aside my fears for now, in hopes of savoring this moment and position myself upright again. "Thank you for my dress and the jewelry. They are really lovely."

Maybe it's the light in the room, but his eyes turn the color of a dark ocean in the midst of a storm, one I completely submerge into. He presses his mouth to mine and takes a dive of his own, his tongue dancing and expertly teasing. When he stops, his gaze becomes lustful. "Jess, the list of things I desire to do to you right now is endless." His words bring to mind his kinky desire to dominate and that causes the heat between my thighs to elevate.

Before Alexander, I could have never imagined submitting to a man in any form, especially sexually. Given my past experiences with the opposite sex, I developed this need to have absolute control, even in the bedroom most times. But I'm stunned to now discover an interest to submit, and not to just anyone, to him. As I sit here on his lap, staring into those soulful eyes, his arms embracing me, I feel something I've never felt with a man before. Security.

I trust Alexander. I trust him with my body, my life… my heart. I'm coming to terms with the fact that, all these years, I never really wanted to constantly be in control. I wanted someone with whom, every so often, I could freely give it up and feel completely safe doing so. It's a profound realization.

"Show me." I whisper.

Hearing my request brings a certain spark to his eye as he sweeps the tips of his fingers over my lips. "Are you sure?"

I nod my head. "I'm ready. I want to experience your world. Everything about it. I trust you."

His face comes to life with a bright smile. He moves and we both stand, then he extends a hand. "Come then. I want you to see something."

He leads me out of the room, down the staircase, and into the foyer of the house's entrance. I almost think he's taking us outside, yet we aren't headed towards the front door. Instead, we walk to a different door, a familiar door. It's the door to the library I had curiously and cautiously entered when I had first come to interview Alex. The library looks exactly the same when we enter, dimly lit, beautiful, though a little ominous. Perhaps because it's so large.

"You want to show me books?" I titter.

"Not quite." He continues to lead me to one of the massive bookcases lining the far back wall, then turns to me. "I have a flair for the mysterious if you haven't noticed." Oh, I've noticed.

I watch in intrigue as his palm presses against a shelf and an audible *click* can be heard. Alex takes a step back as the case opens out toward us, revealing a staircase descending downward to yet another doorway. Okay, a bit more mysterious than I expected. It's a scene straight out of a movie! I've always heard about people having secret rooms like this, but I'd never thought I'd actually see one in real life.

I walk to the top of the staircase, peering below. "What's down there?"

Alexander comes up behind me, grabs my hips and pulls me in close enough that I feel the crown of his erection against my back. He leans his head down till his mouth is level with my ear. With a low, velvety voice, he says, "Let's find out."

<u>20</u>

We stand outside the red door that I anxiously wait for Alexander to open. I don't know what's on the other side, but if the Kink club was any indication of what he's into, I'm imagining some sort of dark dungeon of sexual curiosities, making me extremely nervous. I envision chains hanging from the ceilings, whips lining the walls, cages and all sorts of unusual contraptions. Although I said I was ready to explore his sexual interests, I didn't consider that I could be walking into a potential danger zone.

After unlocking the door, he depresses the handle and I follow him in. My eyes grow wide with astonishment. It's nothing like I imagined at all. Holy fuck! This room is…sexy! It is dark and moody but spacious and classy. The paneled walls have a black matte finish with strips of red LED lights embedded into slits along the top and base, giving the room a very sensual ambiance. There are a few pieces of furniture that I've never seen before and some sort of rail system on the ceiling with thick carabiners. The floor is covered in luxurious black marble shellac, and an elegant white floating tub sits elevated on a raised platform in a far back corner of the room. Another highlight is a gorgeous bed extending from the other corner, fitted with red sheets. There's a mirror built in directly over top of it. It's an elegant red-light den. Modern, classic and so damn suave, just like Alexander.

"Questions?" Alex walks past me as I look on in admiration.

"Um." Do I have questions? I think questions were booted out to make room for processing everything my eyes are absorbing. "No whips?"

He chuckles. "Oh, they are in here. I just have them in a special spot. Follow." I suppose I shouldn't be shocked that he has them in yet another secret location. He leads me to a large, mounted ceiling to floor mirror and places his palm on the bare wall directly next to it, triggering three beeps. The mirror starts to roll back, slowly revealing a very spacious walk-in closet. It is full of all types of neatly organized toys and some bizarre items! I follow him in and realize how much bigger it is inside than it looks on the outside. It is as if he has his own personal adult store!

"I have to hand it to you, this whole place is…pretty impressive. Not at all what I pictured."

He heads straight to the back of the closet. "You should see the play room I have at my place back in London. I had this one specially designed too and it's nice, but that one is something remarkable." His words stir hope within me. Perhaps we really can have a life together after the banquet. He has no idea how much I want that.

He picks up a blue velvet case on one of the top shelves and makes his way back over to where I stand. "Shall we?" He gestures ahead. As we walk out, the mirror slides shut behind us.

He sets the case on the bed, and I sit down next to it. My curiosity peaks. "What's that?"

"Just a small toy box. Nothing too wild. It holds the basics." The basics? He grins at my evident suspicion and nervousness. "Now Jess, even though we won't do anything too intense tonight, I'd like to know what your hard limits are."

"My hard limits?"

"Yes. What are some things, of a sexual nature, that you have no interest in attempting or being involved with? For example, I draw the line at bodily fluids such as urine, blood and vomit." I scrunch my nose in disgust and he laughs. "My thoughts exactly. Though part of the beauty of the kink world is that there's something for everyone and so there are fetishists who are absolutely okay with it. I, on the other hand, consider them hard limits."

"Okay, well, everything you just said are hard limits for me too." Yeah, no way I'm down for any of that.

"Good. What else?"

I think momentarily. "Hmm, I suppose anything that would cause bruising. Doesn't seem appealing. I think that would make me feel like a punching bag and that's a no for me."

"Do you bruise easily?" I shake my head no. "Good to know. How would you feel about spankings?"

"Didn't you spank me yesterday on the way to the room?"

His grin widens. "I'd hardly call that a spank my love, more like a tap."

My eyes bulge and I laugh. "A tap? That tap stung!"

"Did you like it?"

"I mean, I didn't not like it. It was interesting. I suppose I'd be willing to explore that a bit more."

"Okay. And how about bondage?" I've never put much thought into being restrained. The idea of it is alluring though. I'd be lying if I said I didn't enjoy Alex pinning my hands down the other night, preventing me from touching him. It was aggravating yet quite pleasurable. The very memory sends delicious waves of arousal rippling through me. "I'd be willing to explore that more too."

"Okay, that's a good list to work from for tonight. We can go more in depth with hard limits down the road as there becomes more to try. I plan on keeping things on the gentler side with you this evening." I'm interested to see what he considers to be gentle. I don't know much about BDSM, but gentleness isn't what comes to mind when I hear it. Alex hasn't been too rough with me so far, however.

He suddenly pulls his white t-shirt over his head and the sight of him takes my breath away…again. His skin glows red in the tinted light and his muscles ripple with every movement. He smiles at my admiration and reaches in the case, extracting a blindfold. This one appears to be made of lavender colored silk or satin. "Will you hold this for me for a moment?" He hands it to me and my fingers glide along the fine cloth, imagining what it will be like to be void of sight while Alexander touches and teases me however he sees fit.

He takes out a pair of handcuffs next. "And these." I grab hold of them, eyeing the black steel cuffs with intrigue. "Just a moment actually. Let me see your wrists, darling." I raise my wrists up and he grasps them in his hands, turning them over and analyzing them. "Hm, perhaps we'll test the cuffs on you another time. The straps should do fine for tonight."

"Straps?"

He displays a wicked smile and grabs my hand once more. Then, picking up the case, he leads me to the other end of the room to an odd thing that looks like a giant standing X. Sure enough, the X has straps on both ends of the top and the bottom. I look up at Alex, nervous as hell. What the fuck is he planning on doing to me with this thing?

"Don't worry. It's less intimidating than it looks. This is called a Saint Andrew's Cross. It's used for the purposes of restraint…and pleasure of course."

"Um, maybe we should just start with the handcuffs."

"Something tells me you will like this better." He winks. "Trust me."

"Okay, sure, yeah." I hesitantly position myself in front of the cross with my back facing it and begin to take off my sweater.

"Woah, woah, woah," Alexander cautions. I stop, lowering it back down. "Not so fast, Brown Eyes." He gives an amused smirk. My cheeks grow hot with embarrassment. Thank God the light in here is red.

"Let me. Please." His hands glide from my shoulders down my arms. He raises them above my head and then, while making direct eye contact with me, proceeds to lift my sweater up and over. His eyes sweep down my chest in that scorching way that captures my very soul. His index finger hooks under my chin. "I really don't think you have any idea how fucking stunning you are." I don't think he has any idea how captivated he has me.

He reaches around and expertly undoes my bra. In return, I lower my arms and shimmy out of it, letting it drop to my feet, leaving my chest exposed to the touch of his hands. My nipples instantly harden. He caresses my breasts, kneading and teasing them. After a bit, his hands move to my neck and he pulls me into him. His mouth possesses my own. The way his tongue is utterly devoted to pleasing me makes my knees tremble.

While kissing me, he walks forward, and I follow his movement until my back hits the cross. He lifts my arms again, pinning them to the black leather and buckling my wrists into the straps on each arm.

"Before we begin, I'm going to give you a safe word. Are you aware of what that is?"

I remember this from my research on the dynamic. "It's something I say if I want to stop whatever we are doing, right?"

"Correct. If what I do to you becomes too uncomfortable, painful, or you desire me to stop for any other reason, using an assigned safe word will alert me to the fact that it's a serious request, and I will stop."

"Okay, I understand."

His hand cradles my face, and his thumb runs across my lower lip. "Your safe word is Red. Say it."

"Red."

"Red, sir. That's what you will call me whenever we play. Understood?" His firm tone ignites a mighty need within me. I know what he's saying is important, but I really just want him to rip my pants off already and have his way with me.

I bite my lip and flirtatiously reply, "Yes, sir."

"Mm, very good." His mouth overtakes mine for a moment more and I moan. I can tell being strapped to this cross is going to be torturous. I already desperately wish I could touch him. Not to mention, it's abnormal for me to be at anyone's mercy.

"If you behave, I'll keep your legs free." Hmm, how much do I plan on behaving?

He returns to the case of mysterious toys that he set beside us and retrieves another item. This particular one is wild! It looks like a metal handle with a wheel of thin and seemingly sharp spikes at the end. What the fuck is that thing?

It's as if Alex hears the question I'm silently yelling. "This is a Wartenberg wheel. In sensation play, it is rolled across the skin to create a variety of different sensations depending on the pressure differences. It's meant to tease and please."

"Um, that thing looks kind of freaky."

"I will apply it very gently. Over time, I can adjust the pressure depending on your tolerance. It won't hurt."

I'm quite nervous, but equally intrigued. "Okay. As I said, I trust you." A soft smile plays across his lips, and he grabs the blindfold. The last thing I see before he places it on me is the salacious glint in his eyes.

He ties it tight but not too tight. "Does that feel alright?" I nod and notice the absence of his body heat as he steps back. Just as he said to me at the fetish den, the restriction of sight really does heighten every other sense, especially hearing. Currently, it's the only sense I can rely on to let me know what he's doing. I hear the fumbling of clothes and the sound of fabric hitting the floor. I hear the deep breath he sucks in. I hear the quiet impact of his feet on the floor, yet I can't pinpoint exactly where he is.

My senses are tingling. I can practically feel the intensity of his gaze on my bare skin. This is what I'd imagine it would feel like to be hunted, stalked, unable to see a predator who's locked in on his prey, circling slowly and methodically, waiting for the perfect moment to make his move.

I let out an audible gasp as his fingers glide a feather light touch from my left wrist down to my breast. It came as a complete shock, but it's an even bigger shock when I feel a prickling sensation follow the same path his fingers took. My back arches in reaction to the tinge of pleasure the metal instrument provides. The sensation is prickly, but it tickles at the same time, causing my nerves some confusion. When he rolls it to my breast, he runs the wheel back and forth over my nipple and it drives me crazy! "Mm, Alex, wait!"

I feel his breath on my ear as he utters, "What do you call me, Jess?"

My voice waivers as my body struggles to process how I'm feeling. "Sir. Sorry, sir."

I hear his low chuckle and he continues again, moving to my other nipple. "Fuck! Sir, this is– this is– fuck, fuck, fuck!" My wrists strain against the restraints as the wheel continues to roll along my skin, only to then stop and proceed in multiple different areas that I can't predict. It's mind boggling, exciting, extremely frustrating and satisfying. Yes, I think it's satisfying overall. Satisfying to know this pleases him. Satisfying to find that it pleases me too. I love being on display like this, exposed to only him. Available for only his touch. Being pleased in exotic ways I've never experienced before. A sense of pride and adrenaline swells within me.

Alexander stops with the wheel and gives me a quick kiss that he trails down my neck, chest, abdomen, with the last one falling right above the hem of my jeans. I feel his fingers undo the button and slowly pull the zipper down. Then his fingers clutch both the top of my jeans and my black panties and slides them down to my ankles. I step out and he spreads my legs, continuing his kisses from the inside of my knee and up my thigh, stopping just as he reaches my aching pussy.

There's a long pause where nothing happens. I can't hear or feel anything other than the cool air in the room that causes my nipples to remain perked. Intuitively however, I can sense him close, watching me stand here, squirming with need, growing impatient, burning with passion. Suddenly, his finger presses against my clit, sliding back and forth, applying the same expert skill that he does with his cello. "Mmm, you're so wet baby."

Without notice, his mouth envelops my vagina and I groan in utter delight. He grabs both my legs and lifts them, placing them over his shoulders. His tongue plunges between my folds and I thrust into him, reveling in the abundance of worship he gives this part of me.

He stands and kisses me again. The evidence of the arousal he tasted rolls across my taste buds and the sensation of his body flush against mine has me shuttering. His hard member is pressed firmly against my belly, engorged and twitching. "Please." I mutter. "Please, Sir."

"Please what, darling?"

"Please sir, give me your cock."

"Very well then." His hands clutch my thighs, and he raises me up on his hips. He rocks in a subtle motion, allowing his cock to rub against my swollen folds before he nestles the head of it at my entrance. The build and anticipation of this moment is overwhelming. I want him inside me so damn bad!

I suck in a quivering breath as he slowly tunnels into me. My walls contract, gripping him for dear life as if he could get away. He eases out and then impales me with a deep thrust. My toes curl and I release a cry of pleasure. I buck and thrash against the restraints while he ravages me over and over, sending me spinning.

After some time, his palm lands a firm spank on my ass, causing a delicious sting as we breathe heavy and in sync. His thrusts slow and quicken in perfect rhythm. I'm driven mad with lust! He hooks my ankles behind him and then yanks off my blindfold. My eyes adjust to the sight of him, his face hovering inches from mine. Cupping my chin, he brings my face up to look at his. "Atta girl. Cum with me." His pace quickens. I can hardly catch my breath. I shudder as an overpowering orgasm rips through me. I feel his muscles tense, and with one last thrust, he lets out a loud groan as he, too, finds release.

He pulls out and I drop my legs and slide down, barely able to stand. I practically hang by my wrists, breathless. He unstraps me and I'm so unsteady, I slump against him. But he brings us down to the floor and holds me close, wiping strands of sweat drenched hair from my face and smiling tenderly. "You did amazing, Jess. Perfect." He kisses my forehead and I crack a proud grin, closing my eyes and resting my head against his chest.

"That was amazing." I murmur.

A laugh resounds within his chest. "Oh, darling, you didn't think I was done with you, did you?"

My eyes grow wide. "There's more?"

He rises to his feet and I set my sight on the breathtaking view above me. He is still erect. The evidence of our mutual climax glistens along his heavenly shaft, which twitches with need. "On your knees, Jess."

I do as commanded. "Yes, sir."

He reaches down and grasps my chin. His thumb traces the edge of my lower lip. "You know, I really was going to let your lies to me slide." His smoldering gaze has me entranced. "But the more I think about it, the more I believe the most appropriate thing to do is to put that beautiful, trouble making mouth of yours to better use." His finger gently pulls down, parting my lips. I subtly gasp as he proceeds to insert his thumb into my mouth, running it across my tongue. I slowly suck it and he appears immensely turned on by this, which makes me happier than I'm able to understand at this time.

He steps forward. His glistening sword presented in front of me. A bead of moisture has produced on the head. "Clean it, my love."

"Yes, sir."

I cup his sack and run my lips along his manhood, worshipping it with such adoration and appreciation. He inhales a sharp breath as my tongue runs the length of him, cleaning every drop of precious cum that I can. I proceed to envelop him with my mouth, applying the perfect amount of momentum and pressure to coax out the moan of pleasure within him. I look up at him as I slide deeper, trying my best to take him in completely as though I'm competing with myself.

He rakes his hand through my hair and grips a handful. "That's my good girl. Choke on it." As his cock hits the back of my throat, his grip on my head tightens and he slowly draws his hips forward. My eyes water and I gag. He pulls out quickly, crouches down to my level and grasps my neck with his palm. "A much better use for that pretty mouth, innit?"

I display a salacious grin and shake my head in agreement. I love seeing him so pleased by my response and I love the fact that I'm responsible for his immense satisfaction. "Again. Please, sir."

He smiles wickedly. "Hm, I may have underestimated how much of a freak you are, beloved." His lips plant a passionate kiss upon my own and then he stands once more, towering over me like a God. "Open wide." I obey and we dance between him giving me the reigns to please him as I wish and then him restricting my control and taking over. It's quite literally breathtaking.

Eventually he stops and commands me to stand. I do my best, though my legs feel like that of a newborn foal. He takes notice. "Having a hard time?"

I release a quick giggle. "It's fine. I can stand."

He smirks. "Not for long."

He scoops me up and takes me to the bed. As soon as my back hits the mattress, he thrusts himself into me. I cry out in ecstasy, falling apart all over again as he takes and gives, takes and gives. The ebb and flow of pure desire. And it continues like this, until he's fulfilled and I'm once again a dripping, quaking mess.

He rewards me with an abundance of delicate kisses and affirmations. As I lay here, curled up in his sweet embrace, I can't help but think about how much I've lucked out. I never imagined anything like this, or anyone like him. It's a cliché thought, but I really do feel like the luckiest woman on earth. That's how every woman desires to feel, I imagine, truly cherished. Even in his dominance, he doesn't simply fuck me, he makes love to me. There's a certain type of intimacy he provides that is far from basic; it is profound, soul enriching and breathtakingly beautiful. This man has become like air to my lungs. I need him. And that realization alone is scary as hell.

21

For once I'm not the one running late for something. I sit in wait outside Eiffel Inc., stalking the front entrance, hoping to catch Ritter leaving for his usual twelve-thirty lunch break. But it appears he's behind schedule today. I had planned not to come in contact with him again, but Arthur made a good point when he told me I need to take care of this situation appropriately. It's not fair of me to leave the explanation of my sudden absence to him. I may have a sour taste in my mouth for the Chief Editor, but it's the professional thing to do. And I'm really ready to be done with all things Ritter and Eiffel. Time to start fresh and new.

I could have gone up to see him, but I'd rather spare myself a run in with Art again. I can't bear to face him, not with all the unresolved friction between us. I'm still incredibly upset and disappointed by both his actions and his words, but I'm also wracked with guilt. There is a small part of me that believes I'm being too hard on him. Arthur never meant to hurt me; I know he didn't. And though it's true what I said about not needing or wanting him making decisions for me, could I have been too harsh in how I handled addressing him about it? Was my anger warranted? Do I have some apologizing to do myself?

I want to believe there's still a chance we could salvage our friendship. Maybe it doesn't have to end like this. Then again, maybe it's better that it does. I don't know how capable Art is of releasing me from the vision he's had of his future. Can he handle being "just friends"? Can I? I'd be delusional to act like I still don't have feelings for him. Arthur may not be Alexander Marc, but he was the best thing in my world prior to him.

At the end of the day though, I know where my heart beckons me to be and I can't go back to my life in its previous form. I can't go back to him. I've had a taste of freedom; the freedom to be comfortable in who I am, where I am and who I'm with despite the chaos that looms. There's no stepping backwards. I've sampled too much, and I thirst for more.

My mind wanders to the memory of the other night, two souls hot with passion and desire; aching, needy, creating an energetic world where only the two of us existed. Wanton thoughts of Alexander's body entwined with mine dance through my head, and it sends a wave of dopamine pulsing throughout my system. I'm so distracted that I almost miss the sight of Ritter, who's now a good way down the sidewalk! Shit!

I take off after him, pushing my way through the rush of hurried employees who are trying to either get back to work or escape it. I say sorry so many times that it might be a record for most-apologies-in-two-minutes. "Monsieur Ritter! Ritter, un instant, Monsieur!" I finally catch up and hop in front of him, halting him in his tracks.

He eyes me with approval and addresses me in French. "Jess, just the girl I've been hoping to see! You changed your look."

"Yeah, well, there's been a lot of changes lately."

"You are quite the elusive journalist these days."

"About that, I know I haven't been getting back to you but I–" He holds up a palm.

"Before you say anything else, you should know that, effective yesterday, you are no longer needed on the Marc assignment. I received word over the weekend that Mr. Marc has asked that he not be interviewed anymore. Which is a shame, but it means we need to be more covert in our efforts to still put out an effective article. So, I'm pulling you and putting Charles on. Charles managed to obtain an invite to the banquet and Alexander doesn't know him so I think it would be a good idea to have him do some work to try and salvage the story. We've gone ahead and terminated your contract." Little does he know I was prepared for this. Not because Arthur had told me it was coming, but because I know exactly what the hell is going on; the real reason he's so gung-ho about passing this assignment over to Charles. He's desperate.

Yesterday, Alex detailed the reverse blackmail he did to Ritter using the information he obtained. Apparently, Ritter has been involved in some pretty illegal activities, not only within Eiffel, but with a few other major companies that he worked for in the past. Embezzlement isn't a good look for the Chief Editor. I have to hand it to him, he's playing this incredibly calm. He thinks he's standing in front of a clueless girl who failed to do her job and can be easily replaced. But he has no idea that this "girl" is going to show him exactly why you don't play dirty.

I act as though I'm horribly disappointed. "So, that's it? You're dropping me just like that?"

"That's business, Jess. You should know that. Besides, you were obviously too busy anyway. Charles stepped up to the plate. He's proven to me that he can take the initiative. That's what I need. I had hoped that you would be the one to carry the team to victory, but unfortunately you lacked where Charles now has the opportunity to shine."

"You don't even know what I've accomplished."

"The way I see it, if you've accomplished a great deal, you wouldn't be skipping meetings and ignoring phone calls. Arthur hasn't even heard about any of these accomplishments."

"We'll if you'd give me a chance to actually explain–"

"I haven't the time." He glances down at his watch as if I'm unnecessarily keeping him from his onion soup lunch appointment. "The decision is final."

I'm experiencing a mental tug-of-war, debating whether I should keep quiet and just take Ritter's words on the chin, or give him a piece of my mind. I give a half smirk and choose the latter. "I know you don't care, but just on the off chance that you give a shit, here's the real reason I took so long to get back to you. I really wanted to wait for this exact moment, when I could see you face to face to tell you to go fuck yourself."

His shocked expression brings me so much pleasure. "Watch yourself, Jess. You don't know how deep into dangerous waters you're treading."

I cross my arms and step a bit closer to him. "Oh, I know exactly how 'dangerous' your waters are. I'm just not afraid." I let out a small laugh. "You know, for the longest time I practically saw you as a God of this industry. I thought as long as I could please you, I'd be set! I could climb up the ladder of success and all my dreams would come true! But I've recently taken off the rose-tinted glasses and I see you for the filth you are. You think I need *you*? You're about to find out just how much you really needed *me*."

"I want your entry badge and what you've collected on Marc turned in by this evening. You will no longer be doing any business with Eiffel."

I cackle. "Oh, that's fucking rich! You think I'm actually going to hand you a single thing that I've gathered? So, what, Charles can use it to satisfy your hard-on for Alexander's information?" Ritter's face grows redder by the second and I'm loving it.

"The assignment was given to you by *me*! You did a job for *me*! Turn in what you have!"

"Or what? You terminated the contract. You did, not me. I'm no longer obligated to give you a damn thing." I shake my head in disbelief and continue to chortle. "How sad. It sucks to realize you aren't as in control as you think you are, doesn't it?"

"Jess–"

"Sorry, I haven't the time. Like I said, go fuck yourself." I snatch my badge from around my neck and chuck it at him as I walk off, leaving him speechless where he stands.

I meant what I said with every fiber of my being. To know that I am no longer controlled by a need to please or a need to be recognized, especially by the likes of him, is knowledge I now hold sacred. I became a freelance journalist to claim my independence and make a name for myself by any means necessary. But I ended up becoming so hyper fixated on gaining career success that I became too dependent on the praise of those who held such authority, and I lost a part of who I was; I lost some of my integrity. Continuing to try and be the shining light in Dante Ritter's eyes could have taken me deeper down that hole had I not realized the truth and discovered his true colors.

I'm walking away as a woman who no longer just speaks through words on a page. I am a woman who uses her voice, stands up for herself and what she believes in, and carries herself with greater confidence and surety. I walk away as a woman who has liberated herself from the grip of fractured expectations.

I have come to understand that a butterfly is so much more than a pretty creature to be gawked at until the end of its days. A butterfly had to be a caterpillar first and, in its moment of change, had to break down completely in order to transform into a creature with renewed purpose. Purpose far greater than the mere onlooker can fathom.

Like the butterfly, I, too, have finally spread my wings. It's my season to take flight, and it feels so damn good.

$\mathcal{A}$ lexander left this morning for another business trip, this time to London. He said he will be back the day before the banquet which is now a few days away. While he did invite me to go with him, I decided to take the opportunity of not having him around as a delicious distraction, to handle some things here.

In particular, I needed to bring a close to these undercover schemes I've been involved in.

Now that Ritter has been handled, there's just one more person to conclude things with– Aralyn. I want to rid myself of any attempt to procure information from Alexander in a mischievous fashion. I still have no idea why the name of a woman that he loved, or possibly still does, is so important to her, but I am tired of being given run around answers to my questions. I can respect that the topic may be sensitive, I can, but I care about Alexander too much to allow another thing to potentially stand in the way of our happiness together. If she wants her name, she needs to either get it herself, or find another way.

I tried reaching out to Aralyn this morning to let her know that we need to talk, but she's yet to respond. So, I'm sitting in my car in front of the La Chérot salon on a stake out mission. I considered waiting around for her at the cafe but that is a no go because it's past the time she'd usually show. Since I was effectively banished by Madame Chérot herself, this is the closest I can get to potentially seeing Aralyn. I crank the volume up on the radio and let my head fall back on my headrest. There's a chance I might be here for a while. I really have no idea if she's even at the salon today, but I need to talk to her. There's no way I can go another day with this on my chest.

Just as I lean back to relax, I spot Jovana exiting the salon, her long black curls, pulled up into a high ponytail, bounce with each step. Immediately I spring upright. If Aralyn is in there, Jovana will know. I have to go after her. I start the engine and drive forward. The girl walks fast! Then again, she's very tall so her strides are larger.

I pull along next to her and roll my window down. "Jovana!" She looks in my direction, squinting her eyes to get a better look at me. When she recognizes who I am, she walks over to the passenger side and leans in.

"Mademoiselle Rivers, bonjour."

"Bonjour! Is Aralyn in today?"

"No, she said that she has a doctor's appointment, so she won't be in. She might be here tomorrow." That won't do. Tomorrow I'll be meeting up with a couple of the individuals who will be speaking at the charity banquet to interview them.

"Would it be possible for you to give her a call? I really need to speak to her. Perhaps I can give you a ride home while we try to reach her? It's awfully cold out today."

She hesitates before responding, potentially stealing a moment to figure out if it's worth it to get involved with her boss's affairs like this, even if it is just allowing me to use her phone to reach Aralyn. But, after a thought or two, she gives a quick nod and I unlock the door to let her in. She explains that she lives about ten blocks North of the salon. I have ten blocks to get a hold of the woman.

Jovana dials the number, puts the phone on speaker and we wait in nervous silence as the phone rings endlessly. She doesn't pick up. I give Jovana my best puppy dog eyes. "Please, one more time?" She looks extremely reluctant, but she hits the call button again.

After three rings, Aralyn finally picks up. She gives a firm verbal lashing to Jovana in their native tongue. Something like, "Jovana, why do you keep calling me? I told you, if there's an issue, call the Madame!"

I interject quickly so that the poor woman doesn't get any further scolding. "Aralyn, it's me, Jess."

"Jess? What's wrong? Why are you calling me from Jovana's phone?"

"Relax, nothing's wrong, I just needed to reach you and you haven't been answering my calls and texts so when I came across Jovana, I figured you'd probably answer for her. We need to talk."

"I'm not in the best place to talk at the moment and neither are you." I glance over at Jovana who's staring out the passenger side window, as if that would give us privacy. It appears Aralyn really has been quite secretive about this, even to the very staff she's employed to assist with bringing her plan together.

"Okay, so where can I meet you so we can have this conversation? It needs to happen today. I have no time over the next few days and, as you know, the event is Friday."

"I'm aware. Look, just call me back on your phone. I will answer."

Ugh this woman can be so difficult. "Fine." She hangs up and Jovana points out that her flat is two blocks away. "Is she always this hard to communicate with?" I ask. Jovana just looks at me with a weak half smile. "Yeah, never mind, don't answer that. I don't want to get you in any trouble. But hey, I'm truly curious about something. Do you like your job as a Butterfly?"

"A what?"

"A Butterfly. A Diamond Butterfly. Un Papillon Diamanté."

"Ah, oui, no I am not one. I just work at the salon and occasionally Madame Chérot and Madame De la Rue hire me as a personal makeup artist and stylist."

"Madame De la Rue?"

"Oui, Aralyn. Aralyn De la Rue." I find it shocking that after nearly a month of knowing Aralyn, this is the first time I'm hearing her last name.

I drive up to the front of Jovana's complex and prepare to bid her farewell. She turns to me. "Madame De la Rue is tough and, at times, intimidating, but she is also very caring. She'll be there for you in an instant if you need her. I find her inspiring and I respect her a lot. Many of us will be sad to see her go." See her go? Where is she going? She had told me she is Madame Chérot's protégé, so why would she be going anywhere? Before I get the opportunity to ask, my phone rings. Looks like Aralyn decided to reach out to me instead.

"Thank you for the ride, Jess. Bonne journée."

"Of course…au revoir." I wait till she closes the door to answer the call. "Hey, sorry, I was taking Jovana home."

"I won't be able to meet you before the banquet, so you'll have to say whatever it is you have to say now." Quick and to the point I see.

"Okay. I'm out, Aralyn. I can't do this anymore. I don't know why you need the information you're looking for and I get it may be sensitive information but I'm sorry, you're going to have to find another way to get it."

"Why the sudden decision?" she asks. How about I'm sick of doing people's dirty work for starters.

"Ritter pulled me from the assignment."

"So?"

"What do you mean, so? I'm off the assignment. That's it."

"I know you are not the type of woman who would allow something like being removed from an assignment to keep you away from it. So, be honest, what is the real problem?"

Looks like my hopes for ending this without getting too detailed are dashed. I sigh. "I just don't feel like doing this anymore. Alexander deserves better. I don't like feeling like I'm sneaking around behind his back or somehow setting him up."

She's silent for a moment before responding. "You've fallen for him, haven't you?"

Her question throws me off guard. "What makes you say that?"

"You didn't seem to care so much about his feelings before. In fact, as I recall, you were trying to make sure that I was the one who understood the repercussions of our plan. You've become close with him."

"Getting to know someone more and deciding that tricking them into trusting you with personal information isn't worth it does not equate to falling for them, Aralyn."

"Say what you will, but I know you haven't been forthcoming about your connection with him. A friend of mine saw you two in Monaco this weekend. What reason would he have to take a journalist with him there, especially one whose job was simply to cover his event? Apparently, you are now more connected with him than you've led me to believe." Damn right I am! Keeping my growing bond with Alexander hidden from her has been a highlight for me these past couple weeks. I love that Aralyn doesn't, in fact, know all there is to know about me and what I'm doing. I wouldn't have it any other way.

"Think whatever you want Aralyn, I'm serious, this is over. I really hope you get what you're looking for."

"Hm. Yes, I hope you do too." She hangs up and I'm left feeling a bit perplexed. That seemed a little too easy. I expected her to put up a fight, to try and convince me to stay on, but for her to just part ways so casually feels odd. Though perhaps I'm over analyzing things. Afterall, it's a good thing that she's made it quick and painless. No need to make things complicated.

I head back to the house, thinking about the potential the next few days holds. Alex spent some time yesterday answering my remaining questions so, after I conduct my other interviews this week, all I'll have left is attending the charity banquet and I think I'll have crafted a pretty damn good article. Though the banquet is only a minuscule part of the story I'll be telling. Everything that I've come to learn about Alexander has inspired me to write about who he is in a way that people can understand, while also keeping him a mystery. I want people to feel as though they know him but don't know him at the same time. I want to leave something to be desired, as he would say, because his mystique is a large part of his identity. It will be insightful, poetic, and leave the reader yearning for more, much like I do when I'm around him. What I wanted when I set out on this journey was to write one of the most brilliant stories of my career. Today, I'm more confident than ever that I will accomplish that.

22

I'm somehow able to get the zipper up on the back of the stunning dress Alexander bought me. Glancing at myself in the bathroom mirror, I'm once again taken aback by my appearance, in awe of the woman staring back and this time, she doesn't seem so foreign. Just to double check, I ask myself if this is really me. Am I comfortable in this showstopper that adorns my body? To my pleasant surprise, the answer is yes. I have to hand it to Alex, he doesn't just pick any kind of dress for me, he picks dresses I'd love, and I have no idea how he does it. It's not as if I've given him any direction.

I received the sweetest Valentine's Day gift from him the other day too. It wasn't so much the basket of flowers and delicious treats he had delivered, but the endearing letter that was attached to it.

Hey Brown Eyes,

I'll be honest, I had my reservations about writing this, as this day had become inauspicious for me for a while. But I don't think I'd sleep well if I let it go by without acknowledging your significance to me. I have this to say: Your growing presence in my life has reawakened something in me...something that laid dormant and neglected for a while. Something I talked myself into believing I'd be just fine without. A kind of hope. You are an incredible woman. Every day I find myself more in awe of you and I am grateful to have crossed your path. If I wish for anything this day, it's that you know how much you are appreciated and that I care for you greatly.

— Alexander

It means so much that he took the time to not only write something so thoughtful, but allow himself to be a bit more vulnerable with me. I don't believe either of us have expected such feeling and expression to be ignited, especially so rapidly. But, here we are, drawn closer by the day.

I've had this running theory floating through my thoughts for the past few days that maybe whatever is between him and I is deeper, perhaps on some sort of chemical or mystical level. The term "soulmates" isn't something I'd put much thought into before, and I don't consider myself the most spiritual person, but could it be that this connection between us is on a level neither of us can grasp? It's like he's known me long before ever really knowing me. Speaking for myself, I feel like I've known him much longer than the mere three and a half weeks we've been in one another's lives.

"Well, don't you look divine." I twirl around and spot the man on my mind standing in the bathroom doorway. The way his eyes sweep the length of my body brings to mind the way he looked at me back at Jacques Lebrov's art exhibition.

"You're back!"

"I hope you didn't think I'd miss my own event."

I chuckle. "No, but you have to admit you're cutting it pretty damn close." He was supposed to come back yesterday but a turn in the weather made him unable to fly out.

He beams and walks to where I stand, enclosing me in a warm embrace. I look up at him, placing my chin on his chest, admiring this moment. It's only been a few days of his absence, but I've missed him incredibly.

His thumb sweeps over my cheek. "You really do look stunning."

A wide, adoring smile stretches across my face. "You are full of compliments, Mr. Marc."

"Well, that's one thing you'll have to get used to, Ms. Rivers. I will never pass up the opportunity to give you a compliment." He plants a soft kiss on my forehead.

I'm compelled to take this moment to ask him about what comes next. What happens to us after this is all over? The question has been burning in my mind ever since the fear of being without him surfaced. But before I can bring myself to come to an official decision on the matter, he asks, "Did you speak with Ritter?"

I breathe out a sigh. "I did. I'm quite sure he hates my guts now. Might even try to make it harder for me to do my job, honestly. He's probably plotting all the ways he can bad mouth me around town as we speak. Of course, I don't know for sure if he'd be so petty, but if he can use your mother's situation to try and blackmail you into doing what he wants, I wouldn't put it past him."

"Hmm, well, he should really think twice about that."

I giggle. "Yeah? And why is that? Do you plan on doing something about it?"

He shrugs. "I wouldn't not do anything about it."

"Seriously, don't worry. I can handle this. It wouldn't be the first time I've had to make a way for myself through the depravity of the male ego."

"Mm, oh I'm absolutely confident that you can, but you shouldn't have to. Have you thought about taking your business elsewhere?"

"Uh, like where?"

"Like London." I perk up. Is he suggesting what I think he is? Oh God, I hope so. "I know it's a lot to consider right now but I'm just–"

"I do!" The look he gives me is that of perplexed amusement. "I, um, I mean yes, it's a big decision but I'm sure I could make something like that work."

"I know you love Paris. You told me how living here was a dream of yours since you were young, but I'm just not sure Paris deserves you, truthfully. But please, Jess, take whatever time you need to think about it. London just might have more to offer you. And it would be nice to have you there with me."

My chest swells with happiness. Without me even having to say a thing, he knew what I needed to hear. I, of course, will have to take some time to figure some things out before I can move, but I'd do it all in a heartbeat. "I'll take some time, but only to prepare myself. The decision is a no brainer for me. I've traveled to the UK for some assignments before. I enjoyed it. London is a nice city. But honestly even if I loathed the place, it wouldn't matter. I want to be wherever you are." He flashes a brilliant smile that sends my heart a flutter.

"Then it's settled. We'll talk a bit more about it later. Right now, I need to get ready myself. You can't be the only one dressed to impress this evening." He winks.

We release each other and I return to the sink to grab some gloss to put over my dark rouge lipstick. Thanks to the informative tutorial video Jovana sent me last week, my makeup looks top notch this evening. As I apply the finishing touches, my eyes dart to Alexander's reflection still in the mirror. He stands with both hands in his pockets and a look of admiration across his features. "What is it?" I ask.

"Your hair." What's wrong with my hair? I have it slicked back on one side to where it sweeps around in an edgy diagonal angle on the other. He walks up behind me, leaning in as he places his hands on either side of me against the counter, boxing me in. His torso presses against my back and his cheek touches mine as he stares into the mirror along with me. "It's lovely, but it's the one thing I wish Marguerite would have left alone during your makeover."

"Is that so?"

"Mhmm. I don't mind the color so much, but the length…the length you had before was heavenly." His hand glides up my arm and comes to rest around my neck. "Can I tell you a secret?" I'm too busy reveling in his sweet touch to answer. It sends the nerves in my head firing all the way down to my toes and back up again, especially as the warmth of his breath tickles my ear. "The first day we met, when you came for the interview and you sat across from me in the office, that long golden hair all billowed and shining in the light, I had a delicious fantasy. Would you like to hear it?" I swallow and give my head a quick nod. "I had a vision of you bent over my desk after I braided up that hair. All so that I could pull it as I pleased while fucking you mercilessly from behind."

Holy shit! Was that truly the image flashing behind those eyes that gave nothing away that day? It's hard to believe that, as I sat there worried that I was screwing up the interview, he was sitting there fantasizing about railing me!

His words send a rush of lustful sensations throughout my core and the ocean between my thighs starts to swell. I moan subtly and move my hand back behind me, griping his shielded member. I can feel how engorged he is, how intensely his body desires me. In an instant, the hand he had around my throat clasps my wrist.

"I want you." I say rather pleadingly.

After a moment of closing his eyes to regain his composure, he looks back up at my reflection and smirks. "I know, baby. But if I let you, I swear we won't leave this house tonight." The selfish part of me wants that to be a promise. I want to challenge him. To make it hard to resist me. He takes my hand and guides it back to the counter, interlacing his fingers with my own. "And we can't have that." Sarcastically he says, "I'm thinking about my reputation." His grin widens.

I laugh. "Uh huh. Nice one."

He places a lingering kiss on my exposed shoulder. "Don't worry. Tonight, I'm all yours." He stands upright and walks to the door only turning back to say, "See you in a bit darling."

He exits and I'm left reeling, trying desperately to collect myself. Once again, I'm both turned on and frustrated as hell. If there's one thing Alexander Marc is good for, it's a tease. If this is what I have to look forward to this evening, it's going to be one hell of a night.

*a*s we pull up to the Crescendo Hall, my stomach is a bundle of nerves. This is the event I've been preparing to attend for weeks, and yet it seems like it's come upon us too quickly. Quite a few people in formal wear are making their way into the building. I look over at Alex as his door opens for him to exit. "Should I wait a few minutes before walking up?" I ask.

His brows pull together in confusion. "No. Why on earth should you have to wait?"

"I don't know, I suppose I just thought you'd want to go in alone." To my knowledge, Alexander has never escorted a woman to any press event he's attended, much less his own. I had no expectation that I'd be so lucky.

He doesn't respond. Instead, he chuckles softly and steps out of the car. It confuses me, but then after a few moments, my door opens, and he stands outside of it with his hand extended out to me. There's a great sense of joy stirred within me by this simple, yet significant, gesture. I feel so honored that he's choosing to have me by his side tonight. I do realize, however, that this will now draw even more attention to me. Everyone, and I do mean everyone, is going to want to know about the woman who's caught Alexander's attention enough to be seen on his arm in public.

I grab hold of his hand while my other hand does its best to gather the large skirt of my dress so that I don't get tangled up by my own garment as I exit. As soon as I fully step out, I experience déjà vu, recalling my red-carpet entry at the art exhibit. Bright flashing lights consistently go off in front of us. I'm not sure if I'll ever get used to this. I follow Alexander's lead toward the front doors while displaying my boldest smile. Multiple paparazzi clamor and call out to the man of the hour. Their movements remind me of fish during feeding time.

"Alexander! Look over here!"

"Can we have a moment of your time, Monsieur?"

"Who's the beautiful woman you have with you, Mr. Marc?"

Carmyn stands in wait just past the entrance. Like always, she looks amazing. Her hair is pulled up into a high-top bun and she wears a lovely electric blue mermaid style dress with a small train that trails behind her. She walks up and greets us, giving me an eye of approval before providing Alexander with the rundown of who's present and what's been prepared to ensure the evening goes without a hitch.

She accompanies us into the main hall which is beginning to fill up quickly. It's here that I recognize quite a few high-profile faces, as well as a few of the speakers I had interviewed for the article. Alexander greets many of the guests who all stare at me, trying to figure out who I am. He introduces me to a few but, for the most part, he keeps the greetings simple and straightforward small talk, for which I'm grateful.

Glancing around the room, I notice Marguerite and Gregoire chatting with some other guests. I briefly wonder what she'd think seeing me here with Alex. I've had a feeling that she didn't believe I'd ever make it this far. Though, to be honest, I never cared what she thought and that seems relevant now more than ever. I do consider going over to say hello, but then I spot Charles taking a seat at one of the tables.

Huh, so it appears that what Ritter said was true, Deflour did find a way to weasel himself into an invite for this event. Had I spared enough focus on that shared information, I probably could have mentioned it to Alex who would most likely have gotten his name on a banned list of some sort. Then again, I'm kind of happy he's here wasting his efforts. The thought is quite satisfying.

I place a hand on Alexander's arm. "Hey, meet you at our table in a bit?" He nods his head and I head toward Deflour.

When I step next to him, he peers up at me with a cheesy grin. "Bonsoir, Mademoiselle! À qui dois-je l'honneur?"

"Charles, it's me, Jess. Jess Rivers."

He's flabbergasted at first but then he laughs. "No way! Jessy? Magnificent upgrade."

I roll my eyes with agitation. "How many times must I tell you not to call me that? I see you couldn't help yourself but to suck up to Ritter in order to take over my assignment…again."

"Me? Nooo. As I heard it, you quit. I'm simply filling in." He waves his hand in a nonchalant manner, as if to feign innocence. I want to wipe the smug grin right off his face.

"Uh huh. Well, I just came over to say good luck. I wish you the best." I extend my hand out to him and he stares at it, perplexed. Lost in a sense of mass confusion is exactly where I want him. If I'm going to let him continue to believe he's gotten one over on me and won, why not stroke his ego a little more in the process? It makes it all the sweeter to know that ego will only be deflated by the end of the night.

After some hesitation and a bit of side eyeing, he finally takes my hand for a firm shake. "Merci."

"Well, I better settle in. I'll be seeing you."

"Uh, wait. What are *you* doing here?"

I pivot on my heels and glance over my shoulder at him. "Oh, I'm sure you'll figure it out." I wink and walk off, smiling to myself. I don't turn back to see his expression, but I don't need to. I can practically feel his bewildered gaze piercing my back as I continue forward.

Alexander stands and pulls out a seat for me when I approach the table. Such a gentleman. He mentions that he's headed up to the platform to make an opening speech. "Wait, let me fix your tie," I say. He smiles and leans down as I adjust him to perfection. The way he looks at me while I express my care for him in this way makes my heart beam. I get that warm and fuzzy sensation throughout my body that I've heard of but had yet to experience before him. There are a million and one things I'd do to see him look at me like this again and again. When I finish, he thanks me, kisses my forehead and takes his leave.

Looking around at the individuals at our table, I notice that I don't know many of them besides Carmyn. The faces I do recognize are those of Laurent Coultier, the President of Alexander's company branch here in France and his wife, the woman I had to run out on due to the unwelcome appearance of Charles alongside her. "Monsieur Coultier, bonjour!"

"Ah, Mademoiselle Rivers! A pleasure to see you again!" He turns to his wife who's busy chatting with the woman next to them while smoking a cigarette and addresses her in French. "Claire my love, this is the woman I had wanted you to meet at the dinner last week. The one who writes erotic books." I blush at the reminder of my temporary career title.

She gives him an annoyed glare, probably not appreciating having her engaging conversation interrupted, and then surveys me, squinting her eyes and forcing a smile. "Bonsoir."

I greet her in return and she goes back to her smoke and chat. With the interaction having gone not as expected, Laurent straightens his tie and clears his throat. "Eh, perhaps you both will speak on it more at a different time."

I let out a light giggle. "I look forward to it." I, for one, am hoping that it never gets brought up again.

A woman takes the podium and welcomes everyone. After a short speech, she introduces Alexander, and the room claps feverishly when he takes the stage. He thanks everyone for attending and for the contributions that have already been made before the night even kicked off. Then he takes a deep dive into the importance of the charity and the future projects that the organization is taking on.

He really is a brilliant speaker. Alex just has this way of talking that's profound and thought provoking. His words command the full attention of everyone here and we give it, gladly.

I lean over and whisper to Carmyn, "If he keeps going like this, the charity will receive above and beyond what they are hoping for."

She whispers back, "Oh darling, they already have. A few big names handed over checks right after he spoke to them a little while ago. Of course, it's all to impress him. I doubt many are doing it for any other reason." That's not at all surprising. I had often wondered how many individuals who come to these events actually give a crap about the cause they're supporting. I think everyone would like to believe they are involved for the right reasons, even the ones writing the checks. It's a bit sad, but at the same time, it's a delight to know that the banquet is already a success. At the end of the day, the cause really is a great one, and the organization deserves as many resources as possible to see their endeavors through.

I remember what Alexander had told me about his mother being the biggest inspiration for his charitable efforts and it makes me wonder what she'd think of all this if she were here. It would have been lovely to meet her tonight, but I imagine Alex doesn't want her anywhere where she could potentially be inappropriately questioned, judged or ridiculed. Perhaps I'll have the opportunity to meet her when I move to the UK. It would be such an honor to learn about her humanitarian pursuits.

Just as I lean back, a gentleman violently knocks into my chair, causing the wine I'm holding to splash over the rim of the glass and onto the skirt of my dress. "Shit!" I mumble.

"Oh dear, here let me help." Carmyn grabs a cloth napkin off the table and tries her best to dab the wine but, as I fear, it's making it worse. "What a prat!" she exclaims. "As if there wasn't plenty of room for him to walk by without being a total klutz." I chuckle at her crude demeanor.

"It's alright. I'll just quickly run to the lavatory. Perhaps the attendant will have something that can help. If Alex finishes before I return, just tell him I'll be right back." I rise from my seat and do my best to slip out of the room without drawing much attention to myself. This was unexpected, indeed, but I'm just happy that the fabric of the dress is primarily mesh so even though there is a stain, it isn't super visible.

As I hurry down the empty hall, someone calls out to me from behind. "Jess!"

I freeze, my blood running cold at the recognition of the voice. No fucking way. I reluctantly turn to face the last person I expected to run into tonight. "Arthur, what are you doing here?"

He strides toward me. "I could ask you the same question, especially since Ritter took you off the assignment."

"I was invited so I'm here. You and Charles partnering up or something?" Cause how did he even get in?

"I pulled some strings and was able to get on the list. Ritter asked me to come and make sure everything goes smoothly."

"Let me guess. He doesn't actually trust Charles either."

"No, he just knows that this may be his last chance to get a good story out of all this mess so he wants to make sure it happens. He told me what you said to him the other day by the way. Real professional."

My eyes roll to the back of my head. "Oh, please lay off it, Arthur. The last thing I need is to hear you criticize me for standing up for myself. You told me to handle it, so I handled it. End of story."

"You ruined a good thing is what you did. But you know what? I don't even care. It's none of my business."

"Oh good. I'm glad you've had that brilliant epiphany. Enjoy the banquet."

Just as I turn to walk off, he moves in front of me. "Hold on. Wait. What are we doing? Seriously Jess, this is so stupid. This isn't us. I really wish you would just see sense and realize that we are on the same team here."

"No. No Art, we aren't on the same team. You made that very clear when you went behind my back to give your unwarranted approval on removing me from a job you knew I really cared about! Then, you made it that much clearer when you called me selfish for expressing my needs to you! So, you tell me, does that sound like the actions of someone who's on the same team as me?" I cross my arms over my chest in an attempt to keep my hands from shaking. This is triggering me all over again. Why can't he understand how hurt I am by his betrayal? I'm not trying to fight him. Peace between us is the most desirable outcome, but I cannot let what happened go unchecked.

"Look, I get that I may have overstepped, but it wasn't to screw you over, Jess. I honestly thought I was doing you a favor. But don't worry, you won't get any more favors from me."

I huff in disbelief. "Wow. If that was your idea of an apology, you can keep it. I'm out of here." I try to march past him, but he grabs my upper arm and forcefully pulls me to him.

The muscles in his jaw flex and a vein begins to protrude from his temple. "Don't do this. Don't walk away from me again."

I give him a bitter glare. "Arthur, let me go." There's an immense sadness in his eyes hidden right behind the rage. It's the only thing keeping me from clocking him across his jaw for handling me the way he is. That sadness pulls at the threads of my heart that are still connected to the care, admiration and love I have for him, despite everything. But those threads grow thinner every second he keeps his hand gripped like a vice around me.

"For years you have been all I've yearned for, Jess. I care about your happiness more than you seem to realize!"

"Then let me go! Please. You're hurting me, Art."

He leans in close to my face. His voice is laced with distaste. "And still, it's nothing compared to the pain you've caused me." His face contorts with disgust. I've never seen him like this before, ever. What does it mean when the man I had always felt so safe around suddenly has me wanting to run for dear life?

"Is there a problem here?" We both turn our heads to see Alexander approaching, his face marred with concern. Two of his bodyguards follow in tow.

Arthur responds. "Just having a chat. We're friends."

"She doesn't appear to think you're very friendly, mate."

Arthur looks at me and gives an unsettling laugh. "What is this? You somehow managed to convince Alexander Marc to be your knight in shining armor?" I try again to shake myself from Arthur's grip, but he tightens his hold.

Alexander reaches us. "Get your hand off her. Now!" They stare each other down like two lions prepared to fight to the death and I have a gut feeling that things are about to head south fast. I have to find a way to diffuse the situation.

"Please, Art, we can talk about this again later. Not here, not now. This is Alex's event; we don't need to make a scene." Art whips his head my way, his eyes wild with unrecognizable emotion.

"Alex, huh? That's awfully informal of you. You two must have gotten pretty close. You're just so full of fucking surprises, aren't you? I guess that explains the flashy car you got into and why every time I've been to your place this past week, you haven't been there. Whoring it out to the billionaire huh? Classy."

Alex steps closer, his gray eyes turn dark and lethal. "I'm warning you."

"Art, stop!"

"Why? Why stop, Jess? It's true, isn't it? Now I get it. I finally understand. I have been going crazy trying to figure out how the hell you could so easily toss me aside like you have, but I see the truth. All this time I've been pushing myself to do all I can for you like an idiot, not seeing that no matter what, I'd never be good enough!"

"I'm going to tell you one last time. Release her, right now!"

"Oh, fuck you man! Tell me something; how much did you pay her to turn her back on the people she cares about, huh?"

The bodyguards take a few steps toward us, and Alexander throws his hand up, halting them. "Last chance."

Arthur releases my arm as he violently thrusts me into Alex, who immediately moves me behind him. Arthur's cold gaze is still pinned on me, and he says in a low menacing tone, "Once I walk away it's all over. Everything. It's up to you, Jess. Either him or me. Make your choice."

Before a thought can even pass through my mind, Alexander lunges forward, grabs Arthur by the neck and slams him against a wall! His bodyguards bolt to his side as Arthur claws at his hand and arm, struggling to breathe. The guards do their best to pull the two apart but whatever is possessing Alex to latch on in this way, is no match, even for them. I am frozen in complete shock and horror, unable to move or speak. My brain isn't processing what's happening fast enough.

After what feels like an eternity, I gather myself enough to look at our surroundings and see if I can find anyone who can help. My eyes lock onto Carmyn's worried face at the entryway to the hall, which is thankfully not facing the ruckus. She's doing everything in her power to keep anyone who walks up from entering. When I turn back to the scene before me, the guards have managed to pull Alex off of Arthur who slides to the ground, clasping his neck and coughing viciously. Alexander shakes both guards off him, straightening his suit jacket. He's visibly still heated but trying to collect himself.

One of the guards comes up to me and begins to usher me toward a side exit. "No, wait please, I need to make sure he's okay!"

"It's alright, Ms. Rivers. He won't touch Mr. Marc." The way he says it like he didn't just have to stop his boss from choking the life out of Arthur is astounding. Obviously, Alexander can take care of himself; it's Arthur I'm worried about! I may be livid with him, but I didn't want him hurt! I don't want either of them going to bat again, especially not over me.

The outside air is bitter but welcomed. The guard sits me on a bench and uses his radio to request that the car come around.

He takes off his dress coat and lays it across my shoulders. He must know that Alex might have an actual fit if he finds me out here without one. I somehow find amusement in that, despite the horrendous situation we are in. But even that brief deflection doesn't keep my stomach from churning, nor the acid from creeping up the back of my throat.

I jump to my feet when I see Alexander approaching us. My initial instinct is to run to him but, instead, I stand here gauging whether the anger evident on his face is still from what took place, or if it's toward me. He'd have every reason to be pissed. Tonight was supposed to be a night of celebration and people coming together to do good. Now it's soured for him because of my own life drama; drama I had hoped to keep him far away from.

Upon reaching where we stand, he immediately pulls me into him, wrapping his arms tight around my body. I can finally breathe. "Please, tell me you're alright," he says.

I tilt my head back and look up at him. "I'm still a bit rattled but I'm fine. Are *you* alright?"

"I'm better now that I know you're okay."

"And Arthur?" Frown lines bore into his forehead, but there's a look of understanding in his eyes. "He'll be sore tomorrow surly, and he'll suffer from a damaged ego, but he'll be fine."

I'm still finding it hard to fathom that Art had behaved in such a way. It's surreal! I would have never thought him capable of such rage. He'd always been so tender, caring, comical and endearing, even when he was upset. The Art I knew would never throw such a tantrum. Is it possible that he's hidden this side of himself from me all this time, or did his love for me bring that out of him? And could it be possible that what started out as love has become something far more potent– obsession?

*I*n the car there's nothing but silence between myself and Alexander for a long time, both of us deep in our heads. He hasn't stopped staring out his window. I imagine he's probably replaying the incident repeatedly like I am, and I feel so awful. "Alex, I'm so very sorry."

He looks at me with a tender smile and takes my hand in his. "What could you possibly be sorry for?"

"You should be back at the banquet right now, socializing, maybe making another powerful speech, thanking everyone for their amazing contributions to the cause, not getting into an altercation and heading home early. The night wasn't supposed to end like this."

"I'm right where I need to be." He gives my hand a reassuring squeeze and I scoot over, huddling into his side, leaning my head on his shoulder. "It's I who should apologize. I'm embarrassed to have conducted myself in such a manner. I just couldn't unsee the memory."

I peer up at him. "What memory?"

"I blacked out, Jess. When he gave you that ultimatum, it took me back to the night my father was murdered. All I could see was the anger and the gun and I could hear my mother's screams ringing in my ears. It might not have seemed like it, but I was terrified. I was terrified that I'd lose someone else close to me. Terrified that I'd lose you.

"I would give anything to go back to that horrendous day and do something, anything different than what I did. Anything for another chance to save my father. So, when he said what he said to you, I didn't even think about it really, I just acted. I did what I would have done if given another opportunity. My God, I could have killed him." He cups a hand over his mouth as the realization dawns. I sit up and twist my whole body toward him. This was far more serious than I thought. I hadn't even considered how triggered he could have been but it makes so much sense that he was.

His cloudy eyes look at me with such sorrow. "I know he's your friend, and I'm sure that was the last thing you ever thought would happen but I–" My hands reach for his face, and I kiss him. I kiss him with immense depth and passion. I kiss him to let him know how much I understand; to let him know that there is no anger; to let him know that he's safe and that he still has my love and admiration.

His fingers run through my hair while his other hand slides to the small of my back, drawing me onto his lap. We enter back into our world of just us two. Our safe haven. Our place of endless bliss. It's in this space where the only language is the unspoken kind, where our energy speaks loudest in the absence of verbal expression– practically telepathic in nature.

There will be many people who will never understand us. They will question how we ever came to be; the journalist trying to make a name for herself, and the deeply private billionaire who seems to have it all figured out. But I don't mind one bit. Our relationship will be as enigmatic as we already are individually. It wasn't too long ago that I loathed being misunderstood, but now, I'd happily be misunderstood with him.

*W*e arrive at the house just as Alexander receives a call from Carmyn. "Go on inside darling, I need to help her work through the closing." He gives me one last kiss and I slide out. Despite such a grim ending to the evening, I'm on cloud nine. My lips buzz with the lingering memory of Alexander's affection.

Luc opens the front door for me. "Welcome back, Mademoiselle."

"Thank you, Luc!" I enter, making a quick decision that the first stop will be the kitchen. Not only is my stomach insanely upset that we missed out on the dinner portion of the event, but I need to pour myself and Alexander a drink expeditiously. After tonight, we deserve one, maybe three.

As I make my way through the foyer, I'm caught off guard when the library door swings open and out walks, "Aralyn?"

23

"*J*ess? What are you doing here?"

"What am *I* doing here? What the hell are *you* doing here?" She extends her neck past me in order to peer out of the front windows.

"Where's Alexander?"

"He's outside! Aralyn, what the fuck is going on?"

"Merde! He wasn't supposed to be home this early. What happened? The banquet was supposed to go till midnight!" Who gives a crap? Why isn't she answering me?

She grabs my wrist and starts pulling me towards the library. "Jess, we have to go. We have to go now!"

I yank myself from her clutches. "Not until you tell me what the hell is going on!" We both turn, startled upon hearing Alexander's voice echoing right outside the door. He's speaking to Luc.

Aralyn looks at me, eyes wide, projecting worry and dread. She whispers, "Oh my God, you have to hide." She grips my forearm this time and practically drags me into the library. The moment we enter, I once again snatch myself from her grasp.

Alexander's heavy footsteps can now be heard entering the foyer. I speak to Aralyn in hushed agitation. "Give me one good reason I shouldn't blow the lid off this whole thing!"

She takes hold of the door handle, and stares at me, momentarily struggling for words. I haven't seen a look so riddled with a mixture of emotion. Her eyes are filled with pleading, sadness and fear and I realize that I am seeing Aralyn, the true Aralyn, the one without walls, fences and masks for the very first time. "S'il-vous-plaît," She replies in a low tone, "Get through this with me and I will tell you everything. I swear it."

I don't have time to answer before she slips out just as the sound of his footsteps almost reaches our location. I'm left in the dark, save a sliver of light coming through the door she didn't close completely. I peek through and witness Alexander's shock at the sight of her.

"Aralyn?"

My mind is reeling! Aralyn stands frozen in place for a moment, as if unsure of what to do or say. Then she lowers herself down onto her knees, bowing her head in submission to the man who looks almost as shocked as I feel.

"Sir."

He stares at her bewildered and my hand clasps over my mouth as I fall into utter disbelief. I observe him taking a few slow, hesitant steps forward, extending a stiff hand to touch her head, only to pull back at the final moment, clenching it into a firm fist at his side. The look on his face reflects raw pain as he sucks in a long breath and closes his eyes tight, the muscles in his jaw constricting.

His voice breaks when he finally responds with, "What are you doing here, Aralyn?"

"I've come to check on you, Sir." Alexander's eyes shoot open, blazing and dark. Pain has been replaced with bitter rage.

He gives a low command, "Get up." Aralyn begins to rise to her feet, but she isn't quick enough. "I said, *GET UP!*" His roar sends chills shooting through my already shaken body. His face is contorted with emotion, and I can see the glistening droplets in his eyes that he's doing his best to keep at bay.

Aralyn jumps to her feet in no time, her head still bowed. It's bizarre to see her like this. I never took Aralyn to be the submissive type. The woman I thought I'd come to know consistently presented as strong willed; a woman who commanded a room and who expected things to go her way. To see her as she is now, so raw, unfiltered, bare, vulnerable, is hard to grasp. It's as if I've witnessed a whole different person step into her body and relinquish all control.

"You walked out on me, remember? You walked out on three bloody years, Aralyn! No explanation, not even a fucking text, nothing! So, don't you dare show your face in front of me again and lie! I don't know what I did to you, but I know I certainly don't deserve that!"

"You're right, you don't."

After yet another breath he speaks in a calmer manner. "Then answer me truthfully. Why have you come back?"

In a rattled tone she replies, "I didn't plan on seeing you here." She pulls a small envelope from the breast of her dress. "I still had the key to the pleasure room, so I came in hoping to place this letter on your desk before you returned. It's my final goodbye."

Alexander squints at her, irritated. "A goodbye letter. That's why you came back? You really shouldn't have bothered. I already said my goodbyes to you without you present."

Aralyn's head snaps up and she steps toward him, raising her hands to touch his face. "Alexander, please, let me explain." He turns his face away from her touch and her hands withdraw back down to her side.

"You need to leave at once." He brushes past her, but she grabs ahold of his forearm.

"Please Alex, no…" Much as I did, he snatches his arm from her grasp and continues his exit. She cries out to him, "I'm dying!" And I suddenly feel as though my lungs have stopped working and I can't catch my breath.

"I'm dying Alex. That's why I left. I found out my heart is weak. It has a disease and there is no cure." Her voice waivers under the weight of her immense pain and sadness. "I loved you so much, you know that. When I found out, I couldn't subject you to the heartache of such a loss again, not after knowing how much your father's death impacted you. I didn't want you to have to bury me too, so I thought it would be better if you lost me sooner and be upset than later and be broken." Aralyn breaks down into tears. Her sobs reverberate off the walls of the large, empty foyer. Her rosy cheeks fade as her tears wash away the makeup that gave them their color. Her arms cross around her waist like she only has herself for a much needed embrace.

I watch in stunned silence as Alexander's frame enters back into view and his arms wrap a blanket of sincere care and support around Aralyn's hunched body. I listen intently as he whispers in her ear, and though I cannot make out the words, I know they are meant to comfort her. And I see how, for a brief moment, he glances upwards toward the heavens and then closes his eyes as if saying a silent prayer to whomever will listen.

My stomach churns in the darkness of the library. I try hard to process everything I just heard, but the more I try, the more the bitter taste of acid coats my tongue. I am beginning to realize the gravity of what is taking place. Guilt creeps up the mountain of emotions weighing heavily on my chest, because although my heart aches for them both, it shatters for me and I'm not sure whether this is incredibly selfish or justified.

There's no denying the love I have for Alexander Marc. I had hoped he'd formed love for me too. But even if he has, it's become clear that it's not the same. It's not the same as the love that shows itself in his eyes and body language as he holds the face of the woman I envy and plants a gentle kiss on her forehead. Love that inspires even more tears to spring to her eyes and one to his, only because he allowed it. And the fact that he's allowed it speaks volumes. He has proven that around her, he can be completely vulnerable.

As that tear continues its descent down his cheek, reality surfaces with a vengeance and I'm confronted with the magnitude of my foolishness. I was the distraction. Aralyn's plan must have been to use me to get Alexander's mind off of her. Why else would she push me toward him? At this moment, I can't be sure what hurts the most, because everything, EVERYTHING hurts.

"Come now. It's going to be alright." Alex keeps an arm over her shoulder and ushers her away.

When their footsteps no longer echo, I make a mad dash out of the library into the entryway and up to my bedroom. I strip off the dress and toss it to the side like it's going to burn me, and it might as well have, it's brought nothing but bad luck! Like a mad woman, I quickly change into jeans and a t-shirt and then fling my suitcases onto the bed and begin piling in everything I can, with the exception of the wardrobe I had been gifted by Aralyn. She could keep her clothes; I'm done with them. They've served her purpose.

I'm intent on leaving every memory, every feeling, every piece of my life that has any attachment to that woman behind. My chest seizes at the understanding that that means leaving Alexander behind too. I don't want Aralyn's explanation. I don't want the whole story; I just want to go home. I might go as far as to say that I want my old life back, before the black and red, where things were so simple and my heart would have never been put in a position to be broken.

The temperature outside has dropped several degrees since earlier. This frigid cold easily reflects the ice that has formed over my thoughts. I'm bitter. So bitter and so distraught.

I stand outside the red double doors of the mansion, eagerly awaiting Luc to pull my car around. I wrap my coat around me a bit tighter, but nothing can keep the chill I feel from wreaking havoc on my body and soul.

"You're leaving?" Alexander descends down the steps behind me.

I should be embarrassed by the makeup running down my tear-stricken face but I don't care. "I can't stay, not after what I heard…and saw."

"Yes, Aralyn told me you were in the library. She's told me quite a bit of surprising information involving you actually." A mask of pain shadows his face. I see she's caught him up on the details of our scheme and I'm torn between my response coming from a place of guilt, relief or anger. And because I am unsure which yearns to be expressed more, I opt to keep silent. "I'm certain you must have a lot of questions," he says.

"Just one." I let out a sorrowful sigh. "Do you still love her?" I need to hear him say it. I need him to say it so that I can believe it because this night feels like a horrible nightmare that I'm having trouble waking from.

He gazes off in the distance, sucks in an icy breath and releases it before responding. "I loved her once. Then I nearly hated her. Now, I'm not sure." His eyes dart back to mine. "I honestly don't know, Jess. I'm very uncertain about a lot of things at the moment." Without him needing to say the words, I can tell those "things" include his connection with me and can't say I'd blame him for that. To discover that the woman you have feelings for has been plotting with your ex-lover behind your back has to be jarring.

"I'm such a fool to have allowed myself to get caught up in any of this." I bite my quivering lower lip. "I wasn't aware she knew you that way. I didn't say anything about her cause I wasn't sure it would be necessary. And I didn't want to potentially expose anything she relayed to me in confidence."

"I know. She told me that too."

"I am so sorry."

"So am I. I imagine you're hoping to hear something more reassuring, but truthfully, I don't know what to say that will make this situation any better. This is a lot for me to take in. I never expected to grow feelings for you, Jess, but I did. I never expected Aralyn to come back, but she did. And I certainly didn't expect to find out any of the things I've just been told, none of it, but I have. I am terribly conflicted, dismayed, confused and I might be feeling a bit of heartbreak too, which is a difficult thing to acknowledge, but there it is." He looks at me and his voice cracks slightly as he speaks. "In any case, neither makes for a good concoction, and I can see myself spiraling out of control if I don't do my best to reign in my emotions and thoughts surrounding everything that's occurred. For me, that means I need to distance myself for a time. So, I really am sorry Jess. I'm sorry I can't give you what you're hoping for."

There's only one thing worse than a nightmare, and that's a living nightmare. Because nightmares that happen when you're awake are ones you can't escape. They are real, true, they have a permanent placement in the book of your life, never to be erased. That is more frightening than anything you could see or experience in a dream.

Luc pulls around with my car right as another couple tears spill down my cheeks. Alexander clears his throat. "Before you go, I'd like to suggest that when you get to an emotional space where you're able to, you should talk to Aralyn. I don't entirely agree with her actions, but I understand where they were coming from. You may come to understand too." I barely mull over his words. There's no telling how long it will take me to face her again. Along with the fact that she deceived me, I'm having a hard time facing the truth that she's passing. It's hitting me harder than I could have ever expected and I'm not sure why. Hell, I wasn't sure why I was so drawn to her prior to us meeting either. Aralyn is an interesting creature. I suppose that is the one constant in how she's portrayed herself. But she's the last person I want to think about despite her being the one to bring a screeching halt to my desires. I only have room for so much.

Alex follows me over to the drivers' side door while Luc loads my bags into the trunk. "So, this is it?" I ask before getting in. "Will I ever see you again?"

One more tear falls from my tear duct, and he wipes it with his thumb. "I wish I could say, Brown Eyes. I wish so many things."

"Me too." My voice quakes with emotion. "Goodbye, Alex." I don't wait for him to return the farewell. I hop in the car and close the door myself, then take off down the driveway, holding in a gut-wrenching sob for when I'm past the gates.

I'm beyond shocked. I can't believe every beautiful dream I had built up with him had been smashed to pieces in an instant and I was too helpless to prevent it. The loss of control I feel is dizzying. When I reach a point where I am out of sight of the estate, I stop at the side of the road and let out everything left within me. If pity was a woman, I would indeed be her.

I fumble with my keys in a desperate attempt to get into my flat. I left everything in my car. All I want is my bed. Exhaustion has loomed over me for a majority of the night, but I feel it with an intense heaviness at this time, as though I could sleep an entire year away. The minute I make it through the door and lock it behind me, I throw my purse, coat and keys on the couch and head straight to my bedroom, flinging myself on to the bed and curling up in a fetal position. There is nothing and no one that can bring me the comfort I need, a lonely thought that sends me sinking into a deep state of depression I don't think I've ever experienced. I've had breakups. I've been stabbed in the back by people I trusted before as well, but it still holds no comparison.

The truth of the matter is, I have no one to blame but myself and, perhaps, that is why the pain is so severe. I let myself down. I always had my back more than anyone, I made sure of it all throughout my life, but especially after I made the move to Paris. It was me that picked myself up when I was tossed aside. It was me that made sure I was making choices that would propel me forward. I kept myself safe, guarded from chaos as much as possible, even when I had to take a risk to get somewhere. I was very cautious, even overly so at times.

So, how? How did I let myself down this bad? How did I blow past every single red flag that Aralyn was waving? How did I allow myself to believe I could have a happy ending with Alexander Marc, of all people? I dug myself deep into this with such blinding ignorance it's astounding!

I do not know what the sun will bring, nor what the future holds for me now. Within me exists this emptiness beyond the veil, grim and heartbreaking. My whole life has shifted and transformed. My career is in a rocky place, my friendship with Arthur is in shambles, the love of my life is gone and I'm…alone.

Like a fallen angel, I've plummeted straight from heaven and hit rock bottom. The impact was deafening, soul splintering, relentless. The burden of my sorrow sits like heavy black wings upon my back, as my consciousness becomes aware that the world I once knew has been stripped from me eternally.

Is there still a glimmer of hope to cling onto? Because I need a lifeline. I need something to help me crawl from the strong grip of darkness that's consumed my mind. Through shuddering breaths, I do my best to search for it in the chasms of my being, but before it can be found, my body surrenders to the sweet benevolence of sleep.

24

 t's been a little over a month since the night I still cringe reflecting back on. I've spent the last thirty-seven days floating through life while fighting to remain energetically present– an incredibly strange sensation. How does one best describe being here and, yet, absent all at once? Despite the dark cloud that's hovering over my days, I have found a sliver of light that I've clung to tightly, my article. Ritter wasn't getting it, but that didn't mean another publication company couldn't. Needless to say, I didn't completely waste away in my flat, I poured my time, thoughts and energy into a story I can be proud of…I like to think Alexander will be proud of me too, if he reads it.

It was an incredible feat writing about him. Memories constantly danced through my head like a movie reel on repeat and I came close to tossing this story, which would have been the easy thing to do. But, when I realized that no matter what I did, I could not escape the memory of him, the yearning or the visions, it seemed ridiculous not to follow through. If his ghost was going to be that unavoidable, I might as well utilize its presence to bring myself back to life again. I knew the article wouldn't fully be the solution to doing that, but it seemed like a start, and I really needed a start.

As I had suspected, Ritter slandered my name everywhere he could. Thankfully, his attempts to disparage me couldn't keep the company I approached to take on publication of the piece, from growing excited over the thought of being the first to publish an in-depth article on the bachelor. They chose to take it on and I'm fairly content, as they are a company I respect. The article will be published first thing Monday morning and it's making the cover!

I have not heard from Arthur and, for that, I'm honestly grateful. I can't handle any more drama. I heard from another journalist I knew at Eiffel that he resigned a few weeks ago and no one saw it coming. They don't know where he is and it saddens me to think how turbulent his mindset must have gotten for him to abruptly leave a position he loved. I keep hoping that maybe he just came to his senses about Ritter and couldn't bear to work with him anymore.

I'm still quite torn up about our shattered friendship. There's a part of me that clings to the hope of rekindling our connection in the future, or at least bringing some closure to the events that transpired between us, however, I need more time. I'm traumatized from that last interaction and, as of recently, I've begun seeing a therapist to help me process everything that happened, especially what happened with him.

I'd be lying to myself if I say I don't feel on edge every so often, as if I'm expecting him to pop up at any moment. Perhaps I'm being unnecessarily paranoid, but something about how things left off with him feels…open ended and ominous. There was an obsession in his eyes last I checked. Obsession mixed with blinding rage. He quickly became unpredictable. So, as much as I'd like to believe that the Art I knew would never come after me, or even be capable of hurting me, I have to constantly remind myself that I'd seen a side of him I never knew at all. It's that side of him that has me on edge. Wherever he is though, I do hope he's safe, and happy.

Then there's Aralyn. The day after the night from hell, she attempted to reach out to me multiple times. I blocked her, but she sent Jovana to my place. I had to turn her away with a message for Aralyn to leave me alone indicating that I'd speak to her when and if I was ready. She let me be for a while; however, she tried once more to reach me yesterday. I came home to a note stuck to my door that read:

Jess,

I know you need time, but there will only be one last opportunity for us to speak. Please meet me tomorrow morning at the place listed below at eight. I will be waiting. Please, I hope you'll give me a chance to explain and answer any questions you may have, anything at all.

− Aralyn

So, here I am at the Eiffel Tower near the spot where Aralyn suggested we meet, right next to the large field of grass where locals and tourists alike come to chill and stare in awe at one of the world's marvels. It's a lovely morning, and because it's so early, there's a misty morning fog that rolls across the city. The sky is a beautiful display of deep blues, orange and pink.

With a cup of coffee in hand, I take a seat on one of the benches and wait in nervous anticipation. I can't say I'm ready for this conversation. My emotions surrounding the tumultuous events are still raw. I've worked hard to get my mental and emotional space back to some semblance of normalcy and I'm worried that by agreeing to this meeting I will be opening my freshly stitched wounds all over again.

Through the mist, I spot Aralyn approaching with her arm looped around Jovana's. They make it over at a slow pace and it looks as if Jovana is acting as her human crutch. "Bonjour, Jess." Aralyn winces as she's assisted onto the bench. Her face looks thin. There's a fragility about her that's worrisome. However, although she's in the worst state I've ever seen her, she still holds true to her style and poise.

"Hello, Aralyn. Still rocking the heels, I see." The diamond studded butterflies glisten in the light of the rising sun.

"Haha, oui. I haven't been able to wear them as much because I've started to develop swelling in my legs at times, but I refuse to give them up until the day I have no choice." A faint smile pulls on her lips. I wouldn't expect anything less from the feisty and stubborn woman. It's clear that she's not one to give up what she likes or wants. Why should an illness be any exception?

Jovana greets me quickly and walks over to a bench a little way down from us, providing some privacy. "I appreciate your decision to meet me here. Merci. I know it wasn't an easy one."

"Yeah. Well, I suppose if not now I may never get the full story." I gaze at her with sullen eyes. "There's nothing more the doctors can do?"

"I need a new heart. But because of a pre-existing health issue, I'm not eligible for the transplant list. So, unless there's a miracle–"

"There's nothing else to be done."

"Oui, exactement."

"Does Madame Chérot know?"

"She does. She tries not to show emotion about it, which I appreciate. All of this is strange enough as it is. I don't want pity. I want to be treated as though no one knows when I'll die. As if I still have a chance to see sixty." She laughs to herself but, eventually, her laugh trails off and, in the place of her smile, a look of sadness takes over her face as she briefly lowers her head. "Jess, I want to take a moment to apologize before anything else. I did not intend for things to end up the way they did. I really thought I'd have the opportunity to explain everything to you in the way I had hoped, after an outcome I had imagined. You didn't deserve for things to happen like that. You didn't deserve to get hurt."

I interject. "I'm sorry, I'm sure you're about to say more, but the first thing I really want to know is what the hell your game plan was. You're apologizing because it didn't go your way and I didn't find out in the manner you wanted me to, but I don't think I deserved to be dragged into any of this quite frankly. Make it make sense, please, because I just feel used! To me, it seems like I was the distraction, your ploy to keep Alexander from going after you. You lied and manipulated me into believing some ridiculous need for a name!"

"I withheld information, but I did not lie to you. I sent you in search of the name of the woman he loves, and you got it."

"Yeah, *your* name Aralyn!"

"No, Jess. It was your name that I sent you in search of."

Her bold statement puzzles me, and I throw my hands up in exhausted frustration. "For Christ's sake! Stop fucking with me Aralyn!"

"I know you heard every word that was said outside that door. You now know the truth about my situation. I was given a year and a half to live, at best, and I'm already eleven months in. I love Alexander so much and he loved me, maybe he still does, but I sense he's falling for you, if he hasn't fully done so already. I could tell just in the conversation we had that night and that truly was my ultimate goal. He needs a good woman in his life, a solid partner, and I wanted to make sure he had that before I pass. It's my parting gift to the most beautiful man I've ever known." A tear streams down her pale cheek. I keep quiet, continuing to soak in every bit of information she finally provides.

"I had planned to do something like this since I had found out the news of how critical my condition was. My only issue was that I was unable to find anyone that seemed compatible enough for him. That is, until I saw you at his house in January."

Her confession brings confusion, but then it dawns on me, "Oh my God, wait. You were in the library! The first day I came to interview him I thought I had heard the library door close as I was leaving. You were in there, weren't you?" I recall her telling

Alex that she still had the key to the playroom. That must have been where she hid when I went in!

She nods. "Oui. At the time, I had planned to sneak in so that I could speak to Alexander personally and explain why I left because my plan didn't seem to be working. The more time that went by, the guiltier I felt about leaving him the way I did. When he came back to Paris, it seemed like the perfect opportunity to confess. But then, while I paced around the library preparing my speech, I heard your voice, so I cracked open the door and saw you standing in the foyer.

"I recognized you from the café but wasn't sure why you were there until I overheard you talking on your phone about your frustrations with the interview you had just had with him. It may sound strange, but at that moment I had this clear vision. That's when my plan came together instantly. I cannot explain why, at the time, it had to be you, other than I don't believe in coincidence. I was drawn to question you at the café for a reason. You were meant to interview Alexander at that time and at that house for a reason and you left at the exact moment I was in the library for a reason. In my mind, all signs pointed to you.

"After that, I went home and started conducting my research. I went around asking about you and also looked you up online. The more I found out and interacted with you, the more I realized that you were, in fact, perfect for him. Over time, I grew increasingly confident in my decision. You already had the looks and personality that would attract Alexander, you just needed a bit of a makeover and an opportunity to be noticed by him. I knew I could provide those things."

Okay, wow. I'm actually finding it hard not to be impressed by her efforts which is conflicting because I should still be quite vexed. "But you knew that I had only agreed to your plan in order to get ahead in my profession. You knew I was down to set Alex up."

"Oui, and I also knew you wouldn't because I knew you'd fall for him too."

"And what if I hadn't? What if I really ended up not feeling the same way? Was he to be left with two broken hearts? It doesn't sound like you thought that all the way through."

"Despite what you might want to believe, we are just alike. We are strong, determined to succeed, ready to fight for what we want, no matter what…and our biggest weakness is love fused with desire. When we choose to fall in love, it's a serious commitment. It's pure and binding. Whatever and whomever we love, we do so with a burning passion that cannot easily be extinguished and the desires attached to that kind of passion are magnified. That's the type of love that creates yearning. Your heart used to only yearn to succeed in your career and it still does, but now it yearns for Alexander too and everything that comes with a life with him. That, you cannot deny."

I dwell on her words and come to see that she's not wrong. Love fueled desire is indeed my kryptonite. Journalism *was* my everything and Alexander quickly became that as well. I desired the success of both my career and growing relationship with him so much that I lost myself in the fight to obtain the most I could from them. Because of that, I ended up drifting away in a current of despair when the shattering reality of the things I chose to ignore in the process set in.

Aralyn loved Alex so much that she cooked up some insane plan in order to see them both satisfied. Her satisfaction would come in the knowledge that she could depart this life knowing that her partner would still be loved and happy; that his heart would be in safe keeping. Although it's such a beautiful gesture, it was executed in a way that left her picking up the shattered pieces too. Her love-fueled desire gave her tunnel vision; all she could see was the outcome she wanted and nothing else mattered. We both have operated from a place of imbalance and that's a crushing blow to the ego.

"You're right. I can't deny that. He really does have my heart." My voice quivers. "I care about him so much. I may even love him. And I'm angry, so very angry at myself more than anyone, more than you even."

"Because you now feel out of control when you've worked so hard to keep everything together."

"Yeah." My watery eyes meet hers.

"I know," she says, "I've felt the same. I had the perfect life with him. I didn't know how I could be so lucky. I wasn't sure how I deserved it. I kept my heart away from love for a long time before he came along, but my heart didn't stand a chance with him." She giggles and then sighs, her tone becoming dreary. "When I found out how sick I was, my first thought was him. What was I going to tell him? I could feel my control slipping away. My first instinct was to get it back and, at the time, the only way I thought I could do that was to focus on his happiness because I couldn't handle that mine was being stripped from me.

"I wanted revenge on death while I was still alive. I wanted to prove to death that it doesn't get to win. It doesn't get to take my life and his happiness with it. It doesn't get to make me feel weak. I wanted to prove that I have the power to make things different. That even though I may not have the power to change my fate, I could influence his.

"I can't tell you how many times I wished I would have never let myself fall in love simply because of the pain I've ended up with. But Jess, the truth is, I wouldn't change a thing. Not my love for him, nor my hope for the both of you."

There's no holding back the waterworks. I don't know what to say. I mourn for all of us and, at the same time, I'm happy she's opened up like this to me, thankful even. "Oh, Jess." She holds her arms open and without hesitation, I fall into her embrace. She holds me and we stay like this for a time. Two women, barely more than strangers, leaning into each other as if we've been connected for a lifetime.

After a while she pulls back and clutches my face with her hands, wiping away my tears with her thumbs. "Look at us two. Such a mess." She laughs and I choke out a small one too. Her eyes of blue and green with a hint of amber, peer into my own. "No matter what your mind gets caught up believing, you do deserve every beautiful thing your heart desires ma chérie, including him."

I sob. "It's too late, Aralyn. He's gone. I've lost him."

"Then go find him." I'm wrecked with emotion as my head falls forward in defeat of sadness. Aralyn hoists it back up again with her fingers on my chin. "If you leave him too long with his own thoughts and grief, he will retreat so far into himself that you may not be able to get him back out again. I don't want that for him or you. You two belong together, Jess. You must go find him and get him back. Promise me. S'il-vous-plaît, promise me."

With bleary eyes and a woeful heart, I agree to Aralyn's final request. "I promise."

"Très bien. When you get him back, take care of him. Cherish him. Call him out when he's wrong," she chortles and rolls her eyes. "He likes to think he knows it all. Challenge him. Listen to him. Give him encouragement. Be patient with him as he mends his heart. And don't be afraid to love him."

"I will." I'm moved by her dedication to her lover's happiness. I know it can't be easy to do this. The strength it takes to make this request is a strength not easily obtained. This took her many sleepless nights, heartache and tears to get her to this place; to trust the heart she cherished so profoundly in the care of another.

The tears continue to flow, and she pulls me back in for one last long embrace, stroking my hair and comforting me as my heart spills out onto her black coat. "Shhh, chéri it will be alright, you'll see. You'll see." She props me up once more and rummages through her purse, pulling out a red handkerchief with a gold butterfly embroidered on it and hands it to me. It's almost too beautiful for the salt of my tears, but I accept it graciously.

After I collect myself enough to speak, I ask, "What about you? What will you do now?"

"I'm going home to Spain before I become too ill to travel."

"Spain? I thought you were French."

"My father was French, but my mother was Spanish. The only remaining family I have resides in Spain. I'd like to be with them during this time and I wish to be buried there next to my mother." I'm still coming to terms with the fact that this may very well be my last encounter with her.

"Anyway, I'm going to take this moment to say au revoir, Jess, and good luck. I don't think we'll see each other again. I know I didn't always make it easy on you to know me or like me, but I do hope you can find it within yourself to forgive me."

I laugh. "You know, it's funny, the very first time I saw you, I swore I had to know you. There was such an intense need to find out your story. I knew you'd be interesting Aralyn but I certainly wasn't expecting you to be *this* interesting." We share another laugh together. "In all seriousness though, I forgive you and, oddly enough, I thank you. You played a part in helping me become a butterfly, metaphorically speaking." I chuckle a bit at this realization. "Bit by bit you coaxed me out of my comfort zone. You challenged me and, much like Alex, you saw me for me, especially when I couldn't see myself. I'll never forget you Aralyn De la Rue." The biggest, brightest smile I've ever seen her give is plastered across her face and, for a short time, she's glowing.

She waves Jovana over who comes and assists her up. She takes a pause upon standing to catch her breath. "Take good care of yourself, Jess Rivers."

"So long, Aralyn." I smile and hand her back her handkerchief.

"Keep it, I have plenty. Afterall, I don't think I'll have use for it much longer." She winks. Before fully turning away, she stops and shifts back to me. "Oh, one more thing. I will have something shipped out to your flat. I think you might find it useful for your next big story."

My brow peaks with interest. "What is it?"

Giggling, she says, "Learn to leave a little room in your life for surprises, Jess." Huh, that's exactly what Alexander would tell me. I roll my eyes and grin at her remark.

She puts on her sunglasses and says, "Au revoir, ma chérie!"

With Jovana at her side, I watch the auburn-haired beauty strut off into the distance for the last time. It pulls at my heartstrings. Despite the mystery and the drama that had surrounded her presence in my world and still not knowing as much about her as I'd have liked to, I grew to be quite fond of her. She came off cold and uncaring at times but, in the end, it was beautiful to see that she, in fact, has one of the biggest hearts. She loves and loves fiercely. My eyes remain locked on her until she strays out of sight, now officially a memory I shall not soon forget.

I sit on the stoop of my flat and scroll through social media checking out all the buzz on my article. The majority of the readers offer positive praise and feedback. Of course, there are a few negative Nancy's but that's to be expected in this industry– I honestly anticipated more. I'm so fucking proud of this piece. I played on the fact that I was seen by the media with Alexander at the charity event, knowing that there were plenty of people with questions about who I was to him. The article offered a peek into his world through my eyes. I wrote about my experience having personally spent quality time around him. Like Alexander always wanted me to, I harnessed my voice and shared my discoveries with conviction and depth, translating everything I came to love about him in a way most people could understand.

The only details about him that I omitted were the hidden knowledge of the motive behind his father's murder and, well, all things explicitly regarding his sexual lifestyle. Granted, his kink life, in many ways, reflects his lifestyle outside the bedroom, so perhaps elements of his sexual life were reflected in the piece after all. Mm, the bedroom. My mind can't help but drift to the memory of us entwined with one another and now I'm, once again, frustrated by the fact that all I have are the memories.

"Excusez-moi Madame, êtes-vous Jess Rivers?" I look up at the mail carrier holding a package.

"Oui, c'est moi. I'm Jess." He hands it to me and presents a tablet for me to sign off on, then walks away.

I stare at the package the size of a large shoe box and gently shake it. It doesn't have a fragile sticker anywhere and there is, indeed, something clunky moving around inside, maybe a couple things. I look for a return address but there is none. My guess is it's whatever Aralyn said she was having delivered to my house. It would be just like her to not add a return address.

I walk inside my flat, set the box on the kitchen island and begin to open it with a knife. Inside, I find two bundles of books wrapped in plastic wrap. There appears to be about four books total. I unwrap one of the bundles and untie the ribbon binding two of the books before opening the envelope laying on top of them that's addressed to me. It is, indeed, from Aralyn.

Jess,

These journals hold the story of my life. I don't know anyone better to tell it than you. I only ask that you do whatever you can to keep certain locations and the identity of those involved a secret, especially Madame Chérot and the Butterflies. I trust you will. I'd like to think that perhaps others can gain something from my experiences, and I hope for you that this will shed some light on who I am, how I got to where I was and how I came to know Alexander. I told you that by the end of things you would know my story. Here it is. I kept my promise. Don't forget to keep yours.

With love and admiration,

— Aralyn

Oh my God. I drop the letter and race to open the books. Holy shit! They really are her journals! I flip through the pages. There are entries here dating back years, possibly to her teens! My heart swells with gratitude. It's as if I've been waiting forever for these without realizing that I have been waiting for them at all. I think back to the first time I saw Aralyn in her butterfly stilettos with the red soles and how enthralled I was with thoughts of who she could be. To finally be holding the truth of her life in my hands feels inconceivable. To have her blessing to write about her story is…well, an honor. Even though I've always felt she had a story worth telling, I wasn't sure I'd ever come to really know it.

Her last words still linger in my mind as I thumb through the pages. *"I kept my promise. Don't forget to keep yours."* I have been putting a lot of thought this weekend into going after Alexander, but I only ended up teetering on the cusp of uncertainty because I have no idea how he'll receive me, or if he'll even see me at all. It seems irrational to chase after a man who asked for space and time and who clearly felt it best not to proceed further with our connection.

I glance around at my flat, the place that has been my safe haven during my darkest moments for a little over a month and it's now that I'm starting to see the light. A burst of clarity hits me and I take another look at the signature on the letter. Aralyn is the poster child for doing crazy things for love. If she's proven anything, it's that love is wild, unpredictable, powerful and oh so very capable. To her, love is worth the risk.

There is nothing left for me in Paris, so what the hell am I doing here? Shouldn't my life be with the only man I want, the only man I need? Maybe it's time I take a risk for love too. It's time to find Alexander Marc. It's time to keep my promise.

A firm knock on the door echoes loudly through the air. Strange. I wasn't expecting anyone. I haven't had any visitors in quite some time. When the knock comes again, I answer and the sight of the woman on my doorstep leaves me speechless.

"Madame Chérot…"

She removes her sunglasses, revealing her rich brown eyes that sweep my body with heavy critique as she purses her lips. When her gaze meets mine again, she gives a quick smirk and pushes past me through the door.

"Uh, yes, please come in." I murmur to myself, stupefied by her audacity to invite herself into my home.

I close the door and observe as she looks around the living area and proceeds to gravitate to the kitchen island where the journals sit. Her fingertips graze them. "I uh, they just arrived today," I remark.

"Oui. I know," she says, still staring down at them, as if they've pulled her deep into thought and heavy contemplation.

"So, then you also know she's asked me to write about her?" She says nothing in response, and I begin to worry that she's here to give me another lecture or, perhaps, even threaten me. "If you're worried about me writing about you or the Butterflies, I swear I won't say anything that will jeopardize any of you."

"I know you won't. You aren't stupid." I sense a subliminal warning hidden in her tone. She looks up at me and I cautiously walk over to meet her at the island, as if at any moment, this fierce yet intimidating woman could strike. "I'll be quick and to the point, as I don't like exchanging useless words. Now that Aralyn has resigned, I need a new protégé. So, I need your answer."

"I'm sorry, my answer?" There's no way she's asking what I think she's asking. "I get that you need a new protégé, but you can't possibly mean–"

"You, Jess. I mean you."

Holy shit.

ACKNOWLEDGEMENTS

This book is my baby! There are so many individuals to thank for their assistance in bringing it to life! I'm very blessed to have such a tremendous support team in friends and family and that can't go unacknowledged.

Ngozi Magena, the magician, you truly create magic! Such insight, skill and attention. I honestly couldn't imagine having a better editor. You've taken the time to really immerse yourself in this book. You endeavored to understand the ins and outs of these characters and made sure their individual voices held strong throughout, adding suggestions on how to highlight the biggest aspects of who they are so that they shine even more. You took time to listen to me, you understood my vision, and you helped shape a great book into an even better one with as much enthusiasm as I had. I truly believe this book wouldn't be as amazing as it is without you. Thank you!

Brittany J, my home skillet biscuit, my sounding board, you're absolutely incredible! You were the one who continuously kept my motivation high while finishing this book. Your voiced anticipation as you waited for me to send the next chapter (I know you wanted to hurt me for leaving you on cliff hangers at times) pushed me to keep going. Your honest feedback and suggestions were most helpful and whenever I felt like pulling my hair out, stressing over something I needn't stress about, you'd bring me back to center and remind me of what I'm capable of. I appreciate you more than you know!

Angel Velasquez, the princess, my vivacious cheerleader, you are a ball of love and amazing energy that I adore! Thank you for being such an amazing beta reader and an epic friend. You were one of the people who motivated me most when I finished this book and I'll never forget you for it. I knew you were a keeper the moment we sang Disney songs on the jump seat during final decent hahaha. There was no going back from there.

Mom, my rock, you have been my biggest supporter in life. You have led by great example and paved the way so that I'd have the best chance for success. Life hasn't always been kind to you, yet, despite it all, you aimed to provide us kids with all the tools necessary to be good people who make a positive change in the world. People who make an impact. You showed me that it does not matter how many times you get knocked down, whether in life, love or passion, never give up. You instilled that in me. And I believe that's one of the reasons I never gave up on pursuing my dreams of being a published author. I love you!

Amanda Harper, my longest friend, the love is real! I think back fondly on my love for writing and how you were the first to really see my ideas on paper. I remember how as middle school girls, in the multiple pen pal letters we'd write to each other, I'd tell you all about the stories I was writing. I remember there was a time we both wrote a story together, taking turns to write our piece within each letter. You were the first to witness my love of words. And here you are, twenty years later, still supporting me, still rooting for me, and you've even greatly assisted me by being an epic beta reader! You're amazing! I appreciate you so much.

Sydney Hertel, the sunshine, gosh you're just the best! I can't tell you how much I appreciate you taking the time to proofread this book. Our friendship formed over a love of adventure. How fitting that you also take part in this grand adventure too! You provided such honest feedback that helped smooth this beauty out and you've provided so many words of support. Don't ever stop being the quirky, beautiful, brilliant woman you are!

Bryant Vega, my twin flame, my soul thanks you! I will never experience the kind of connection I have with you with anyone else. It's on a different level. It's complex, yet beautiful and profound. In being your twin, I came to understand the true definition of unconditional love. I've taken that understanding and poured some of it into the creation of this book. Thank you for your unyielding support, your constant words of encouragement and your love!

To all my friends and family who in some way or another provided support, assistance and rooted for me. There aren't enough words in the world to express my gratitude. I thank you all from the depths of my soul. Know that you made a positive impact. You all have my love!

ABOUT THE AUTHOR

Besides her adoration for the world of romance novels, A. M. Darling is a lover of all things creative. A self–proclaimed Jill of trades, she lives for artistic expression in a variety of mediums–creative writing, fine art and photography being her favorites. She's also an avid traveler, a mentor and life path guide.

Her love for creative writing started at age ten. With her head often in the clouds, she spent a lot of time reading books and creating the characters she envisioned. Writing was her first and most profound form of self-expression and has remained one of the greatest constants throughout her life.